A PERFECT MATCH

SUGAR SPRINGS
BOOK 3

ALEXA ASTON

Published by Oliver-Heber Books

0 9 8 7 6 5 4 3 2 1

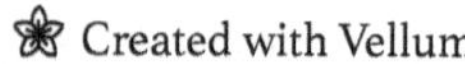 Created with Vellum

PROLOGUE

OCTOBER—SIXTEEN YEARS AGO...

Quit texting. Ace is dead.

Nova stared at the screen, dumbfounded by the words she read. Even if she weren't pregnant—and she definitely was—her stomach would've done exactly what it was doing now.

She raced across the hall to the bathroom, barely making it to the toilet. She vomited what little she'd been able to keep down today. Cold chills ran through her, her mind racing.

Ace was dead.

No wonder he hadn't replied to her texts. Or answered her desperate calls.

Had the person who'd just texted her back from his cell listened to the myriad of voicemails she'd left?

Nova flushed the toilet and rinsed her mouth with water, trying to get the bitter taste to leave. When it didn't, she brushed her teeth, though even that nauseated her nowadays.

Because she was pregnant. Going to be a mother in seven months or so.

And the father—a guy whose last name she didn't even know —was dead.

Or was he?

Nova, despite her religious fundamentalist background, wasn't a very trusting person. Her parents were—as they called themselves—good Christians, but she had found that they were hypocrites worse than the esteemed Pharisees in the Bible. They didn't like anyone who wasn't exactly like them. They barely tolerated people of other denominations, even thinking Catholics were children of the Devil. And they believed anyone who was gay was someone out to destroy society.

She accompanied her parents to their church each Sunday, where they spent a majority of the day. The love the preacher and elders talked about was certainly lacking in the Turner house- hold. Her father ignored his daughter for the most part. Her mother criticized Nova for every infraction, real or imagined. If charity began at home, it was definitely absent in the Turner household.

Deciding she had to know for certain about Ace, she sent a text.

I'm pregnant. Call me back now—or I go to the police and report you.

WHEN SHE'D FIGURED out she was pregnant a few days ago, after missing two of her periods, she'd gone to the library, telling her mother she had homework to do for a research project and needed the resources available there. The Turners had no computers or Internet in their home. They'd homeschooled Nova through eighth grade and then allowed her to attend the local high school in their Dallas suburb because she was so academically advanced, and neither her mother nor her father knew how to cater to her educational needs. Not that they wanted her to go to college. Neither of them had, and they didn't plan for their only child to, either.

Still, they couldn't have her getting married at thirteen, so they'd agreed she could attend the public high school. After graduation, it was understood that she would be married to someone in their congregation. She'd already eavesdropped on more than one occasion and knew some of the men her parents were considering for her were in their thirties and forties, which totally freaked her out.

Maybe that's why she'd decided to sneak out when her next-door neighbor suggested it. A traveling carnival had come to town, sponsored by the neighbor's Catholic church. Nova had gone—and met Ace there.

His arms were covered in colorful tattoos. He had curly blond hair and mischievous blue eyes and was tall and had biceps that were the largest she'd ever seen. He told her it was from being what he called a roustabout, a worker who erected the rides and tents of the carnival and set up the various booths for the games of chance.

Ace had given Nova her first kiss. When he kissed her, she was no longer Nova Turner, inexperienced, sheltered teen. She became, in her mind, strong and powerful and sexy. A woman who could do and be anything. And after her third time of sneaking out, all to see Ace, she lost her virginity once all the rides had shut down and the carnies had bedded down for the night. It hurt—but Ace told her how beautiful she was, so she didn't dwell on the brief pain.

After that, they'd done it twice more before the carnival moved on. She'd never even thought to use any kind of protection. Nova hadn't a clue how sex worked.

Then the early morning nausea set in. She had to face the fact that she was pregnant. Not having any confidant to ask, she had gone to the library to read every book she could find and scour the Internet on what was happening to her body and what could be expected.

She'd also starting texting Ace like crazy, calling when her texts remained unanswered.

Her cell dinged. She wasn't supposed to have a smart phone. It was an older model, what they called a flip phone, which she'd gotten from the same neighbor who'd helped her sneak out that first time. It took forever to send a text, unlike the kind she'd seen kids at school send. They not only typed texts quickly on a keyboard, but some of them even talked into their phones, and the texts magically wrote themselves.

Call again in ten minutes. I'll answer.

NOVA DECIDED to trust whoever was behind that text. It might be Ace, finally agreeing to talk to her. Or if Ace really were dead, it could be someone who could tell her what had happened to him.

She waited, leaving the house's lone bathroom because if she were in there too long, Mama would beat on the door and want to know why. She returned to her room and quietly shut the door. She wasn't supposed to close it. Papa didn't believe in privacy for anyone in their household. But he was at work, and Mama was in the kitchen frying chicken for dinner. Nova only hoped she could have this conversation without interruption and get some answers.

Either way, she was going to have to tell her parents that a baby was growing inside her.

They would want to go to the police. She didn't know exactly why, only that another girl at church had gotten pregnant a few years ago. The elders had met at the Turner house to discuss the situation, and Nova had listened to the conversation, perched in the hallway. She learned a little from what she heard, mainly that a girl had to consent to have relations and if she didn't, that was called rape. Even if she did consent and she was under a certain age, the boy—or man—could be brought up on criminal charges.

That's why she'd made the threat in the text she'd sent, not knowing exactly what that involved, but hoping it would get Ace to call her back. After all, he was nineteen.

Nova was fifteen.

The phone rang, and she answered it quickly, her gut churning. "Hello?"

"You're the pretty one," a young female voice said. "You've got the medium brown hair with the gold highlights, right? And hazel eyes?"

"Yes, that's me," she said, disappointed that it wasn't Ace on the other end of the line. "I'm Nova."

"I'm sorry, Nova," the voice said, choking. "Ace really is dead."

"Are you lying to me?" she asked, her voice full of steel, knowing she had to be strong not only for herself—but for the baby she carried.

A sob sounded. "No."

She could hear crying and wished she could comfort whoever was on the other end of the line.

"What happened?" she asked quietly.

"It was a motorcycle accident. Two weeks ago."

When she'd figured out the baby was inside her.

"We were north of Houston. The carnival had stopped for a three-week stay. We've got cousins there. One of them had just gotten out of the army. He had a new motorcycle. He and Ace were always daring each other to do crazy shit."

She flinched at the curse word but remained quiet.

A pause. More sobs. "Ace ran a redlight. On purpose. My cousin said the bike was fast enough that Ace could blow through any light and not get hit. It was awful."

The girl on the line began crying again. Nova recalled seeing her because she resembled Ace so much. He had told her it was his little sister, who was twelve. He'd called her a brat but said he loved her anyway.

"I'm sorry you lost your brother," she said, her throat closing up with unshed tears. She didn't want to start crying because she was afraid if she did, she might never stop.

"I'm sorry you're gonna have his baby, Nova, but I can't help you. My dad won't care. Ace was from two marriages ago, and he despises that wife. He had another one and then married my mom. He doesn't give a shit about me and barely even liked Ace. You're on your own."

"I understand. Thank you for calling me back. And letting me know."

"Are you... are you gonna be okay?" the girl asked.

"I'll be just fine. And I promise I won't call again. I'm sorry you lost your brother."

Nova hung up. She swallowed hard, trying to force down the painful lump. She prayed for the courage to tell her parents about the trouble she was in, trying not to think how the other pregnant girl at church, after the elders had met, had been beaten by her parents. They'd hit her so much and so hard, she had lost the baby. The man she was supposed to marry the next year had said he didn't want damaged goods.

That girl had killed herself.

It had been a huge scandal in their small, religious community. Everyone whispered about it, but no one acknowledged the fact the girl had needed love and understanding. Instead, she'd been shamed and humiliated and physically abused until she'd lost the child she carried.

Leaving her bedroom, she went to the kitchen and set the table. She helped place all the bowls of food on it as she heard her father come in the front door and head to the bathroom to wash up.

They ate in silence. They usually did. Occasionally, Papa would tell a story about one of the houses he'd serviced that day. He was a plumber. Mama rarely contributed anything to the conversation. No one ever asked Nova about her day or what was happening at school, so it didn't surprise her when she cleared her throat and saw the startled expressions on her parents' faces. In their world, children were to be seen and never heard.

"I have something to tell you. I'm... going to have a baby."

They stared at her as if she'd turned green, their jaws slack.

"How?" Papa demanded, his hands balling into fists.

That frightened Nova, but she needed to say her piece.

And do everything she could to protect her baby.

"I met a boy. We made it. Together." She was not going to neglect her part in this. She might not have exactly understood what was going on, but she had contributed to the circumstances as much as Ace had.

"No," Mama said, her mouth hardening. "This is wrong. You're only fifteen."

Papa's eyes narrowed. "Old enough to defy us. You sneaked out to meet this boy, didn't you."

Nova nodded solemnly.

"It's that school. We never should have let her go to high school with all those heathens," Papa declared. "We must go to the principal and the authorities. This boy must pay."

Mama gasped. "No! We can't do that, you fool. You will lose your position as head elder in our church. I will no longer be able to lead the sewing circle. Think of our positions. We will be outcasts, Father Turner."

"You're right," Papa agreed. "I was letting my tongue run away with me. The Devil was speaking through me." He glared at Nova. "It doesn't matter who this boy is. We cannot have you here. You are only fifteen. You will ruin our reputations."

Papa looked to Mama. "We must be careful what we say, Mother Turner. We cannot tell the congregation she has run away. That would reflect poorly on us." He thought a moment. "We can say we went to visit our sister congregation in Arkansas. That we had a car wreck. And Nova was killed."

"Yes," Mama agreed, her head bobbing up and down. "Arkansas is far enough away. Of course, we won't actually arrive there. The accident can happen before we get there. We can sell the car. Take the bus back to Texas."

Papa nodded, satisfied with the lie being spun. "It will bring much sympathy to us, Mother. Why, it could elevate both our positions in the church," he declared, now beaming.

Startled by the direction things had turned, she asked, "Where am I supposed to go?"

"Anywhere but here!" her mother shouted at her, beginning to say horrible things, calling Nova a Whore from Babylon and far worse.

"But Mama—"

"I cannot stand the sight of you," her mother proclaimed, scooting her chair from the table and storming out of the kitchen.

The bedroom door slammed, and Nova and her father locked eyes.

"I will drop you at some shelter in Dallas," he said stiffly. "We can't have you in our home ever again. Surely, you understand that. You have disappointed us beyond words, Nova. Your actions have humiliated us. We mustn't ever let anyone know. You must never contact us—or anyone from the church—for help. You made your bed. Now, you must lie in the sin of it."

Anger now rose within her, and she wanted to defend herself.

And her baby.

"What kind of Christians are you?" she demanded. "You and Mama talk about being disciples of Christ and loving and acting as he did. I am your own flesh and blood, Papa, and I need your help. Your support. Your *love*." She shook her head. "Then again, I have never gotten anything from you, have I? You would help a stranger before you would your own daughter. I have never meant anything to you, have I?"

"You are nothing like a child of ours should be," he said, his jaw tightening. "You always have your head in the clouds. You are far too smart for your own good. You waste precious time, drawing and painting, just like my sister did. Art is not practical, Nova. It will not feed you. I hope you will learn some skill so that you might support yourself. The people at the shelter will help you. They will see that your baby goes to a good home."

"No!" she cried. "I am not giving up my baby. How could you even think that?" she asked, her voice hysterical. "This has never been a home to me. You have never been good parents, despite what you think. I will go and have this baby and care for it and love it and never see you or Mama again."

"Go pack your things," Papa said sternly. "I will be waiting in the car. Five minutes. And then I will take you somewhere. A place where they help wayward girls such as yourself." He shook his head. "Thank goodness it is already dark, and no one will see us leave."

Nova hurried to her room. She didn't own a suitcase, so she crammed some clothes into her backpack, telling herself over and over not to cry. Not to show weakness in front of anyone.

She slung the backpack over her shoulder and picked up the flip phone before deciding to leave it behind. She had no one to call—and no one would be calling her. Snapping it in two, she dropped in her trashcan.

Making her way to her father's car, she climbed inside. No conversation occurred as he drove from their suburban neighborhood and headed toward the interstate that led into Dallas.

Forty minutes later, he pulled the car to the curb and looked at her. "Get out," he ordered.

"You said you would take me to a shelter," she said defiantly, her chin rising a notch.

"I don't really know who takes girls like you," he said, his voice laced with venom. "I just want to be rid of you. Don't contact us, Nova. You can never come home. As of this moment, you are dead to us."

"I never want to see you again," she told him. "I have more courage in my pinky than you do in your entire body. You are a hypocrite, just like the Pharisees who belittled Jesus. I don't want to be anything like you. My baby will have a good mother. And I'll make a wonderful home for him or her."

Getting out of the car, she slammed the door. Her father sped away. Nova watched his taillights until they disappeared.

She was truly alone now. It was dark, the early October evening cool. She hadn't even thought to put on her jacket when she left. From what she had learned on the Internet, she was about two months along. Her baby would come in May.

Nova might freeze to death—or starve to death—before then.

Tears began streaming down her cheeks. Fear now enveloped her as she looked about and saw a homeless man sitting on the sidewalk staring at her. He grinned malevolently, and she rushed in the opposite direction, tears now blinding her. She kept walking, though, her head down, when she suddenly crashed into someone.

"Hey, are you all right?" the woman asked, gripping Nova's upper arms so that Nova didn't fall. Seeing her tears, the woman asked, "What's wrong, honey? Do you need me to call someone for you?"

She shook her head vigorously. "No."

After a long moment, the woman said, "Would you let me buy you a meal? There's a diner two blocks from here. I was on my way there to grab a bite to eat. I could use the company."

Not knowing where her next one might come from, Nova nodded. She had the baby to think of now.

"Okay," she said, her voice small.

They reached the diner, and the woman ordered soup and

sandwiches for the both of them. As Nova ate, she suddenly knew who she could call.

Rain...

She'd only met her aunt a handful of times, but they traded letters a few times a year. Rain's real name was Reba, and she was what Papa called the black sheep of the Turner family. She was an artist and had encouraged Nova in her own artwork.

"May I borrow your phone, please?" she asked.

"Of course." The woman handed her cell over.

Just as she had Rain's address memorized, she also knew her aunt's phone number by heart. Rain had asked her to memorize it, telling Nova that one day she might need her—and Rain would be there for her.

Even though the woman across from her would hear everything, Nova didn't care. She dialed the number and swallowed, gathering her courage.

"Hello?"

"Rain, it's me. Nova."

"Nova! How good to hear from you. I was just writing a letter to you."

"I need... help."

Nova explained how she had sneaked out and met Ace. How he'd been a carny who'd moved on and left Nova with a baby in her belly. How Ace had been killed in an accident.

"They told me I would embarrass them. That their church friends would say bad things about them," she revealed, tears streaming down her face now. "Papa drove me to Dallas and left me." She sniffed. "I'm scared, Rain. I don't have any money. I didn't know what to do."

"I'll come get you, honey," Rain said, no hesitation in her voice. "Where are you?"

"In a diner." She looked to the woman, who provided the address, which Nova passed along to Rain.

"It's about a ninety-minute drive from Sugar Springs to you," her aunt said. "Stay there. I'll pay the bill when I get there. Don't leave, Nova. I'm coming for you."

"I knew you'd help me, Rain."

"I plan to do more than help, honey. You're going to live with me for as long as you'd like. I'll see you soon. I love you, sweet girl."

"I love you, too."

Nova handed the phone back to the woman. "Thank you. My aunt is going to come get me."

"I'll stay with you until she comes," the woman said. "I heard what you told her. I'm so sorry your parents tossed you out." She took Nova's hand. "But you have someone who cares for you. I think you're going to be just fine. Now, try and eat something, okay?"

True to her word, the stranger kept Nova company, even buying her dessert. Nova's appetite returned, and she ate the apple pie, enjoying every bite.

When Rain arrived, she came straight to their booth, thanking the woman for taking care of Nova, saying she wouldn't soon forget the kindness of a stranger.

In the car, Rain said, "I meant what I said. You have a home with me now, Nova. As an artist, I've learned one man's trash is another man's treasure. Well, your no-good parents threw you out like trash, but you are someone I cherish. You have a home now, Nova, a true home where you'll be loved and coddled and even spoiled a bit. You can keep the baby or not. That will be up to you. You don't have to decide anything right now."

"I want this baby," she said fervently.

Rain smiled. "Then he—or she—will have the best mom in the world."

1

NOW—AUSTIN, TEXAS

Nova continued thinning and raising the walls of the pot she was working on. Once the walls were completed, she evened out the top, the last step in throwing a pot. She'd already set her electric kiln to eight hundred and fifty degrees and quickly snapped a picture of this work in progress before she placed her latest creation inside the kiln for the initial twelve-hour firing to produce the bisque pot.

This was a new design she was trying out, hopeful that it would lead to another line. She'd recently held a show and sold every single piece. Now, she was back at the drawing board, toying with the direction she would head with her new series. She texted the picture to Rain and then used her cell's voice recorder to send a lengthy text about the picture and what she was thinking about as far as this design went.

No reply came, which wasn't a surprise. When Rain was sculpting, making pottery, or painting, she would turn off her cell, hating any interruption during the creative process.

Her aunt was still Nova's biggest supporter and cheerleader. Nova was grateful Rain had taken her in all those years ago. In all this time, Nova had never had any contact with her parents. They never knew anything about the birth of their grandson and what an amazing kid Leo was.

He'd been such a good baby and was still a good kid, despite being a teenager. Leo had been smart from the beginning and had gone to a Montessori preschool, where he'd thrived. Nova wouldn't have been able to afford the school during those early years. It had been Rain who paid for the doctor and hospital. For the pediatrician and preschool. For everything Nova and Leo had needed.

But she owed her aunt far more than money. A debt which could never be repaid. Rain's kindness had meant the world to Nova. She'd been able to keep her baby even as she worked toward her GED, all the while soaking up the art lessons Rain gave her. Painting. Pottery. Sculpting. Jewelry-making. Nova had taken all those lessons to heart, thriving with each process and technique she learned, happy she was using her talent wisely.

She had left Sugar Springs when Leo turned five because she had the opportunity to apprentice under Zayden, a renown potter and friend of Rain's. Zayden's wife, Medora, was a painter and also guided Nova's early works. The Austin couple was two decades older than Nova, but she was comfortable around them. Childcare fortunately hadn't been an issue because Leo had started kindergarten, freeing Nova up for the bulk of the day.

The artistic pair rented the garage apartment above their house to her and treated Nova and Leo like family. Eventually, she started doing small shows of her own, consisting of both pottery and painting, and then adding in various pieces of jewelry at craft fairs and shows around the Austin area. She made enough to begin paying Rain back a little each month, and she continued to do so even now, years after Leo's birth.

For the last three years, Nova had lived with Stuart Jones, known professionally as Jagger. Jagger was in his mid-thirties but never shared his exact age with her. The moody painter said age was unimportant, as was marriage. While she agreed about the marriage part, she did insist upon monogamy. While she loved Jagger, he exasperated like no one else could, due to his frequent mood swings. Nova also tried to get the artist to do more with Leo, but Jagger told her that he wasn't interested in children. She had recently overheard him tell one of his fellow artists that Nova was perfect—except for the baggage she brought along with her. It wasn't her emotional baggage Jagger referred to.

He meant Leo.

She had pondered long and hard the past few days since she'd heard that cutting remark, wondering if she should stay with Jagger. Doing so made her feel disloyal to her son, and Nova believed Jagger would never change.

It was time to have a come to Jesus meeting with her lover.

Nova went upstairs. They shared studio space and the rent for it, with her taking the downstairs and Jagger being upstairs. It was more convenient because of her kiln for her to be located on the lower level.

He wasn't there.

She hadn't heard him leave. Then again, Jagger came and went at odd hours as the spirit moved him, while she was always focused on the project in front of her and kept regular hours so she could be home when Leo got home from school. She pulled her phone from her pocket and texted her lover.

No response.

That wasn't unusual since she and Rain did the same thing when they worked. Still, something nagged at Nova. She decided to head home since it was almost noon. Sometimes, Jagger would take a break and go to their apartment to eat or out to lunch with a friend. She liked that the apartment was only six blocks from their studio and walked the short distance home.

When she entered, she froze. The sounds of sex—loud, lusty sex—came from their bedroom. Immediately, hurt filled her. Then denial. Then anger.

Nova steeled herself for what she would see and went to the

bedroom, shocked to discover her close friend Anastacia, another artist who worked as a glassblower, riding Jagger.

"Stop!" she shouted, blinking rapidly to keep the tears of anger and frustration from spilling down her cheeks.

Anastacia stopped rocking, gliding off Jagger and sitting on the bed, facing Nova. Jagger pushed up on his elbows. Neither had an ounce of guilt or shame on their faces, which immediately told her things she was loath to deal with.

Still, through gritted teeth, Nova said, "The one thing I asked of you was for you to be faithful to me. You promised you would be loyal. That you would love only me."

Her now-former friend laughed. "You really think someone with Jagger's looks and temperament could be tied to one woman?"

A sinking feeling filled her. "We might not be married—but we made promises to each other."

Anastacia laughed even harder. "I'm one of many, you stupid cow." She started reeling off the names of people Nova knew.

Men and women.

"Is this true? You've been seeing a parade of others behind my back?" she accused, her stomach now churning painfully.

Jagger shrugged. In that moment, Nova realized he didn't care enough about her to even deny her accusation, much less fight for her.

"Leo and I will be gone by tomorrow," she told him. "Don't come home tonight so we can pack in peace. I'm sure Anastacia would be happy to entertain you at her place. Now, get dressed and get out."

They did so as she glared at them. Nova ached at the loss of the life she had thought she had. Both humiliation and embarrassment filled her as she figured everyone in their circle of friends had known about this. Except her. She remembered how Leo had tried to warn her about something of this very nature, and she'd shut him down, one of the few times she hadn't listened to her own child.

That brought guilt and remorse to the hodgepodge of emotions running through her although anger was now the strongest emotion inside her. Nova believed she might never get over this betrayal. Jagger was the only man she'd been with since Ace. She had devoted a dozen years to Leo before becoming involved with the temperamental painter. This incident told her she would never trust another man again. She would be destined to live a life alone once her son left home.

That thought brought despondency, losing Leo and being lonely.

She couldn't stay in Austin. The art community was thriving but small enough that everyone would know about this betrayal by tomorrow, if they didn't already.

Her heart told her it was once again time to flee to Sugar Springs. Rain would be there. Rain could help fix what was broken.

The two lovers brushed past her, causing nausea to rise within her, the scent of sex still heavy in the air. Once she heard the front door slam, Nova raced to the toilet and threw up. She hoped she expelled all the horrible things in her life as she flushed and then rinsed her mouth.

She started packing and tried texting Rain again, to give her aunt a heads up that she and Leo would be arriving tomorrow by noon. Rain didn't reply, but her phone rang a few seconds later. Seeing it was her aunt's number, she eagerly answered the call.

"Is this Nova Turner?" a stranger's voice asked.

"Yes," she said carefully. "Who is this?"

"I see where you've been trying to reach the owner of this phone."

"Yes, I'm her niece. Rain Turner's niece. What's wrong? Where's Rain?"

"I'm sorry to inform you that your aunt was struck from

behind on a freeway in Dallas by a drunk driver. She was part of a seven-car pile-up and rushed to the hospital. Miss Turner, I'm so sorry. Your aunt died in surgery an hour ago."

The woman went on to explain how she was a nurse at the hospital and was going through Rain's things now to look for next of kin information and whom to notify regarding her death.

"I'm her only family. My son and I," Nova said, her heart shattering into a thousand pieces. "I can contact Rain's attorney. She lives—lived—in Sugar Springs. That's where he is, too."

Nova suddenly recalled Rain had mentioned going to Dallas to see an art show and that she would stay overnight with a friend before buying art supplies and heading back to Sugar Springs.

"Please do so," the nurse said.

They talked a few more minutes, with the nurse advising Nova to arrange with a funeral home to collect Rain's body from the hospital's morgue, saying the funeral home would hold it until they received further instructions.

"You should come to Dallas if you're in a position to do so, Miss Turner. I'll hold your aunt's personal effects, and you can collect them when you come. I'm very sorry for your loss."

Nova hung up, grieving not only for the loss of her relationship with Jagger, but now dealing with the huge hole in her heart and her life with Rain's permanent absence. Still, she was grateful to have Leo in her life. She couldn't fall apart. She had to be strong for him.

She had thought to go to Sugar Springs and would still do so now, certain that Rain's house and the studio in the back yard would be hers. Her aunt had told her of the will Campbell Cox, a local attorney, had drawn up years ago, naming her as heir to everything Rain possessed.

Taking time to compose herself, she looked online and found the website of the lawyer and called the phone number listed. After being put through by his receptionist, Nova gave Cox the few details she had regarding Rain's death and the hospital her aunt had been taken to.

"I can handle things for you, Nova," Cox assured her in a calm voice laced with concern. "I'm assuming you know Rain's property and possessions go to you. Your aunt's will stipulated that she be cremated. It would be easier to do so in Dallas. I can have my receptionist go to Dallas in order to pick up Rain's effects and her ashes. I think you're living in Austin now if I remember correctly."

She swallowed. "I was about to move back in with Rain. My son, too. Can I do so, Mr. Cox?"

"That won't be a problem. I've pulled up a copy of Rain's will as we've been speaking to confirm everything will go to you. I can work on getting probate started immediately, but I don't see a problem with you coming to Sugar Springs and taking possession of the house."

She thanked him and continued packing in a daze. It was difficult to believe she would never see Rain again. Her aunt had been so full of life.

Leo came home two hours later from the part-time summer job he was working at a local tennis center. When she heard him bustling about the kitchen, she went to talk to him.

He took one look at her and asked, "What's wrong?"

"Everything," she said, shaking her head.

Nova explained about Rain's death, and Leo teared up, having always remained close to his great-aunt and FaceTiming often with her.

"We're leaving Austin."

"For the funeral?" he asked, confused. "I thought you said she was being cremated and Mr. Cox would take care of having Rain's remains brought back to Sugar Springs. I know she'd like her ashes spread across Sugar Lake. We spent a lot of fun times there."

Nova took a deep breath and slowly expelled it. "What I

meant to say is we're leaving Austin permanently. I think we're done with Austin—and Jagger."

Relief filled her son's face. "About time, Mom. He's such an asshole."

Leo hugged her tightly.

"Rain left everything to me, so we have a place to stay. To live."

"This will be good for both of us, Mom," Leo said, obviously trying to reassure her.

She ruffled his hair. "When did you become so wise?"

He grinned. "I was born that way. Rain always said so. She called me an old soul."

"Go pack your things. We're leaving as soon as you do."

"What about all the stuff in your studio? The kiln, even if it is ancient. Your wheel. That's only a couple of years old."

She frowned. "You're right. We need to rent a small U-Haul." Then she changed her mind, thinking of her aunt's equipment in her studio. How everything was top of the line. "No. I know an artist—a potter—who would love to buy my stuff. With the show I just did, my studio is almost bare. He'll buy the kiln and my wheel. Let's leave it all behind and start fresh, Leo."

While Leo packed, Nova made a call. Twenty minutes later, she walked to the studio for the last time and met her fellow potter, an up and comer she'd mentored some. She took him inside and showed him the kiln and wheel, and he agreed to pay cash. He went to a branch of his bank to make the withdrawal, and Nova packed up her jewelry-making equipment in the duffel bag she'd brought while he was gone.

Half an hour later, she and Leo loaded the car and gassed it up. When they hit the interstate in her ancient sedan, she watched Austin recede in her rear-view mirror, and her anger slowly began to dissolve. She knew she was leaving it behind— and she was ready to start a new chapter in her life with Leo in Sugar Springs.

2

———————

SUGAR SPRINGS, TEXAS

Cole Johnson answered his cell phone, seeing it was Aunt Ju on the line, the woman who had meant the most to him because she had made him the man he was today.

"Hey, Aunt Ju," he said. "I'm almost to Sugar Springs. Should be there in the next fifteen minutes or so."

Her warm laughter bubbled up. "I'll bet East Texas looks a lot better than West Texas."

"You know no matter where I land, West Texas will always be home."

"You just do you for this interview," his aunt advised. "If they're smart, they'll want you as their head football coach. If not, you have a great job as it is. Or there'll be other positions which open up down the road." She paused. "You know I think you can do anything, Cole."

"And where did I learn that from?" he asked.

Aunt Ju—Julia Johnson—had been both mother and father to Cole. She'd only been nineteen years old and a freshman in college when her sixteen-year-old sister Penny turned up pregnant. Aunt Ju had been working two part-time jobs, as well as attending college fulltime. She took in her pregnant sister, who had been living in foster care, the same as Aunt Ju had been until she turned eighteen and was no longer the state's obligation. The foster parents had kicked Penny Johnson out, telling the State of Texas they wanted to be removed from responsibility of the pregnant girl.

Aunt Ju had slept on the floor of her dorm room, giving her younger sister the bed. Thank goodness she'd had an incredibly understanding roommate who'd kept her mouth closed and allowed Penny to remain in their dorm room the rest of the semester.

When Penny went into labor on the last day of finals that spring, Aunt Ju had taken her sister to the hospital. She'd returned to take three finals and work the late shift at her convenience store job. The next day when she arrived to visit, the nurse informed Julia Johnson that Penny had discharged herself and left.

Without her infant son.

After a ton of paperwork, Aunt Ju took Cole, giving him a name and raising him as her own. She had given up her college plans and never had the opportunity to go back. Instead, she took a job as a cook on a large cattle ranch, explaining to the ranch's owner that she had a small nephew she was raising, and they were a package deal. If he wanted her, he would take the boy, too.

Cole had grown up on the Triple R Ranch, almost like a mascot to the cowboys who worked it. Aunt Ju made sure Cole went to school and taught him all about manners and how to treat others the right way, but it was the cowboys on the Triple R who taught him how to ride and rope.

One of those cowboys had given him a football for his seventh birthday, and he had slept with it every night for years. He did his chores and also helped Aunt Ju in the kitchen, where she fed not only the cowboys three meals a day but also the family who owned the ranch. Cole became an excellent student with a deep love of learning, encouraged by his aunt. Aunt Ju had never let him call her *Mom*, saying he already had one of those, even though she had abandoned him. While his aunt held out hope that one day her sister might mature and return to claim Cole, he had written his birth mother off before he hit double digits.

Cole had been the smartest kid in his grade each year, his reading level far above the other students. He also had a knack for numbers and a love for football, which burned deeply inside him. He played Pee Wee football from the time he was eight and continued playing the sport through high school, where his team won district every year and went to the playoffs, making it to the state championship game his senior year. Though they lost on last minute field goal, Cole garnered plenty of attention and received several scholarship offers. He wanted to play closer to home so that Aunt Ju could come to an occasional game, but she told him to take the scholarship offer from the University of Texas in Austin. Not only did they have a strong football program, but their academics were second to none among the state's public schools. Aunt Ju told Cole he could be whatever he wanted to be with a degree from UT.

All he wanted to do, however, was play football.

He excelled at linebacker for the Longhorns, becoming a starter his sophomore year. He was all-conference that year and all-American by his junior year. On the way to a stellar season his senior year until he tore up a knee during the first conference game of the season. A grueling rehab followed. Cole never abandoned his teammates, however. He stood on the sidelines every Saturday, propped up by his crutches, absorbing things that became life lessons to him.

While he had a final year of playing eligibility left once he graduated, he knew his speed and cutting ability was gone, thanks to his bum knee. He was lucky to have his health and mobility and still be able to walk without pain. He had a long talk with the head coach and after it, Cole enrolled in graduate school at UT and was named a graduate football assistant. He worked with the defense, especially the linebacking corps, which he'd been a part of so recently.

After two years, he left the university with his master's degree, as well as a teaching certificate in his back pocket. He was offered a job coaching defensive backs at an Austin area high school and took the position, teaching biology during the day and coaching after hours.

He had switched schools four years into his coaching career, moving up in the ranks to serve as the defensive coordinator at a large Dallas suburban school, which went to the playoffs every year and had a bevy of state titles.

Now, at thirty-two, he was eager to run a program of his own. That's why he was headed to Sugar Springs, a small town in East Texas with a winning football tradition. Their coach was retiring and had been the one to recommend Cole to Joe Bob Milton, the principal of Sugar Springs High School. Cole had run into Coach Reynolds at THSCA, the annual Texas High School Coaches Association, held in mid-July each year. Bubba Reynolds had given no one an indication at that event that he was about to walk away from coaching. It was only after THSCA ended that Reynolds called Cole and asked if he might be interested in the head coaching position at Sugar Springs. With the high school being a perennial favorite to capture the district title in football each year, he would have been a fool to turn down the opportunity to interview.

The only thing which troubled him was how late in July it was for something like this to occur. Most high schools who changed coaches did so in the spring to very early summer. With the third week in July almost gone now, that could cause problems for whoever took the job.

But he wanted it. Badly.

Cole told his aunt goodbye and promised to let her know how the interview went. He cruised into Sugar Springs more than half an hour before his scheduled interview at the high school and drove around the small town for a few minutes, familiarizing himself with it. Having been raised in a small town, he was eager to get back to those roots. While a majority of coaches would have waited and put in more time at a larger school, hoping to move up in the ranks, Cole didn't mind moving to a lower classification if it meant being in charge of the entire football program.

The attraction in Sugar Springs was not only its winning ways, but he would not be teaching in the classroom. He had taught biology in Austin and currently taught chemistry in his present assignment, but he always felt he was shortchanging his students. He had to limit the hours he tutored, and he didn't always have time to grade every assignment he gave.

The Sugar Springs' position involved not only being the high school's head football coach, but it was accompanied by the title of athletic director. That meant Cole would be in charge of all sports teams in the district, not only at the high school, but the two middle schools, as well. For football, it would be ideal, because he could work with the middle school coaches to implement a similar type of offense which the high school would run. Exposing seventh and eighth graders to an offense and then allowing them to continue in that same offense when they reached high school would make for a smoother transition for those student athletes. Cole would also work with the other head coaches of various sports, male and female teams, and oversee their programs and budgets. It was a lot of responsibility for a man of his age, but he was ready to meet that challenge.

He parked in front of the school, where only two pickup trucks stood. He knew teachers and counselors had already finished up their work for the past school year and assumed he would be interviewed by the owners of these two trucks—Milton, the principal, and the current football coach and AD, Bubba Reynolds.

Entering the school, he made his way directly to the office, opening the door and finding the place deserted of clerks and secretaries. He followed a long corridor and heard voices at the end of it.

Reaching the office at the end of the hall, he stood in the doorway and said, "I'm Cole Johnson. Here for my interview."

The man seated behind the desk had to be the principal. The one seated in front of the desk was Bubba Reynolds. Not only had Cole known Reynolds from the annual state convention of football coaches, Reynolds was also an alumnus of UT and had played defensive back for the Longhorns two decades before Cole landed at the school.

Both men stood, and Milton said, "Come on in, Cole. I'm Job Bob Milton, principal at Sugar Springs High School. Bubba was just telling me all about you."

He shook hands with each and took the seat Reynolds indicated.

For the next half-hour, Reynolds outlined the football program he had created over the last fifteen years and discussed his athletes' expectations, along with those of the town, when it came to football.

Milton then told Cole a little about the school district and the student population, asking if he had any questions.

Cole asked a few, and both men took turns answering them.

The principal said, "We've told you all about Sugar Springs. Now, tell us a little about yourself."

"I'm from a small town in West Texas, so I know how small towns operate and what football means to the people living in them," he began.

He elaborated on his athletic career and talked about coaching both at the collegiate level and at the two high schools where he'd held positions. Cole outlined the program he was interested in installing and how it would be run.

"I'm eager to take the next step in my coaching career, gentlemen. That means being in charge of a program. As Jerry Jones once famously said when he bought the Dallas Cowboys years ago, I want to be involved in everything from jocks to socks. I've elaborated on the ideas I wish to incorporate with the traditions already present in Sugar Springs. The offense I wish to install is complimentary to the one Bubba has run here for years. I am my own man, though, and I plan to do things my own way—but that doesn't mean I won't seek or listen to input from others."

"You won't be getting any from me," Bubba interjected. "I know what it's like to have a retired coach hanging over your shoulder, whispering in your ear and getting inside your head. My wife and I are moving to Arizona. Our daughter and three grandchildren are there, and a golf course is waiting for me. You can do whatever you wish with the program, Cole, and I wish you the best of luck with it."

"Does this mean I'm being offered the job?" he asked bluntly.

Joe Bob Milton guffawed. "Hell, Cole, you had the job before you walked through the door. We've just been shooting the breeze, letting you know about Sugar Springs and hearing a little bit about you and where you plan to take things. You come with the bona fides to do this job better than most. I also know you're young and working your way up the football ladder. While I would love to have you for two decades or more, I'm hoping to get five years out of you before you move on. Bubba here tells me you're the best fit for the job, and he's never steered me wrong."

"THERE IS A BIG *BUT*, THOUGH," Coach Reynolds said, throwing cold water on the elation building inside Cole. "A kind of roadblock."

"What kind of roadblock?" he asked warily.

"You know it's almost August, Cole. When someone is hired as a head coach, he usually has time to put together his own staff. Those coaches have to resign from their current positions. Others have to be hired in their place. It's a lot of dominos falling."

Reynolds paused. "Two-a-days start in a little over a week. Because of that, you're being offered the AD slot *and* the head football coach position. The drawback is you'll have to keep my current staff intact."

He let out a slow, long breathe, thinking as he did so, his wheels spinning rapidly.

"It's too late to let go the football coaches we have," Milton continued. "And the ones you want? Their head coaches wouldn't release them from their contracts so close to the beginning of the school year. It would mean too much movement too late in the game. Master schedules are set."

Reynolds looked at him. "I've assembled a terrific staff, Cole. They will know *you* are the head coach. They would also know that they're under the gun to produce—else you'll get rid of them next spring. I figure you'll want to bring a few of your people in anyway, no matter how this upcoming season goes. At least this way, you can see what my guys can do and who's worth keeping around and whom you'd like to jettison."

"Think of it as renting a car for a year," the principal suggested. "If you like it, you can buy it. If you don't, you can replace it."

"Won't their loyalties be to you?" Cole asked Reynolds. "And won't at least a couple of them think *they* should be the ones running the program once you're gone?"

The coach scratched his chin thoughtfully. "Maybe. But if you accept, I'll promise I'll meet with each of them individually and then as a group, so they understand you are my choice. That they'll need to perform, or you'll cut them loose next spring." He looked hopefully at Cole. "So, what do you say?"

It wasn't an ideal situation. Despite Reynolds promising to speak to his coaches, the old man would be gone. Cole would be left holding the bag, responsible for the program and how his staff performed. And there had to be a couple of them who would resent a young newcomer being brought in, thinking they should have been the one chosen for the position.

Still, this kind of opportunity didn't manifest itself often. He was in his early thirties. He had a lot of energy and drive. It was everything he wanted, including returning to his small-town roots.

"I'm in," he said firmly.

Milton stuck out a hand. "Welcome to Sugar Springs, Coach Johnson."

3

———————

Cole awoke before his alarm went off and silenced it, throwing on clothes for his daily jog. He had jogged every morning since he was twelve years old—in season or not—and this ritual was the perfect start to his day. He could think about things that troubled him. Clear his head. Prepare himself for what the day would bring.

He downed a protein shake and was out the door by three-thirty, running the same route he had run the last few days he had been living in Sugar Springs. He was renting an apartment which didn't have hardly anything in it beyond his clothes and a toothbrush. His first coaching position he had rented a room in a fellow coach's house and hadn't needed any furniture. His last post in Dallas, he rented a garage apartment from an assistant principal at the high school he taught at. It, too, had come furnished.

Since he'd had to move quickly to Sugar Springs, he had found an apartment only two blocks from the school. Since it was unfurnished and he had no time to think about furniture, Cole had bought a sleeping bag and lawn chair at Target on his way to his new job. His clothes hung in the closet, while things such as socks and underwear were in stacks along the wall. Once things slowed down—if they slowed down—he could think about furniture at that point. It really didn't matter because he was spending pretty much every waking hour at school.

Good to his word, Bubba Reynolds had called his staff together and given them the news of his retirement and shared who his replacement would be. Bubba hadn't come to any of the early morning practices held this week. Practices in Texas were governed by the University Interscholastic League—UIL, for short. The first two days allowed student athletes to practice in only T-shirts, shorts, and helmets. No physical contact was permitted. The practice was limited to three hours, with a one-hour break factored in at the head coach's discretion, though a one-hour walk-through was permitted in addition to that practice.

Yesterday and today, no person-to-person contact was allowed, but players wore their helmets, shoulder pads, and girdles. The team was still limited to the same hours. Cole looked forward to tomorrow's fifth day of practice. While most of the parameters were the same, on this fifth and final day of the acclimatization period, person-to-person contact was finally permitted. No full contact, but he could start getting an idea of each player's set of skills and how to build on them while addressing any deficiencies.

The staff had been welcoming. At least, most of them had. The two men he would depend upon most were his offensive and defensive coordinators, brothers who had played their college ball at the University of North Texas. Ben Peterson, the older of the pair at forty, was the offensive coordinator, and Cole had worked with Ben closely on the changes he wanted to implement in the offensive scheme. The coach had been openly receptive to Cole's ideas, noting the changes weren't huge but that they could make a big difference in the team's attitude and play. Ben was also high on Jake Fletcher, the junior quarterback who would be starting for the first time.

Fletcher had stepped in late last season when the senior starter had gone down with a knee injury and led the Sugar Springs Knights to a final victory in district play, along with wins in the first two rounds of the playoffs. Cole liked everything about Jake Fletcher. The teenager was a natural athlete and already showed excellent leadership in the previous three days of practice.

The younger Peterson brother, John, was known for being a defensive genius. From what Cole gathered, John also assumed when Bubba Reynolds did retire, the top spot would go to him. While he had not been openly hostile to Cole, Cole sensed an undercurrent running between them and hoped John wouldn't undermine him with either the coaches or student-athletes. Most likely, he would need to have a one-on-one with the defensive coordinator and air what differences they had.

Soon.

Completing his established loop, he headed now for the high school. It was easier to get ready there instead of at home and saved him time. Cole hit the locker room and after showering and shaving, he dressed in a blue and gold coaching staff shirt and shorts and went to his office. He had been in it by five every morning this week, with a called coaches' meeting at five-thirty. Then practice had started at six. With the Texas heat in August and the limit the UIL put on practices at this time of year, Cole thought it best to go from six to ten in the mornings and avoid as much of the heat as possible. It also allowed the players who had summer jobs to get in some last days of work before the start of school.

Unfortunately, he would have to leave practice early today and tomorrow in order to attend the teacher training sessions the district required of their new employees. It wasn't anything he hadn't heard before and absolutely a waste of time, but he knew the hoops had to be jumped through. Joe Bob Milton had told him that there were two other new hires, both from the Social Studies Department. That's where the Peterson brothers taught, both of them covering freshmen world geography classes.

Cole reviewed and printed today's schedule on his computer and made copies of it using the small copier in his office. When he finished, he went to the conference room off the locker room, where the coaches met for their meetings. It was also the place where they reviewed film. Ben was already there and greeted Cole.

"I want to talk about a few plays," the coach told Cole, elaborating on an idea he had.

He listened, nodding. "Yes, I think you've hit on something. With that left side of the offensive line being larger, it could easily work."

Both his left guard and tackle were oversized cousins. Luke and Lyle Smith were seniors and bucking for athletic scholarships. Cole would do everything in his power to help these players land one. He knew the pressure was on him because the Knights had a winning tradition under Coach Reynolds. He also knew how some small town coaches might be run out of town when they didn't produce.

Cole planned to win. Period.

The other coaches began drifting into the room, coffees in hand, and he started their meeting promptly at five-thirty. He passed out the sheets with today's schedule, and they went over this timeline. The rest of the time they discussed the grades given to various players after yesterday's practice.

With his eye on the clock, knowing they needed to head out to the field now, Cole said, "I'm going to miss part of practice today and tomorrow. From eight to ten. Today, Ben will be in charge after I leave, and tomorrow, John will take over running the practice."

"Already weaseling out of practice, Coach?" John Peterson ribbed.

The others chuckled, and Cole did too, but he sensed the dig in the words.

"I've got to attend new hire training," he explained. "I'm sure you and your brother will do a fine job of running practice during my absence." He looked to Ben. "I finish up at three this afternoon. I'll head to the conference room, and you can brief me on what I missed at practice, Coach."

Ben smiled easily. "Be happy to do so, Coach."

"All right, gentlemen. Let's roll."

Cole led them out to the football practice field, where their team, members of both varsity and junior varsity, were already lined up. The four captains, two from the offense and two from the defense, faced the group. He blew a whistle, nodding to the captains to start practice.

Jake Fletcher took the lead and began running the group through a series of calisthenics. Once those had been finished, they split up into offense and defense units, by position. Cole rotated between groups, observing and occasionally voicing a recommendation. He could tell the student athletes were still feeling their way, trying to figure him out. That was okay. He was doing the same with them and his coaching staff, and he would know more about them once contact drills were allowed.

When the time came, Cole went back into the building, deciding to check his mailbox in the office before he reported to the library, where the training session would take place today. He pulled the thick stack of mail from his box and started flipping through it, tossing a few items in the recycle bin below the boxes, and then opening a letter.

As he read through it, he heard the door to the office open and a voice said, "Hello, I'm Nova Turner. This is my son Leo, and I need to enroll him for the upcoming school year. We just moved here from Austin."

He glanced over and saw Rilda O'Riley, a clerk who had been very friendly and helpful to him, moved to the counter to help the woman and her son. From the back, the mom had a nice figure, while the son was tall and rangy. Immediately, Cole wondered if the boy played football and decided to hang around a moment.

Rilda handed over a clipboard. "Here you go, Mrs. Turner. You'll need to fill out this paperwork and then we can have you and Leo meet with our counselor regarding his schedule." She smiled. "It's so nice to have you at Sugar Springs High School, Leo. Are you a sophomore? Or maybe a junior?'

"I'm a sophomore, ma'am."

"If you are in any extra-curriculars, Leo, be sure and tell the counselor about that when you're planning your schedule." Rilda looked back to the mother. "Do you have any of Leo's prior records or the transcript from his former school, Mrs. Turner?"

"It's Miss Turner," the mother corrected. "And no, we just came in the last two days rather quickly. My aunt passed away, and we'll be living in her house."

"Oh, are you Rain's niece?"

"I am. Did you know my aunt?"

"I certainly did, honey," Rilda said. "I'm so sorry to hear about her accident. She was well-loved in this community." She looked to Leo. "Are you an artist like your great-aunt was?"

"I like to draw," the teenager said. "Graphic novels. But I want to do more than draw. I want to play football."

Cole turned now, ready to walk over and join the conversation.

Before he did so, the mother looked at her son, surprise filling her face. "Leo, you've never played any sports at all. And of those you could choose, football is the last one I want you to participate in."

"Mom, you said this is a fresh start for both of us. I *want* to play football."

"Well, I can't allow that," the mom snapped. "Football is a brutal activity. Players just slam into each other, deliberately trying to hurt one another. Haven't you heard about all the concussions that occur in football? And what about TBI—traumatic brain injuries? No, Leo, I can't let you play football."

Cole strode toward the pair and said, "Excuse me, Miss Turner. I couldn't help but overhear your conversation. I'm Coach Johnson, the head football coach and athletic director here at Sugar Springs. And let me tell you, there is far more to football than athletes hitting one another. Football helps improve coordination. It's a great physical activity, helping growing teenagers condition themselves. It teaches leadership skills. Discipline. Character. If Leo here wants to play, I welcome him to my team."

She flushed, whether in embarrassment or anger, Cole didn't know.

What he did know was that she was one attractive woman.

He wondered if she truly were this boy's mother, because he saw no resemblance between the pair. She was about five-five, with curly, medium-brown hair that glistened with golden highlights. Her hazel eyes showed flecks of green and brown in them. Leo, on the other hand, was an inch under six feet, with dirty blond hair and blue eyes.

Moreover, this woman looked no more than thirty years old. He thought maybe she might be an older sister functioning as Leo's guardian, and the boy had slid into the habit of calling her Mom.

Or maybe Nova Turner was like his own mother, a teenager who had gotten herself knocked up and had a baby when she was no more than a kid herself. If that were the case, despite her negative feelings about her son playing football, Cole had to admire her.

Because she hadn't cut and run. She had raised this polite kid, who seemed to be a very good one.

Turning his attention to the boy, Cole stuck out a hand.

"Coach Johnson, Leo. I'll tell you now that it will be tough coming out for a sport for the first time, having never played it, but if you've got drive and determination, I think you could learn quite a bit."

"Oh, Coach Johnson, I know football inside and out," the teen declared. "I watch every college and pro game on TV that I can."

He chuckled. "Being an armchair quarterback is different than being a player on the field, Leo," he gently chided. "Do you have an idea what position you might be interested in playing?"

The boy was lean and all arms and legs. He would never survive on the line or at tight end.

"I'd like to be a receiver, sir," Leo told him.

Leo launched into telling Cole who some of his football idols were and discussing the various offenses run by the schools these college athletes played at. As he talked, Cole realized Leo did know quite a bit about football. Still, knowledge was one thing. Practical experience was another.

"We have an open policy here at Sugar Springs High School, where anyone makes the team if they come out for it," he continued. "It doesn't mean you'll get a lot of playing time, though. You'd be assigned to the junior varsity and would have to earn a starting position on that team. If you're riding the bench and we get ahead in a game, you would see a little bit of action. Juniors can volunteer to remain on JV if they won't be starting on varsity, but seniors move up to varsity regardless of their starter or non-starter status."

"That all sounds good to me, Coach." Leo turned to his mom. "Please, Mom. You know how much I enjoy watching football. I've wanted to play for a long time."

"You never told me that," she said quietly. "I still believe football to be a dangerous sport, but if it's what you really want to do, we can give it a try."

Leo threw his arms around her, hugging her tightly. "Thanks,

Mom. You're the best." He turned back to Cole. "When and where do I report, Coach?"

Cole laughed. "I like your enthusiasm, Leo. Practice this week is from six to ten in the mornings. Next week, we'll shift over to three-thirty to seven-thirty because my staff and I will be in faculty sessions to prepare for the upcoming school year. I'm new to Sugar Springs myself and about to head over for some new hire training. I finish at three this afternoon. If you want to meet me back here in the office at three, I can take you down and give you a tour of the locker room. Let you test yourself on the weights. Issue you practice clothes and get your jersey number assigned. Sound good?"

The boy beamed. "It's sounds awesome, Coach. I'll be here."

"And I will, too," his mother said. "I want to see these facilities and what kind of measures you have in place to keep my son safe. I don't care if you believe I'm overprotective or acting like a helicopter mom."

"I don't think that at all, ma'am," Cole said honestly. "I think you love your son a great deal and want to make sure I'll watch out for him when he's in my care." He paused. "I need to get going, and I know you have paperwork to fill out and a schedule to register for. I'll see you both back here at three o'clock."

"Thank you, Coach Johnson," the woman said.

He turned and walked out of the office, his heart hammering wildly in his chest. The last thing he needed to do was get involved with the mom of one of his players. Hell, he didn't want to date anyone, much less start up a relationship.

But the sweet curves on Nova Turner and that angelic face made his knees go weak. He would have to watch himself around her.

Cole headed to the library, where he found Joe Bob Milton seated at a table with two other women.

"Sorry I'm a few minutes late," he apologized. "There was a new student registering in the office, and he wants to play football. His mom had a few questions for me, and I felt I needed to stay and answer them in order to assure her that we'd take good care of her son."

He sat and added, "I'm Cole Johnson, the new head football coach and athletic director."

The auburn-haired woman to his left, who looked vaguely familiar, said, "I'm Rory Addison. I'll be teaching history. World and U.S." She offered her hand. "Nice to meet you, Coach Johnson."

Having heard her name, he had to ask, "Are you the figure skating Rory Addison?"

Something flickered in her eyes. "I was once upon a time. I'm just a teacher now."

"And I'm Pam Holland," the woman across from him said. "I'm also in the Social Studies Department and will cover gov and econ classes."

She named the Dallas suburb she used to teach in, and he grinned. "We were rivals once upon a time. And your school actually beat mine last year." Cole extended his hand and shook with Pam. "Nice to meet you, too."

Joe Bob passed out a notebook to each of them and went over campus policies in this handbook, asking to see if they had any questions. The school's two assistant principals joined them, and Milton introduced both. The librarian came over and met them, taking charge at that point and giving the trio a tour of the library and media center.

When that was done, the librarian told them to go to the teacher lounge, where a boxed lunch from the local diner awaited them. Cole took time to text Ben and explained they'd have to push back their meeting because of his meeting with the Turners.

The afternoon was filled with another session of meeting counselors, the school nurse, and the three faculty members who would serve as their mentors throughout the school year. Cole was glad to see he was paired with Stan Watson, the basketball coach. A fellow coach would have valuable insight and the kind of special knowledge that a regular teacher wouldn't have access to.

"Nice to meet you, Coach Watson," he said.

The basketball coach then took them on a tour of the entire school, pointing out everything from the ice machine used exclusively by the faculty to explaining what to do when the copier jammed.

Three o'clock arrived, and they were dismissed for the day, Joe Bob telling them that tomorrow would entail some district and state training, as well as meeting people in various positions at the administration building.

Cole told Pam and Rory goodbye and hurried down to the office. As he expected, the Turners were waiting for him. While Leo wore the same T-shirt and shorts from this morning, Nova Turner had changed into a lemon yellow, sleeveless dress which struck her a couple of inches above the knee, showing off a spectacular set of tanned, toned legs that made his mouth grow dry.

"Ready for your tour?" he asked brightly, focusing his attention on Leo as he tried to breathe slowly and get his heart rate back under control.

"Yes!" Leo said enthusiastically.

"Then let's head down to the wing where the gym and locker rooms are housed."

Cole held the door, and mother and son exited the office. Leo fell into step on one side of him, while Nova Turner walked on the other. A light, floral scent emanated from her, causing his pulse to speed up.

They reached the gym, where several students were shooting baskets, including Freddie Otts, captain of the basketball team. Cole introduced Leo to the teens, and Freddie offered to give Leo the grand tour.

"I'll have him back in fifteen minutes, Coach," Freddie said.

"I'll show him the locker room and the weight room. The whole nine yards."

The pair left, with the other players trailing along, leaving him alone with Nova Turner.

He indicated the bleachers. "Want to sit?" he asked.

She nodded and took a seat. Cole sat next to her, not knowing what to say. He hadn't been this tongue-tied around a woman since he'd passed a note to a girl in eighth grade, asking if she wanted to go to the upcoming dance with him.

Suddenly, Nova turned to him, tears filling her eyes. "Please don't let anything happen to my boy," she pleaded, grabbing his hand. "Leo is all I have."

4

———————

Nova felt the electricity as she touched Coach Johnson's hand. The sexual spark was something she had never experienced. While she had been excited by Ace's touch when she was a teenager because it was something new and forbidden and she'd been physically attracted to Jagger, neither man had caused her to grow dizzy the way this man now did.

Quickly, she released the coach's hand and apologized. "I'm so sorry. I'm all over the map emotionally." Collecting herself, she added, "I hope I didn't make you uncomfortable by taking your hand. I wasn't trying to be forward."

"I didn't take it that way, Miss Turner."

She smiled. "Why don't you call me Nova?"

"I will. If you tell me a little about yourself. And Leo. Obviously, you were a very young mother."

Heat filled her face. Stiffly, she said, "That is none of your business, Coach Johnson."

"My mom was barely seventeen when she had me," he said softly.

Her anger cooled instantly. "She was? How did she handle it, becoming a parent as a teenager?"

"Badly," he said, a wry smile crossing his sensual lips. "She left me in the hospital a few hours after she gave birth. Her sister Julia took me in and brought me up as her own kid. She was only nineteen herself. Both of them had been raised in foster care. Poor Aunt Ju gave up on college and all her dreams and went to work to keep a roof over both our heads."

"That's... awful that she abandoned you. And yet, I can understand how frightened your mother must have been because I remember how scared I was," Nova said, sympathy filling her for his situation. "Your aunt must be a wonderful person."

"She's a salt of the earth type. Stressed to me to get an education and taught me hard work pays off. Aunt Ju never married. Never even really dated that I can recall."

"Where does she live?"

"In West Texas, working as a cook on a ranch." He paused. "So, I get where you're coming from. You're obviously alone. Except for Leo, who is the world to you."

Nova nodded. "He is. Best kid ever. He was a great baby. Always smiling and cooing. Even when he was teething, he was all drools and smiles. He was a happy baby—and he's made me happy all these years."

"I overheard when you were speaking to Rilda in the office that your aunt had died. That's why you'd come to Sugar Springs."

Laying all her cards on the table, Nova said, "I just broke up with someone. A very messy breakup. He was screwing around with... more than one person. Rain—my aunt—let me move in with her when I was fifteen and pregnant. Kicked out of the house by my fundamentalist parents. I decided to leave Austin. Make a clean break. Thought Leo and I could come and stay with Rain while I got my act together."

Tears welled in her eyes. "That's when I was notified that she was in an accident and had died. I was her only heir."

His hand slipped around hers, warm and comforting. "I'm really sorry to hear that, Nova. If I lost Aunt Ju, I don't know how I'd feel."

"Rain was my rock. She was an artist and taught me about art, as well. Started Leo drawing when he was barely able to walk. She could make me laugh when I was down. She was... home."

"I get that. Aunt Ju will always be that for me, no matter where I go."

"It's just so hard," she said. "Not getting to tell her goodbye." Nova cleared her throat. "At least Leo and I have a place to stay. I'm an artist myself, so I'll be able to use her studio to complete projects."

"What kind of art?" he asked, and she could see he wasn't just asking to be polite. He seemed interested in her answer.

"I've concentrated on pottery and jewelry-making the last several years, but I also do a little painting. I may want to try more of that now that I'm back in Sugar Springs for good."

Conscious of his hand still holding hers, she withdrew hers carefully. "I'm feeling raw and vulnerable right now with Rain's death and leaving Jagger behind."

"Jagger? Like Mick Jagger?" Coach Johnson bit back a smile.

"My boyfriend just went by Jagger. His real name is Stuart Jones." She giggled. "He thought Jagger sounded cool."

Now, the coach roared with laughter. "I think you're better off without him, Nova. Jagger sounds like a pretentious asshole." He paused. "Sorry. I shouldn't be so judgmental."

"No, he *was* an asshole. And a pain in the ass to live with, truth be told. Leo never liked him. He didn't trust Jagger. I just didn't listen. I hadn't been involved with anyone since I was expecting Leo. I let Jagger's charm turn my head. I can see now my own son was a better judge of character than I was."

"Leo seems like a pretty mature kid," Coach Johnson agreed.

"And I *will* take care of him. It's hard to move and make new friends. Sugar Springs seems to be a friendly place, though. With him going out for football, he'll be around a lot of other kids. He'll find things in common with them. It'll be good for him, being part of a group."

"I lived here with Rain until Leo was five. That's when he and I moved to Austin. The arts community is thriving there. But I always did miss the small-town feel of Sugar Springs."

"We'll make sure Leo is taken care of, Nova," he promised.

"I'm sorry I said horrible things about football," she blurted out.

"Do you watch it? Understand the game?"

"No," Nova admitted. "But Leo lives for it. He's always watching games, dialing back and forth between them. Talking about stuff I have no idea what it means. I should have realized he wanted to play."

"Maybe I can give you a few lessons about football," he said. "So you can understand the game better and know what to look for when you come to see Leo's games. At least, I assume you will."

"Of course. I always go to his school events. He's acted in plays and sung in the choir. I've been to science fairs and STEM competitions. I'll definitely go to his games. Probably even the Sugar Springs Friday night football games, as well. Rain and I use to take Leo. He loved everything about those football games. The pageantry. The band and cheerleaders. The players."

"Good. I hope you will come to see the team play." He grinned. "And me coach."

"You're awfully young to be a head coach," she pointed out. "I don't know much about any sport, but to me, coaches are gray-haired and have craggy faces and beer bellies."

He laughed. "I'm thirty-two. This is my first head coaching position. It also involves being the district's athletic director."

"What does that even mean?" she asked, baffled by the title.

Coach Johnson told her a little about what his additional duties entailed, outside of football. As he spoke, Nova found she liked the timbre of his voice. His expressions.

And his wicked good looks.

But she was just coming off a failed relationship and had no business getting involved with another man this fast. Maybe she could simply be friends with him.

The thought was laughable. He would be fresh meat in a small town where single, eligible bachelors rarely appeared. Every woman under forty would be setting her sights on the handsome newcomer.

"Have you gotten settled into your aunt's house? Your house, I should say."

"Yes, we didn't bring much with us. Campbell Cox, a local attorney, handled having Rain cremated and brought her personal items over to me yesterday."

"Will you keep her ashes, or do you have a place you're going to scatter them?" he asked.

"Leo thought Sugar Lake would be a good place to do that. We've spent some good times at the lake over the years."

"If you'd like some company doing that, I'd be happy to go with you and Leo. Unless you'd prefer your privacy."

"No," she said quickly. "That... would be nice."

They exchanged cell numbers.

Leo appeared, his face flush with happiness. "Freddie and the guys showed me everything, Coach. It's a really nice set-up."

He stood, so she did the same. "Let's see about issuing you clothes and equipment, Leo. Tell me, what did you sign up for on your schedule?"

Nova listened as her son and his new coach talked about what classes he'd be taking in the fall. The counselor had placed Leo in Pre-AP English, World History, Geometry, Biology, Spanish 3, and Drama, along with an athletic class at the end of the day.

"That's a tough schedule," the coach said. "Remember, we've

got no pass/no play, so you'll need to keep up your grades in order to hit the field."

"Piece of cake, Coach," Leo said. "I pretty much ace all my classes."

"But you've never played sports before, Leo. Football practice will drain a lot of your time and energy. You'll have to be careful. Eat right. Get plenty of sleep. Designate time for homework. Get the tutoring you need if you require help. Your teachers can help with that, or I can also tutor you in math or science. Those are my strong points."

"Thanks, Coach. I'll let you know if I need any help."

She paid attention while Coach Johnson talked to both her and Leo about what position her son should play. He called in another coach, one who was head of the offense, whatever that meant. Coach Peters asked Leo several questions, and the coaches recommended that Leo play wide receiver for the Sugar Springs Knights.

"Your heroes seem to be receivers," Coach Johnson pointed out. "We'll have you study some film of previous receivers for the Knights."

"Will you be at practice tomorrow, Leo?" Coach Peters asked.

"Yes, sir. Six o'clock sharp," her son said, his smiling face looking so happy.

Nova couldn't remember the last time Leo had glowed like this. It made her realize how unhappy he'd been in Austin, living with Jagger. She only hoped he would find his niche and make friends in Sugar Springs.

"I think that'll do it," Coach Johnson said. "Let me walk you out."

Leo went ahead of them, carrying his assigned athletic bag, stuffed with his practice jerseys, as he balanced his gear.

"Thanks for allowing Leo the opportunity to play ball for me," Coach Johnson said. "I hope this move to Sugar Springs will be good for both of you." He hesitated. "Do you know when you'll be scattering your aunt's ashes?"

"We can do so anytime," she said. "I know this is a busy time for you, though."

"How about tonight?" he suggested. "I'll probably leave campus before six. It's light for another couple of hours."

Nova texted him Rain's address. "Why don't you come for dinner, Coach Johnson, and then we can head to the lake? There'll be plenty of daylight even after we eat."

His gaze held hers a long moment. "I'd like that, Nova. I'll be at your place at six. And call me Cole."

"Cole," she said, her voice low and unsteady, her heart racing.

He glanced at her son, who stood at the locked car. "Good meeting you."

"Nice meeting you, Coach," he called.

Cole turned to her. "And I'll see you for dinner, Nova," he said, his voice husky.

She could only nod, words escaping her as Cole gave a brusque nod and left her. Shaking her head, trying to gain control of her senses again, Nova joined Leo at their car, euphoria filing her, even as she warned herself to be careful. She was a hot mess emotionally. Her life was in transition. She had Leo to think of. He needed to be her priority now.

And yet all she could think of was Cole Johnson's solid build. The broad shoulders and muscular chest. The dark-blond hair and sky-blue eyes. The smile that drew her in, making her feel special.

Nova cautioned herself to be wary. She was vulnerable now. In no position to become involved with any man, much less her son's football coach.

But the thought of being kissed by Cole Johnson, long and slow, caused her skin to heat and tingle.

"Come on, Mom. This is heavy," Leo complained, standing at the locked sedan.

"All right," she said, unlocking the car as she pulled her head from the clouds and back to reality.

She wouldn't think about him. She had a thousand other things to focus on. To do. To arrange. To rearrange. Cole Johnson needed to be placed on a back burner.

But even back burners simmered.

5

———

When they reached home, Leo brought all his new athletic gear into his bedroom, trying it on and showing off to her. Nova had to admit he did look good in it.

"Just remember to do everything the coaches tell you to do," she reminded.

"I'm in good shape, Mom," Leo said, slight exasperation in his tone. "I run and do yoga. And I *know* football."

She laughed, doubting any other boy on the football team practiced yoga, something much more common for a teenager in Austin.

"I know how much you *watch* football. I was hoping you might do something like become a sports announcer if you didn't follow up on your acting. I'm glad they have a drama program in Sugar Springs. You need a little creative arts to balance out all this he-man roughness that's coming your way."

"I just wish I could've worked art into my schedule," he lamented.

"Well, the counselor said you can swap drama for art next semester, so there's that. Also, she said if you didn't like playing football, you wouldn't have to be in the off-season program. That would open up your schedule even further."

"Hey, let me at least go to my first practice before you have me leaving the program," her son teased.

"I'll admit that I'm not wild about the idea of you participating in something so rough, but Coach Johnson promised me he'd keep an eye on you." She paused. "I hope you don't mind, but I asked him to come to dinner tonight."

"Mind?" Her son's face lit up. "Not at all. Coach is cool." Then he frowned. "Why did you invite him?"

She shrugged. "We got to talking about Rain dying and us coming to Sugar Springs to take over her house. He has a lot of empathy. When he heard we were going to scatter her ashes at Sugar Lake, he asked if he could come along. I thought he needed to eat, and so I asked him to do so before we drove to the lake."

"Huh," Leo said thoughtfully. "Okay, I guess. Even if it's a little weird he wants to say goodbye to someone he doesn't know."

Nova didn't tell her son that Rain sounded an awful lot like the kind of woman the coach's aunt was, taking in a baby and raising him, even as she had to give up on going to college.

"If you don't want him to come with us, tell me now," she said. "I'll just text him and say—"

"No! Don't text him. He can come. To dinner and the lake. Geez, Mom." Leo left the room, shaking his head.

Not knowing if she had done something right—or very wrong —Nova went to check the chicken she'd placed in the slow cooker hours ago. Rain had been a big fan of crockpots, tossing this and that into them in the mornings and providing some pretty heavenly dinners after a long day in her studio. The barbe-cued chicken smelled amazing. She had some fresh okra she could fry up and ears of corn to boil. It was the exact same supper she would have put on the table for Leo and herself.

Except for the brownies. How could you invite a guest over and not serve dessert?

Rain was a chocoholic and always had chocolate in her pantry and freezer. She'd taught Nova to make all kinds of brownies, from cream cheese brownies to marshmallow crunch and white chocolate raspberry ones. Nova could make them from a mix. Improve the mix with a few ingredients. Or even start from scratch. She hoped Cole Johnson would like brownies with nuts because Rain had some wonderful walnuts that would go well in a brownie mix.

While the brownies baked, she took up her sketchbook, working on a jewelry line she had fiddled with for months. Leo finally came out of his room, showing her the latest pages in the graphic novel he was currently working on, and then she had him set the table as she began preparing the vegetables.

He offered to put together a salad, and she allowed him to do so, thinking she would have two hungry guys at the table this evening and didn't want to run out of food for either of them.

Rain's grandfather clock began to chime six as the doorbell rang.

She tossed the cup towel over her shoulder and went to answer the door. "Right on time," she said and then stopped.

Cole Johnson had changed from his coaching attire. He wore a navy golf shirt and khaki pants with a sharp crease. She gazed into his tanned face, taken aback again with how truly nice-looking he was, with cheekbones that could cut glass and a smile that made her glow inside.

He pulled a bouquet of flowers wrapped in tissue paper from behind his back and handed them to her.

"Aunt Ju always told me to bring flowers or wine when I was invited to dinner. Since I didn't know if you drank and Leo would be with us, I thought flowers was the better choice."

Nova dipped her head, inhaling the scent of the pink peonies. "Thank you, Cole, but you didn't have to bring anything."

"And you didn't have to invite me to dinner after I invited

myself to the spreading of your aunt's ashes. I didn't mean to muscle in like that, Nova. I usually show better manners."

"No, Leo and I are happy to have you accompany us to Sugar Lake." She stood back. "Won't you come in?"

He passed by her, and once more, she was struck with how large he was. At least three inches over six feet and broad everywhere.

Closing the door, she asked, "What position did you play in football?"

"Tight end," he told her. "And don't check out my ass."

She felt her face grow hot at his teasing, mostly because she'd done that very thing as he'd entered the house.

"I never heard of a tight end," Nova admitted. "I know nothing about sports."

Rubbing his hands together in glee, Cole smiled. "We'll have a little tutorial during dinner. Just to get you familiar with what Leo will be up to on the field."

"Will there be a quiz after?" she asked, flirtation in her voice.

"What kind of teacher would I be if I didn't test you on your knowledge?" he asked, his voice dropping.

Leo entered the room. "Hey, Coach."

Her son's appearance broke the curtain of innuendo hanging over the room, and Nova went to the kitchen, finding a vase to put the flowers in and setting them on the kitchen table.

"Can I do anything to help?" Cole asked.

"Not a thing. You can have a seat at the table," she replied. "I had just taken up the okra when the doorbell sounded. The corn is ready, I'm sure."

Quickly, she dished out things while Leo poured iced tea for the three of them. They spent an enjoyable half-hour, Cole and Leo explaining the rules of football and the various positions to her.

"It's not as hard to understand as I thought it would be," Nova mused. "Actually, it makes sense."

"The next game that comes on, you can watch it with me, Mom," Leo told her. "Maybe even Coach could come, too, and help explain things."

Her gaze met his. "Would you have time to tutor a parent? I know your season is coming up."

His smile made her toes curl. "I'll make time. You'll need to come watch our first scrimmage. And you definitely need to join the booster club."

"Sounds like I might be getting in over my head," she complained cheerfully.

"It would be a good way to meet the other parents," he told her. "Being new to town—or at least after leaving a decade ago—it'll be nice to make some friends, as well as get to know the parents of the guys Leo hangs out with."

"I do plan to come to all his games," she said, seeing the look on her son's face. "And yes, Leo, I know you might not get a lot of playing time. I can still watch and learn and meet new people."

Nova looked at their cleaned plates, both having eaten second helpings of everything. "Ready for dessert?"

"We are," Cole said. "But you'll have to earn yours." He glanced to Leo. "We need to quiz your mom now. Dessert for her, at least tonight, will need to be earned."

He grinned. "I'll go type up a few questions, Coach. Be right back."

She watched her son leave and then said, "I haven't seen him this happy in years. I thought he liked Austin and his school, but he did spend the first five years of his life in Sugar Springs. Maybe he heard the inaudible call of the town, whispering for him to come back to her."

"That's a very romantic notion. Are all artists romantics?" He reached and took her hand, his thumb circling lazily, bringing a rush of chills down her spine.

"I think some are," she said carefully, not wanting to sound as breathless as she was. "But that's a generality. Could you say all athletes are pragmatic?"

His thumb now rubbed back and forth, the motion lulling—and exciting—her. "I think a good portion of them are. But the great ones? They're the dreamers. They dream of the opportunities they want to grasp and go after them. They push themselves to their limits and beyond, urging their teammates to do the same. And when they taste victory, they know they have made it to Valhalla."

"Valhalla? Are you sure you aren't a history teacher instead of a coach?"

He moved his hand away, returning it to his lap. Disappointment flooded her, but then again, Leo could come back at any moment. She didn't know how her teenager would react to his new coach touching her as she swooned.

"I've always enjoyed history. I was a terrific student. Liked reading and history. Good at math. Was attracted to and taught science because of its practical nature, which just made sense to me. What classes did you enjoy in school?"

"I was actually homeschooled until I started high school, so I had no classmates and no true classes. I was pretty advanced, though, which is why my parents gave in and let me attend the public high school. They couldn't teach me anymore. I'd outgrown everything they knew."

"Did you meet Leo's father there?" he asked quietly.

"No." Thoughts of Ace left a bad taste in her mouth. "I'd rather not talk about him. He's dead. He died... right before I learned I was pregnant."

Sympathy filled Cole's eyes. "Oh, Nova. I'm so sorry. You really were alone, weren't you?"

"I had Rain. Rain was all I needed," she said stubbornly.

"Does Leo know anything about his dad?" Cole prodded gently.

"He knows we weren't married and only knew each other

briefly. That we were both teenagers when I got pregnant. He does know his father was killed in an accident. I owed him the truth. That's the very least I could give him." She paused. "What about you? You said your mom left. What about your father?"

He shrugged. "I know nothing about him. Penny and Aunt Ju were in foster care. Their parents died when they were so little, they couldn't remember them. No relatives to adopt them. They became wards of the State of Texas. Grew up in foster homes. Aunt Ju had started college and moved to the dorm, while Penny was still in high school."

He paused, and she asked, "You don't call her Mom?"

"How can I? She abandoned me a few hours after I was born. We've never heard from her in all these years. When I do think of her, she's this vague, shadowy figure. Aunt Ju didn't have any pictures of them growing up. I guess foster parents don't really care to preserve their charges' memories."

Cole tossed his napkin on the table. "Aunt Ju is my mother in every sense of the word. She's just never wanted the title. We're all we have, as far as family goes. Now that I have a head coaching position, I'd love to sweet talk her into moving to Sugar Springs. I doubt she'll do it, but after I get established, I'm going to ask her to do so."

"Okay, I've got ten questions for you, Mom." Leo entered the kitchen. "Look over these, Coach, and see what you think."

Nova watched Cole Johnson read the page, his brow furrowing slightly. Her attraction to him was off the charts. She told herself to rein it in.

For Leo's sake.

He smiled up at her son. "Looks good, Leo. Ask away."

"I started easy, Mom, but they get harder. I hope you were listening carefully."

She answered questions about how to score different kinds of points and what needed to happen to earn a first down. When a team should punt and the situations when they should go for it instead of punting. Her final question was about timeouts, and she answered it with confidence.

"Way to go, Mom!" Leo praised. "You aced your test."

Hearing that caused her heart to ache a bit. She had never shared with Leo that his dad was called Ace. She'd only known that nickname and never learned what his given name had been.

Still, smiling brightly, she said, "Then I suppose I earned my brownie. Maybe two?"

"Definitely two," Cole said, laughing.

"I'll get them," Leo volunteered, bringing back the pan and a knife and then retrieving plates while Nova sliced them generous squares.

Cole sank his teeth into one and sighed. "That is one amazing brownie," he said. "I mean, it's *really* good."

"It's Rain's recipe," she shared.

"I'm sorry I never met her," the coach said quietly. "You both must miss her a great deal."

She gestured around them. "Rain is everywhere in the house. Her imprint is in the color of paint on the walls. In every rug and piece of furniture. Living here, I think we'll feel wrapped in her love."

They finished dessert, and Leo said, "I'll go get Rain, Mom. It's almost seven. We need to get to the lake."

Once Leo vanished, Cole said, "You have a lot to be proud of, Nova. Your boy is a good one. I've been around kids a lot, both in the classroom and on the playing field. He's definitely first class."

"Thank you," she said, her eyes misting with tears. "I meant what I told you earlier. Leo is all I have that's worth anything to me. I just want the best for him."

Cole looked at her a long moment. "I hope you both find what you're looking for in Sugar Springs."

6

—————

After Leo mentioned they'd need to take the canoe and oars, Cole offered to drive them to Sugar Lake in his truck. He was venturing into new territory with Nova and Leo. While he'd gotten to know a good number of his student athletes' parents, he had never considered dating one of the moms.

And yet that's what was on his mind right now.

Cole had never been a big dater. He'd put a lot of hours into athletics and academics as a student, as well as doing chores for Aunt Ju on the ranch. High school dates had been more group gatherings, where a half-dozen to a dozen friends would grab a meal or drive around together. Yes, sometimes couples paired off. He'd been among them from time to time.

College meant even longer hours at football practice, from team and position meetings to actual practice and reviewing film. Once that was done and he put in the hours needed to study for his classes, not much time had been left over for socializing. The closest he came to a relationship was his senior year in college when he was rehabbing his injured knee. One of the trainers at the campus rehab center had been cute and friendly. He'd spent long hours in her company at the health facility, which had turned into steady dating for the rest of his senior year. When they both graduated the following May, though, she'd taken off for a master's sports program in California at UCLA, and Cole had never had any further contact with her.

He'd gone out every now and then when other coaches set him up. Usually, that was with a sister or cousin or some friend. He'd never dated a parent before, though. Then again, the high school kids he coached didn't have parents as young as Nova Turner.

Was he crazy to even think something could work between them?

Leo placed the last of the oars into the bed of Cole's truck. They'd already secured the canoe. Nova stood watching them, holding a small urn which contained the ashes of her aunt and the bouquet of flowers he'd brought. She had asked if he minded if they used the flowers as a send-off to Rain, and he had quickly agreed to the idea.

Leo climbed into the back of the truck, leaving Cole to open the passenger door for Nova.

"I can take those," he said indicating the urn and flowers.

"Okay." She handed the items to him as she got in and buckled her seatbelt. "I'll hold them now."

He returned both to her and climbed behind the wheel of his truck. Nova gave him directions to Sugar Lake, and they reached it fifteen minutes later. Cole helped Leo retrieve the canoe and oars, and they took everything down to the water's edge, Nova following behind.

Cole climbed into the canoe with his oars and explained to her that he and Leo would take the bow and stern seats in order to row, while she would sit in the middle.

Offering her a hand, he helped her into the canoe, and she settled on the floor of the small boat. Running a hand through his hair, he said, with second thoughts, "Maybe this is something just you and Leo want to do. After all, I didn't even know Rain."

She gazed up at him. "No. Come. Please."

"All right," he said, glad she had agreed to him accompanying them onto the water.

Leo pushed the canoe deeper into the water and jumped in, beginning to paddle. Cole did the same, and they maneuvered the small boat toward the center of the lake.

After a few minutes, Nova said, "This is good. No one is around. We should have privacy."

They pulled the oars into the boat and floated in silence a few minutes. Cole had only been to a handful of funerals and nothing remotely like this, so he would take his cues from his companions.

Then Nova began singing in a low voice, and he recognized the song as *Over the Rainbow*. Leo joined in, and their voices blended together well, harmonizing as he'd guessed they'd done many times.

When the song ended, tears stung at Cole's eyes. He'd never been moved by a song before. Until now.

Leo nodded. "Rain would've liked that." He looked to Cole. "*The Wizard of Oz* was her favorite movie. We must've watched it hundreds of times together. Mom always said Rain stayed an innocent child her whole life."

"You both did justice to the song. I can't remember the last time I heard it, but your version moved me."

"Rain always encouraged people to express themselves in any way they wanted," Leo continued. "Whether it was singing. Painting. Dancing." He grinned sheepishly. "Or naked dancing."

Nova laughed. "Leo went through a stage where all he wanted to do was tear off his clothes and run through the sprinklers in the back yard. Of course, Rain let him." She smiled wistfully. "I'd forgotten about that until now."

"You'll probably recall a dozen more things as the days pass and you think of her," Cole said. "You might want to write them down, so you don't forget."

She nodded. "That's a good idea." She sighed. "I guess we should finish up."

Nova bowed her head a moment, and he knew she was collecting her thoughts.

"Rain, you were a new beginning for me," Nova said, lifting her head, her eyes peering across the water. "I remember the first time I saw you was at a funeral. Your mother's funeral. I overheard someone say, 'That Reba Turner was the death of her mother.' I didn't know what that meant. All I knew was that Grandmother had been very sick for a long time. I was frowning, trying to understand how you could have made someone sick when you weren't even around. You came up and sat next to me. Introduced yourself. I was taken by your long, braided hair and beautiful face and clothes that were different from any I'd ever seen."

She sighed. "You became my first friend, Rain. You taught me about art. You saved me from everything and everyone when you took me in. You changed just as many diapers of Leo's as I did and told him more stories than I ever could. You are so woven into the fabric of my life that I'm not sure where you end and I begin."

Cole reached to cover her hand when a small sob sounded. She smiled up at him through watery eyes.

"Thank you for being my friend. My aunt. My mentor. My sage. Thank you for letting me see there was more to this world and exposing me to so many new and wonderful ideas. Thank you for making Leo and me part of your family. Part of your world."

Nova fell silent, and Leo took up the mantle. "Thanks, Rain, for answering all the silly questions I had and making them seem not silly at all. Thanks for encouraging me. Believing in me. Telling me I could be anyone I want and go anywhere I wish.

Thanks for showing me how to draw and how to think about things. Thanks for... just being you."

Nova turned, handing the urn and bouquet to her son. "There's a small scoop inside. Scatter her ashes and these peonies while I sing Rain's favorite song."

As Leo dispersed the ashes from the urn, his mother began singing a song Cole recognized, though he hadn't heard it in many years. Aunt Ju was a film fanatic and had exposed him to a number of movies over the years. *Beaches* had starred Bette Midler and *The Wind Beneath My Wings*, the song Nova now sang, came from that film.

He listened to the lyrics, the song taking him back to the many times he'd sat next to Aunt Ju as they'd watched movies together. He couldn't imagine the loss Nova and Leo now suffered with Rain's death and felt fortunate Aunt Ju was in perfect health. Still, he could put himself in their shoes and think how he'd feel if his aunt had died suddenly, with no chance of a final farewell. His throat grew thick with unshed tears.

The last note in the song ended, but they stayed on the water, watching the sun slowly set. Once it had, he and Leo took up the oars and rowed them back to shore.

They drove home without conversation, but he could feel a peace had settled over the truck's occupants.

Cole pulled into the driveway and Leo hopped out, gathering the oars. Nova looked at Cole intently.

"Thank you for going. Rain would have liked you."

"I have a feeling I would have liked her, too."

She started to get out of the truck, but he touched her arm. Turning to face him, she gave him a quizzical look.

"I don't know if I should do this, but I'm going to anyway," he said. "Would you... that is, if you're not busy... would you like to have dinner tomorrow night?"

A slow smile lit up her face. "I'd like that, Cole."

He blew out a breath. "Okay, then. Okay. Well, I'll text you tomorrow. To see when. Or where. I haven't been here long. I don't know what Sugar Springs has to offer."

"We could go into Tyler if you'd like," Nova suggested. "If you don't want anyone to see us, that is."

"No, it's not that. Well, maybe," he said. "I've never dated a parent. I don't how that's going to go over in Sugar Springs."

"Then definitely Tyler," she said and then frowned. "Actually, a Friday night in Tyler? We might run into people from Sugar Springs. Why don't you just come for dinner again tomorrow night? Leo told me he's going to eat with some of the new friends he made today. We could have dinner. Watch some TV. Talk."

"Yeah. Okay. That." He raked a hand through his hair. "It sounds like I'm flustered. And I am."

"I fluster you?"

His gaze met hers. "You do."

She blushed. "Okay."

"Let me help Leo."

Cole got out of the truck as the teenager returned and helped him carry the canoe to the back yard.

"Your mom said you made plans with some of the guys you met today."

Leo nodded. "A few of the ones who were shooting hoops. We're going to some pizza place tomorrow night. And maybe I'll make a couple more friends at football practice tomorrow."

"I'm glad you're already fitting in."

"It'll be easier for me than Mom. It's not like she goes to a job every day and meets and sees people. She'll just work from Rain's studio. I want her to get out and have friends. Do things. Not mope about Rain or Jagger." Leo paused. "That's her stupid, cheating boyfriend. He was a huge jerk."

"We'll try to get her involved in the booster club," Cole said. "I've also met a couple of teachers who are close to her age. Maybe I can introduce them to her."

"That would be great, Coach."

Leo accompanied him back to his truck and shook hands with Cole. "Thanks for going with us. I hope it didn't weird you out since you didn't know Rain. But it was nice having you there."

"It was nice being there."

He got into his truck and saw Nova standing on the porch. She raised a hand and waved goodbye, and he did the same.

As Cole drove back to his apartment, he felt on the brink of something. Not just his new position in Sugar Springs.

More like jumping into the deep end with Nova Turner—and not having a clue how to swim.

7

———

Cole was up and out the door earlier than usual. He hit the pavement full-speed, throwing everything he had into his run. Questions kept floating through his head.

Why was he attracted to Nova Turner?

Why was he acting on this attraction?

Would it mess with his head when he needed to focus on his team?

He had always had a great work ethic, courtesy of Aunt Ju. She was organized and could have five projects going at one time, with everything streamlined. He'd learned to do the same. His twenties had been all about establishing himself in his chosen career. Learning as much as he could from the men who taught and mentored him. Going where the most challenging job was and giving it his all, which in Cole's case, meant putting in extremely long hours.

In Sugar Springs, he'd obtained one of several goals he'd mapped out for himself a decade ago, by landing the head football coaching job. The fact the position came with athletic director attached to it made it even sweeter. His love of crunching numbers would come in handy as he helped the staff under him prepare budgets for their athletic programs. In fact, he had wondered if the administrative side to sports might wind up appealing more to him than the day-to-day coaching chores. Being Sugar Springs' AD would give him his first glimpse of that side of athletics.

He'd turned thirty-two almost three months ago and wondered if that had triggered some emotional response in him, the natural response of a man wanting to have a family and home. He had so few material possessions to his name. He hadn't had the time or inclination to have a lasting relationship with a woman. Did men have an internal clock ticking down, making them aware the years were passing and if they were going to start a family, they better do it before it was too late?

Cole liked kids. A lot. He was the kind of guy who naturally got along with everyone. He had enjoyed his time in the classroom almost as much as he did when teaching on the practice field. Teenagers were an amalgamation of so many different things coming together. He liked being there for them. Talking things over with them. Guiding and advising them.

What would it be like to do that for his own children?

He increased his pace as his questions to himself became more difficult, pushing himself to his limits.

Was he meant to be a husband and father? Was Sugar Springs the place he'd take those next steps in his life and find a woman? Fall in love? Have babies?

The pull toward Nova Turner was overwhelming, unlike anything he'd ever experienced. Yet he was reluctant to become involved with her. She already had a child and had gone through all those stages with a baby, toddler, pre-teen, and now teen. Even if he did eventually get together with her, Nova was not just Nova. She was a packaged deal, coming with a teenager. He might have been around and taught teens for a decade, but becoming an instant father to one?

He had no business doing that.

Maybe he should cancel their date.

Or maybe he should go and tell Nova he was just too busy to begin a relationship at this time. Spare her feelings. After all, she was coming off a broken relationship. She probably didn't want to get involved either.

Then why did the thought of pushing her away bother him so much?

No, he would go to dinner tonight. Let things unfold. Take it slowly. Not commit to anything long-term. Tonight would be one of those test the waters and see if going with the flow would work or not.

Cole looked up, not realizing where he was, and had to run another few blocks before he spied something familiar. He never got that deep into his head on a run.

Then again, he'd never been taken with a woman as he had Nova Turner.

He ran toward the high school and quickly showered, shaved, and dressed for the day. He'd already met with Ben Peterson about Leo and brought up the kid's name in the coaches' meeting now.

"We have a new player reporting to practice this morning from out of town," he informed his staff.

"This late?" Ray Barker, his line coach, asked. "Where's he coming from? We have to worry about transfer rules."

"They won't apply in this instance. Name is Leo Turner. Sophomore. Has never played sports before."

A loud round of laughter filled the conference room, and John Peterson said, "You take him on offense, Ben. My defense doesn't need some snot-nosed newbie."

Irritated by the remark, Cole said, "Leo is new in town. He just lost his aunt, Rain Turner."

"Oh, Rain was a nice lady," Ray said. "She's done some really great art pieces for people in town."

"I met Leo and his mom when they were registering him yesterday," he continued. "He may not have played before, but the kid knows football. I met with Ben about yesterday's practice, and he and I agreed that Leo will go out for wide receiver."

"I hope you told him he'll be a benchwarmer," John said.

"He knows he'll need to earn his playing time. I just wanted all of you to be aware of his situation when we start practice today. It's tough being uprooted and moving at that age. He was close to his aunt. We're here not just to teach Leo and the other student athletes about football. We're here to be good role models for them and to teach them life lessons."

John Peterson rolled his eyes. "If you say so, Coach."

"I say we take care of this kid—and all our kids," Cole said firmly, glad that Leo hadn't been interested in playing defense. He would be in much better, more patient hands with Ben Peterson.

Cole went over the practice schedule today, reminding the staff that today was the first person-to-person drills, even though no full contact was allowed yet by UIL rules. He clarified when the breaks would occur and what would be accomplished during the walk-through before dismissing the players for the day.

Ben stayed behind. "I seem to do this a lot, Cole, but I wanted to apologize for my brother. He's been a pain in the ass ever since he came into this world. I know you have to have figured out that he thought Bubba would turn the program over to him. That's why John needles you about everything."

"You have nothing to apologize for, Ben. You've been an exemplary coach. I've enjoyed our meetings and really look forward to working with you this year and beyond. Your brother and I will be meeting after practice today, however. I want to make sure the air is cleared between us, and he knows exactly where he and I stand."

Ben shook his head. "Good luck with that." He hesitated a moment. "Will you keep John on? After this year? I know when Bubba met with us and broke the news about you taking his spot, he told us you were hamstringed because he'd made his decision to retire so late in the year. I know you inherited all of us, and we're not your choice of a staff. Bubba said we'd have to prove ourselves to you by next spring, when you'd be deciding who stays and who goes."

"As to your brother staying?" Cole shrugged. "I don't know him well enough yet to make that kind of call. I'm thinking he'll be the one to pull the pin, though, Ben. I'm sure he already has feelers out now, asking for friends to keep their ears open about new openings."

"Sounds exactly like John," Ben agreed. "I just want you to know I'm happy doing what I'm doing and doing it for you. Frankly, my family is settled here in Sugar Springs. We've been here for ten years. Coaches are usually nomads, traipsing all over the map. My wife and I like this town. I enjoy what I'm doing. I have no aspirations of being a head coach, Cole. I like the responsibility I have."

He slapped Ben on the back. "Let's go have a good practice, Coach."

The two men headed to the practice field, where the morning exercises had already commenced. Cole scanned the field and found Leo. He hoped the kid would fit in and give Nova one less thing to worry about.

When exercises finished, he nodded to Jake and the quarterback said, "Listen up. Coach wants to talk to you."

He stepped to the front and looked out at the JV and varsity players before him.

"Today's our first day of contact in drills. Go easy. Don't kill each other. Remember, we're all on the same team."

A chuckle rippled through the student athletes.

"Come Monday, the pace picks up, gentlemen. We move into the full equipment and full contact period of practice. That means we coaches expect you to be at a competitive, full-speed pace. Walk-throughs will merely be for teaching purposes, to learn the ins and outs of a play. When a play is being run, it's the real deal. Players will be taken to the ground in full tackles."

Cole paused, looking across the field of players. "We'll also switch to afternoon practices since we coaches will be in staff development training for the upcoming school year. If you're working a summer job, I advise you quit it this weekend—because you'll have dead legs when you wake up on Tuesday morning. Practice will run from three-fifteen until seven-fifteen each day. The weightroom will be open for an hour, though, at six every weekday morning if you choose to make use of it. The coaching staff will rotate being present during those early mornings so that you will be supervised. Any questions?"

No one raised a hand, so he finished with, "Two things. We have a new player joining our squad today. Leo Turner. Leo? Where are you?"

Though Cole knew exactly where the teenager was, he looked around and pretended to find him. "Welcome to Sugar Springs. Leo is coming from Austin and will be playing wide receiver on JV for us."

He turned back, scanning the entire group. "Second thing. I want to thank you for welcoming me this week. Bubba Reynolds is a heckuva coach. A legend in the Texas high school coaching world. I am honored to be following in his footsteps and a little bit scared, if you know what I mean."

Cole saw several players nodding. "Sugar Springs has a winning tradition. I plan to build on the foundation Coach Reynolds created. You know from our team meetings that we're keeping a lot of what he did and trying a few new things. What I want you to know is that we're in this together. We are a team. We are a family. We are brothers. Watch out for one another. Take responsibility for your actions. Contribute everything you have—and we can go far this season. Knights on three! One, two, three!"

The team erupted with the yell 'Knights,' and Cole added, "Break into offensive and defensive units. Now!"

The rest of his time at practice went smoothly and when it came close to eight, he moved toward John Peters.

"You've got practice now, Coach. I'm heading in for the last of my new hire training. Meet me at three in my office so we can talk about today's practice. And a few other things."

His defensive coordinator grew defensive. "What other things?" he growled.

Cole smiled. "See you then, Coach."

He spent the rest of his day with Rory and Pam, again eating a lunch delivered from the local diner, which both women praised for its menu variety and reasonable prices. Since they'd been in town longer than he had, he would take their advice and try eating at Ida Lou's in the near future.

He did mention Leo Turner being a new sophomore student, and Rory promised to look for him on her rosters once they received those next week.

"I met Leo and his mom, Nova, when they were registering yesterday," he said casually. "With her being new in town, maybe you two could help welcome her."

Pam laughed. "I can tell you've already forgotten about being in the classroom, Cole. Don't you remember what this time of year is like? Getting your room ready. Making copies. Doing lesson plans. I barely have time to comb my hair—or that of my three-year-olds."

"You're right. This is my first year with no teaching assignments. I do remember how much pressure there is to be ready to go on opening day. No problem. I'm sure Miss Turner will find some people to hang out with."

"Your booster club should be good for that," Rory said. "Lots of parents join those, I hear."

He didn't tell them the problem was that Nova would be so much younger than any other high school parents. He thought now how ostracizing her age must have been while Leo was growing up and how other moms had probably gossiped viciously about her.

They finished with their mandated training, and Joe Bob said,

"Thank you again for taking the job you did at Sugar Springs High School. We'll get you introduced to the entire faculty bright and early Monday morning. See you then."

Cole left for the fieldhouse. He found John Peterson already waiting for him when he reached his office.

"Give me a rundown about practice after I left, Coach."

Peterson did so, with Cole asking several questions, wanting the other man to elaborate more.

"I'm cutting to the chase and telling you what you need to know," snapped Peterson. "If you wanted a minute-by-minute replay, you should've filmed the thing."

Cole rose and closed his door, returning to his seat.

"Oh, boy, I must be in trouble now," Peterson said mockingly.

"Cut the shit," he ordered sternly. "Or I'll cut you lose right now."

Peterson's nostrils flared in anger. "You wouldn't dare let me go. You need me too badly, Johnson."

"What I need are team players," he said sternly. "I expect one hundred percent from my staff and my players, Peterson. We plan together. Practice together. Play together. Sweat together. Succeed—or fail. All together. I won't have anyone—coach or student—being disruptive to my program. And yes, it's *my* program. Bubba Reynolds left the Sugar Springs Knights in my hands. Not yours. Think on that. He must've had a pretty compelling reason to do so."

Anger sparked in the other man's eyes. "You're an outsider. You're in over your head. You're going to ruin this program. Run it into the ground."

"I came from a small town," Cole said evenly. "I *know* small towns. And I know when I see a cancer. You can finish out this school year, but I will replace you as defensive coordinator in the spring, Peterson. You might want to get out your résumé and polish it up because you'll be looking for a new job come next year."

The other coach leaped to his feet. "I—"

Cole stood and cut him off. "You don't want to quit. That won't look good on that résumé. Abandoning your team a week before school starts? Practices already underway? You'll look like a spoiled kid who didn't get his way and stormed off."

He softened his tone. "Stay, John. You're an excellent coach, else Bubba wouldn't have had you on his staff in the first place. See this season through. If you want to leave at semester, I won't stop you. I'll even give you a good recommendation—if you put in the time and energy needed." He paused. "What do you say? Can we be mature about this and do our best over the next few months and then agree to part ways?"

Thrusting out his hand, Cole waited a moment. With some reluctance, John Peterson took it and shook.

"My defense will mop the field. Our opponents won't know what hit them."

"I like the sound of that," he said, hoping Peterson was now on the same page as he was. "And the further we go in the play-offs, the more attractive you'll be to another school district. Maybe even a head job of your own."

Peterson eyed him. "I can go along to get along. But I don't have to like you, Johnson."

"Just don't let it spill over anywhere. In practice. In our coaches' meetings. I don't want these football players or anyone on staff to know of our mutual dislike of one another."

Peterson snorted. "So, it's mutual?"

Cole smiled breezily. "Since the day I walked in, Coach."

That caused the other man to laugh, and he hoped when they parted, it was now on better terms than they'd been during this past week.

He stayed in his office, working on a few things, but keeping his eye on the clock. When it hit five, he left to go home and shower and change clothes. He stopped and picked up a bottle of pinot noir, taking a chance that Nova might drink it. It was light enough, so it would go with practically anything. If she didn't want it, he'd simply bring it home.

His heart hammered in his chest as he eased his truck into her driveway and got out, bottle in hand. Going to the front door, he knocked on it.

Something told Cole whatever happened tonight might change the trajectory of his life.

8

———

Nova changed clothes. Again. She had no idea what to wear on a date.

Was this a date?

Yes. It wasn't a going out in public date. More of a stay in and eat and watch TV together kind of date.

Hell, what did she even know about dating?

Absolutely nothing.

Dating hadn't been part of her world when she'd lived with her parents. The understanding of them choosing a husband for her—despite it being the twenty-first century—had always lingered in the air. She had watched as young women in their congregation had been married off to other members of the church. No dating was involved. Just both sets of parents talking things over between them—and sometimes the groom—and then telling their children what the outcome would be. Some-times, though, it was older men who weren't married and seeking a bride. Those were the ones who had scared her, especially when she saw them talking with her parents after church services and looking in her direction.

Nova had kept to herself when she'd started at the public

high school. Her mother had specifically told her not to encourage friendships with the heathens that attend the school. She didn't sit with anyone at lunch, instead going to the library and reading novels she knew she couldn't bring home. The only interaction she'd had with other students occurred when teachers placed her in a cooperative learning activity. She always pulled her weight in a group and usually more than her weight since others quickly figured out she was smart and would do whatever work needed to get a good grade.

Meeting Ace at the carnival hadn't meant dates. The few times they were together, she would hang around, watching him run a carny game until everything shut down for the night. Then they would talk. And do other stuff. That short week she'd known Ace still seemed like a made-up dream—but Leo was the proof that it had happened.

As far as Jagger went, they just fell into a relationship. The Austin arts community was tight-knit, and she had gone out with groups of artists over the years, for coffee or art showings. Jagger was around a lot. They'd gotten to talking. And then somehow, they'd wound up together. Nova couldn't remember a single time they'd dressed up and actually gone somewhere. To a restaurant. A movie or a concert. Jagger was more about sitting around with a bunch of other artists, drinking, smoking, and talking. Especially since he had very little money, saying he hadn't hit his artistic stride yet. Nova's art and jewelry had paid the majority of their bills.

Why had she wasted her life on a man so self-centered?

"Back to tonight," she said aloud, trying to focus on what to wear when Cole Johnson came over. The football coach had good looks and then some. She thought he would be an excellent coach, one who truly cared for his players. The fact he was coming for dinner again had almost thrown her for a loop. But she wanted to be around him. Talk with him.

Maybe even kiss him...

Nova wondered if kissing might be on tonight's menu for the Sugar Springs coach—or was he even interested in pursuing a relationship? After all, he was new to the town, which meant he had a lot to prove. Having grown up in Texas, though she'd never followed football, she knew most Texans took the game very seriously. Football was jokingly referred to as the state religion.

If they did kiss?

She was sorely out of practice. Ace had been the first boy—man, really—whom she'd kissed. That was so long ago. Jagger hadn't been into kissing much. He was more about touch. Truth be told, Jagger was all about what made Jagger feel good. He'd skimped in the foreplay department with her, letting Nova do most of the heavy lifting when it came to lovemaking.

What if she'd forgotten how to kiss?

The thought horrified her. Yet Cole Johnson *was* a coach. Maybe he could coach her through the experience. That is, if he wanted to kiss her. Which he probably didn't.

"This is so frustrating!" she complained. "What are you thinking, Nova Turner? This is purely crazy talk. The man is coming over to share dinner with you. And talk. That's it. We're both new in town. Just some food and conversation. No expectations beyond that."

She heard the shower go off and thought she better get her act together once her son toweled off and dressed.

By the time Leo appeared in a Knights T-shirt and shorts, his hair still damp, Nova had talked herself into calming down by gathering ingredients for making a salad.

"Hey, Mom." He sniffed the air. "Is that lasagna? Didn't you remember I'm going out?"

Chuckling, she said, "You might be going out, but I still need to eat. I'd already planned for lasagna tonight. I know how you like leftovers. I'm sure by the time you get home, you'll be starving again, and you can pull some out and heat it up for you."

Or not. Cole Johnson was a big guy. He'd probably eat half the pan. How would she explain that to Leo? Or even explain about his coach coming over a second night in a row?

This time to see her.

"About coming home," Leo began. "What's my curfew? I've never really had one before."

That was true. In Austin, her son had been a homebody for the most part. The only times he'd been out late were when he was in a drama production and stayed after to help clean up. The rest of the time, he came home by ten at the latest.

"I suppose we need to set one," she mused.

"Freddie—one of the guys who's a senior—said I needed one. But I don't need to be out late because of football practice."

"You don't have practice over the weekend."

"Jake told me I should keep the same hours during the week and weekends," Leo explained.

"And who is Jake?"

Leo's face lit up. "He's our quarterback. He's a junior and really awesome. He worked with me some on my patterns after practice today. He'll be coming tonight to eat pizza with us, and then he asked me if I wanted to come over after and maybe watch a movie."

"Do you happen to have Jake's parents' phone number?"

"Mom!" he protested. "It's not like I'm five and you're arranging a play date for me."

"But I don't know them, Leo." She paused. "Compromise. Have Jake's mom or dad call me once you get there. Just so I can introduce myself and say hi. Besides, I'll need to know where to pick you up."

"Jake said he could take me home. He has his own car since last spring. A vintage Mustang he and his dad restored."

Nova wavered. "Okay. Jake can bring you home. By eleven at the latest. But I still want you to call me when you get to his house, okay?"

He smacked her cheek. "Okay, Mom. You're the best."

His phone dinged and he pulled it from his pocket. "The guys are here. Gotta go, Love you."

Leo was out the door in a blur. She went to the window and watched him amble toward the car sitting in their driveway. She could see a driver and someone in the passenger seat. Leo waved and then reached the car, getting in. As the car pulled out of the drive, she could see another boy in the back seat.

"My boy's growing up," she said softly.

She hadn't seen much of him during this past summer, thanks to the job he'd held and the play practice he'd put in for a local community theatre group. Leo hadn't had a part in the production, but he'd been on the lighting crew, so he'd attended every rehearsal and performance.

Nova wondered if this was how high school would be. Leo, coming and going, headed to school or clubs or football practice or games. Maybe even dates. He'd never had a girlfriend before, but he was a good-looking kid. Some girl here in Sugar Springs would be lucky to land Leo Turner as her boyfriend. Nova figured he'd spend most of his waking hours away from the house and when he was home, he would be studying. He always made top grades, and she couldn't see his interest in school lessening because he now played football.

Tears filled her eyes. Only three more years until he would go off to college. She was determined to see him do so. She still wished she could have had the college experience. Not just taking classes and earning her degree but the social aspects of college. Meeting new people. Making lifelong friends. Dating. Learning about herself.

Yet despite missing out on that typical life experience, Nova wouldn't trade a thousand chances at colleges for what she had experienced in raising Leo. While being a young mother had been difficult, Rain had coached her through the rough patches. Leo had been a joy to raise. Happy and carefree and curious.

Though she had never toyed with the idea of having another

child, especially since Jagger didn't want any, Nova felt the pull of it now. To hold a baby in her arms again. To nurse again. Play peekaboo. Watch as they learned how to walk and talk. Those had been glorious days. Now that she knew what they consisted of, she was better prepared.

Would she ever have an opportunity to have another child?

If so, it would be here in Sugar Springs. This town would be where she put down permanent roots, ones which would last long after Leo went out into the world on his own. She hoped she would become a part of this community. Find friends and clients.

Find herself...

Nova wondered if she really knew who she was. As an artist, yes. As a person? Not so much. For so long, she had been Leo's mom. Then the last few years, she'd been Jagger's partner. Who was she, away from her art?

She was ready to find out.

The doorbell rang, and she took a deep, calming breath as she went to answer it. When she opened the door, the breath whooshed out of her.

Cole Johnson was freakin' hot.

The midnight blue T-shirt he wore only made his sky-blue eyes pop in his tanned face. She caught the light scent of cologne, which revved up the desire that zipped through her like lighting. His jeans were probably a decade old and molded to his muscular legs.

"May I come in?" he asked.

She realized she'd been standing there, gawking, and heat filled her cheeks. "Please do."

Stepping aside to let him pass, she could feel his body heat, which made her own temperature rise a few notches. Quickly, she closed the door, turning and smiling brightly, trying to cover all the multitude of feelings rushing through her.

Spotting wine in his hands, she said, "I see you brought something for us to drink."

"Yeah. A pinot noir. I never did really find out if you like wine."

"I do. A pinot will be great with the lasagna I made. And I was about to toss a salad. Let me finish putting it together for us."

Nova went into the kitchen, telling herself to breathe and slow down, thinking she'd been talking too quickly.

As she began slicing black olives, she said, "No bread tonight. There are enough carbs in the pasta to last me a week. I'm sure you don't fight that problem."

Cole leaned against the counter, his arms crossed, watching her work as she moved to cutting cucumbers. She stole a glance at his forearms, cutting her eyes back, her pulse pounding.

"Actually, when I hit twenty-five, I had a bit of a metabolism slowdown. Friends tell me another one sneaks up on you around forty. But I run daily and lift weights a few times a week. Right now, I can still eat pretty much whatever I want, but I know the day is coming when I'll have to cut back."

The timer went off, and she asked, "Would you grab the oven mitts and set the lasagna on top of the stove? It's supposed to rest a few minutes before it can be served. We can work on our salads in the meantime. And the wine."

She washed her hands as he removed the glass casserole dish from the oven, and then she picked up the corkscrew, opening the wine and pouring glasses for both of them.

He had taken the initiative, carrying the salad bowl and tongs to the table.

"I would've thought Leo would have set it before he left."

Nova worried her bottom lip. "Leo didn't know you were coming."

She set their wine glasses on the table and went to the cupboard, pulling out plates for their entrees and bowls for the salad. Then she removed a homemade salad dressing from the refrigerator.

In the meantime, Cole had located silverware and napkins

and placed each beside their plates. He held her chair for her, causing her pulse to beat faster. The gesture was one no one had ever done for her before, letting her know what a true gentleman this man was.

After she was settled, he seated himself, eyeing the table. "Everything looks terrific, Nova."

He reached for the serving utensil, but she latched onto his wrist. "Wait a minute. Let me explain. Or let's figure this out."

"Leo? Or us?"

She shook her head helplessly. "I am such a novice at this, Cole." She released his wrist. "I feel awkward around you."

"Have I done something to make you feel that way?" he asked gently, his eyes searching hers.

"No. Not at all. I've never really dated. I explained to you about Ace. Leo's father. And the man I was with for a couple of years? We were both artists. We hung out with other artists. We just fell in together somehow. We never really had a date. So being here with you, now, is a totally new experience for me. And the way you reacted before, saying you'd never dated a parent? I didn't know if you even wanted to be seen with me. If it would make things awkward for you. That's why I didn't mention anything to Leo."

She felt tears sliding down her cheeks. "I just don't know what this is. And now I'm acting all high maintenance and you're wondering how fast you can get out of the crazy lady's house and I—"

Suddenly, she found herself in Cole's lap. Her arms went around his neck as she buried her face against him, the tears coming fast and furiously now.

"It's okay," he repeated several times, rubbing her back, smoothing her hair.

Nova lifted her head. He wiped her tears with his napkin and said, "Let's talk it out. So that we're both clear. This is a date. And yes, I did feel a little funny asking you out and then acting weird about it. This is my first head job. I have a lot riding on it, especially in a town where winning is the tradition and trips to the playoffs are expected every year. But I don't want to hide anything. I also want to make clear to everyone that I won't show Leo any favoritism just because I'm seeing you."

She sniffed. "Seeing me implies... well, it makes it sound as if we're dating. This is just a first date tonight, Cole. With me falling apart on you, it's probably going to be a last date, as well."

He tucked a lock of her hair behind her ear. "Don't jump to conclusions. I think it's gone really well so far."

He looked so earnest and serious—and then she realized he was teasing her. Nova burst out laughing.

"Get 'em laughing. That's what Aunt Ju always told me. Looks fade. But funny is forever. If I could make a woman laugh, she said that was the real deal."

Nova stopped laughing, feeling shy around him, and awkward sitting in his lap.

"Let me get up," she said, but his arms tightened about her.

"Stay," he urged. "Let's finish talking. I was saying we'll be transparent. People will know we're seeing each other. Hell, I'm from a small town. You can't keep anything quiet, especially a relationship."

Nova arched her brows. "So, we're now having a relationship?"

"If you want."

His words hung in the air between them. Then she didn't know if she moved toward him, he moved to her, or they met in the middle—but they were kissing. A soft kiss. A sweet one. One which lingered. One which spoke of unspoken promises.

Cole broke the kiss. "I like you, Nova. A lot. And I barely know you. I feel a connection between us. I did from the moment we met. Is that crazy?"

"No," she whispered. "I felt it, too. And I never have, so I didn't know if it was only me or if it might be real."

He grinned. "Oh, it's real. Definitely real." He kissed her softly again. "I'd like to do more of that, but the smell of your lasagna is about to make my stomach growl."

She laughed, an open, free laugh that made her feel young. Pushing off him, she picked up the server and cut him a generous portion.

"I hope you like it. Another recipe of Rain's which Leo and I enjoy quite a bit."

While she served herself a piece, Cole filled their bowls with salad.

"Do you think Leo will feel awkward if we're seeing each other?" he asked, taking a bite of the lasagna and then moaning. "Oh, this is amazing."

"Thank you. Leo is a really chill kid. As long as we don't make out in front of him, I think he'll be fine."

Cole smiled lazily. "We're gonna make out after dinner. Just to let you know."

Her heartbeat doubled. "As long as you don't eat too much lasagna and fall asleep on me."

Reaching for her hand, he entwined their fingers. "I don't think you'd ever put me to sleep. Not the way my heart is racing now."

"Is it? Mine is, too," she admitted.

He brought her hand to his lips and tenderly kissed her knuckles before releasing it. "Let's do justice to this meal."

After that, they talked easily. He liked country music. She liked rock and pop. He was fascinated by history and numbers. She loved all the performing arts. They both enjoyed movies, though he preferred going to the cinema and she liked watching at home from her own sofa.

"But you miss all the big screen wonder," he chastised. "The sound surrounding you. And, of course, the movie theatre popcorn."

Nova countered with, "The seats are never comfortable, and I always wind up in one which squeaks. The popcorn is so over-priced. I pop a way better batch."

"I'll hold you to that," he said, his eyes darkening. "Let's clean up."

"Don't you want seconds? Or dessert?"

"You need to save something for Leo. When does he get home?"

"He's eating pizza with a big group of guys and then going to Jake's house to watch a movie."

Cole nodded in approval. "Jake is our quarterback. He and Leo got along really well. They stayed after practice and ran a few routes, working on their timing. They really seemed to click. If I hadn't known Leo hadn't played ball before, I would never have guessed from what I saw on the field today." He paused. "As for dessert?

"I'm looking at it."

9
____

Nova shivered at those words. She'd almost forgotten how attracted she was to Cole as they'd eaten dinner because the conversation had been quick and fun. They had several things in common and those where their interests or opinions varied? It didn't seem to matter. Cole Johnson was someone she wanted to hang around with. Be friends with.

Be more than friends.

Obviously, he was now thinking about seeing if they had chemistry together. At heart, she was a rom-com fan, always loving how those films tugged at her heartstrings and put her in a sentimental mood. She had never thought that was real life, though.

But could it be?

She stood. "I'll clean up. You're company."

He rose. "I'll help. I don't want to be treated like company. Company only comes around every now and then." His gaze intensified, causing heat to rush through her. "I plan to be a frequent visitor."

Flustered, she nodded, picking up her plate, salad bowl, and silverware and taking them to the sink. Cole followed with the same, stacking his items on top of hers.

"You rinse and put 'em in the dishwasher the way you like. If I learned one thing from Aunt Ju, it's that women have their own system of loading a dishwasher—and men have yet to crack the code. I'll clear the rest of the table."

He retrieved the lasagna and salad, covering the lasagna with foil and placing it in the fridge. Nova directed him to a smaller container, and he placed the remaining salad in it and popped on the top, putting it away.

"I'll take our wine glasses into the other room," he said, skillfully grabbing the stems of both in one hand and picking up the bottle with the other.

By the time she finished up and washed her hands and joined him, he'd already poured them both another glass of wine.

"Two's my limit," he shared as she sat next to him, and he handed her a glass. "There's a little more in the bottle. You're welcome to it."

More than anything, she wanted to keep her head and said, "I'll be fine with this."

Cole tapped his glass against hers. "To us—and whatever lies ahead."

"To us," Nova echoed, growing still as she gazed at him.

"Do you feel it?" he asked. "It's... something different."

"I do," she said, nodding her head. "It's a little weird. I don't mean that in a bad way."

"I hear you. Dinner was just so enjoyable. It wasn't like a first date. Nothing's been strained. None of those awkward silences where you're thinking about how soon you can extricate yourself from the situation."

He took her free hand. "I mean it, Nova. This is uncharted territory for me. For us both, if I'm reading you right." He took a deep breath. "I plan for us to go slowly."

"I'm fine with that. Better than fine." She took a sip of her wine. "And I want this to be the first relationship where I don't hold back. Total transparency. Total honesty." She hesitated. "With Jagger, I was always walking on eggshells. He possessed that famous artistic temperament. I kept bad things—sad things—to myself. I didn't want to rock the boat."

He squeezed her hand and she added, "Not that I'm a boat rocker. I'm usually a go with the flow type of person. Very flexible. I think it's the artist in me, always knowing things can change and mutate, and I simply adjust."

"I don't want you to hide your feelings around me," he said. "If you've had a bad day, I want to hear about it." He grinned. "I'm sure I'll have some doozies that I'll want to bitch about. But I always want to know what you're thinking. What you're feeling."

Cole washed down about half the wine in his glass. "I haven't dated much, Nova. I'm not a novice. I just haven't had the time to do so since I got into coaching. Coaching consumes you. It seems like there isn't a minute to come up and breathe and take a moment for yourself. But that's in the past. Yes, I'm going to put in long hours, but I'm going to make a life outside of football, too."

She placed her wine glass on the coffee table and removed his from his hand. "I already think we've made a good start. I've never been this open with anyone in my life. I'm pretty scared going in, but at the same time, I feel safe. Because of you. You make me feel like everything will be fine."

His hands moved to cup her face. "It will be."

He touched his lips to hers gently, feeling his way. She breathed in the tang of his cologne. Felt the calluses on his fingertips against her face. Leaned in, wanting to feel the heat that radiated from him.

Then her cell rang.

Nova leaned back, breaking the kiss. "It's Leo."

"Does he have a nanny cam on us?" Cole joked.

She got up to retrieve her cell from where it sat in the kitchen and caught it on the third ring.

"Hey, Leo," she said, walking back into the room and returning to the sofa.

"Hi, Mom. Just letting you know I made it to Jake's. The pizza was fantastic. It's a place called Romano's. We've got to order from there." Her son paused. "I told Mrs. Fletcher you wanted to talk to her. Hang on."

She whispered, "Leo calling from Jake's. I wanted to speak to one of Jake's parents."

"Good idea," Cole said.

"Hello?" a voice said.

"Hello, Mrs. Fletcher," Nova responded. "Thank you for chatting with me a moment. Nova Turner."

"Jessica Fletcher. And not the detective from Cabot Cove. My husband and I own the local bakery. Leo told me you wanted to touch base with us. He's a lovely boy. Jake came home talking about Leo and his work ethic on the football field."

"Well, it's his first time playing football. Leo's an excellent student. He does love football. I just wanted to meet you, even if it is over the phone. Being new in town, I know Leo will be making friends. I want to keep up with where he is and who he's with."

"Jason and I are the same way, Nova. Jake is our only child, and I can be a bit overprotective. The boys tell me they'll be watching a movie, and then Jake is going to drive Leo home. I promise he's a good driver. I taught him myself."

"I appreciate that, Jessica. Thanks for chatting with me."

"I'd love to meet in person. Please stop by Rolling Scones, our bakery, anytime. It's on the square. I can always take a break and sit and have a coffee and pastry with you, especially if you'll come after the morning rush."

"I'd like that," she said, feeling good about the impromptu invitation. "I'll take you up on that soon."

"Good to hear. I'll give you back to Leo. Bye."

"Hey, Mom. So, we'll watch the movie and then I'll be home. Probably ten or a little after."

"I'll see you then, honey. Have fun."

Nova ended the call and placed her cell on the table. "Jessica Fletcher sounds lovely. And Leo seemed over the moon. He said he'll be home around ten."

Cole glanced at his watch. "Then we've got a couple of hours of kissing ahead of us."

She thought he might be exaggerating—but Cole Johnson was as good as his word. Nova experienced every kind of kiss imaginable with the handsome football coach. He started gently with light kisses on her lips, teasing, tempting her. His hand settled against her nape, steadying her, as the barrage of kisses came. Some slow and delicious. Some fast and hard. Some insistent. Yet never once did Nova feel pressured to go beyond kissing.

Even if her body was willing to do so.

Cole pulled her into his lap and leisurely explored her mouth, tasting, teasing, showing her he was in no rush. She found herself pushing her fingers through his thick hair, holding onto it, afraid he would let go. Responding to his kisses seemed the most natural thing in the world. Her entire body tingled as she felt the urgency build, the sexual tension growing between them. Her pulse and heart rates skyrocketed. Every nerve in her body seem to light on fire.

Yet he took his time and never once pushed Nova from her comfort zone. He broke the kiss several times, nuzzled her neck or cheek, moving his lips to her ear and teasing her lobe with his teeth and tongue. His hands moved up and down her back without straying to other places. When his mouth returned, fusing to hers, adrenaline shot through her, bringing energy and enjoyment.

Finally, Cole broke the kiss and rested his forehead against hers a moment, reluctant to end the contact between them.

"I'm worn out," he admitted, raising his head and gazing into her eyes. "I've never kissed anyone so long. But it was worth it. You are one helluva kisser, Nova Turner."

Her face flushed. "I followed your lead. I... well, I haven't done much kissing. I've only been with one man besides Leo's dad. Neither of them took much interest in kissing." She touched his cheek with her fingers. "I have to say, I really liked it. Kissing you."

"I liked kissing you," he said, his voice husky. He grazed his lips against hers again and smiled. "I like kissing you a whole lot."

Then he grew serious. "We need to talk before Leo gets home. I'm laying my cards on the table, Nova. I want to continue seeing you. Date you exclusively. But I am at a really busy point in my life. With this being my first head position, it's going to be time intensive. Football season always is, from the summer drills and practice to scrimmages to actual games played. My days will be full and very, very long. I'll need to devote a lot of time to my team and staff. Even on weekends."

She crinkled her nose. "Weekends? I thought games were on Friday nights."

He chuckled. "They usually are, with a few on Saturdays thrown into the mix sometimes. But coaches need to do a post-mortem after a game. Look at game film. Grade each position and know what needs to be worked on with that athlete. Watch more film of the upcoming opponent. Come up with a game plan for the next opponent."

She blew out a breath. "That sounds like a lot of work."

"It is." Cole took her hand. "What I'm trying to say is, I'm interested in you. In seeing you. But I'm not going to be a guy who will be around a lot. If you're looking for someone to come over and hang out with you several nights a week, that's not going to happen. I have a ton to prove to the school board and this town. My entire professional career is riding on how this season turns out."

He shook his head. "I'm saying this all wrong."

She squeezed his hand. "No, you're not. You're letting me know you don't have time for a needy, clinging woman. You have an important job to do. A lot is riding on your team's performance —and yours. You're interested in me but can't be around as much as either of us might like."

He smiled. "You do get it."

"I'm a private person, Cole. I need space. A lot of space. And I've never been clingy. I'm one of the most self-sufficient people you'll ever meet. If anything, I go overboard the opposite way and keep too much to myself."

"I hope you understand that I *will* make time for you. And while it won't be quantity time, I plan for it to be quality time."

She returned his smile. "I can live with that."

He captured both her hands in his and raised them to his lips, kissing them tenderly. "I've dated sporadically. Nothing ever too serious. My twenties were devoted to establishing myself in my career." He paused. "My thirties will be about taking on more job responsibilities—but I'm also interested in achieving a work/life balance. The free time I have, I want to spend it with you, Nova. And Leo."

His words touched her, especially the fact that he was interested in including Leo. Already, her feelings for Cole Johnson were probably stronger than they should be. Yes, she was very much physically attracted to him, but it was also the person he was that made her want to spend more time with him.

"I value honesty. Integrity. Communication. You've shown me tonight the kind of man you are, Cole. If you are willing to give me at least some of your time, I'm happy to explore a relationship with you."

Suddenly, his mouth was on hers, hard and possessive, his arms around her bringing her close. It surprised her—and thrilled her—at the same time.

Breaking the kiss, he said, "I always want to be open with you, Nova. If at any time, this isn't working for you, let me know. Give me a chance to remedy what's wrong. And then if you wish to walk away, I'll understand."

Thinking that was only fair, she said, "I'll ask the same of you. I think you're a man who can teach me what a true relationship can be like." She paused and grinned. "And also teach me about football, of course."

He laughed, kissing her again. Then she heard Leo's key in the lock, and she broke the kiss, smoothing her hair.

Her son entered the room and spotted them on the sofa, a quizzical look crossing his face.

"Coach?"

"Hey, Leo. Would you have a seat, please?"

He looked from her to Cole. "Am I in trouble?"

"No, honey," she quickly reassured him.

Leo sat in a chair. Cole looked to her, and she nodded, sensing he wanted to take the lead.

"Leo, I enjoyed dinner with the two of you last night. So much that I asked your mom to have dinner with me again tonight. We've hit it off pretty well, and I would like to start seeing her."

"Like... dating?" Leo asked, gulping.

"Yes. Exactly. But I want you to be comfortable with that. This is a small town, and I have no intention of sneaking around. Even if I tried, we'd get caught. I want people to know I'm seeing your mom. I need to know if you have a problem with that."

Leo grew thoughtful. "No. I really like you, Coach. And Mom needs someone to be good to her. She's never had that before."

"You may get some teasing from the other guys on the team. Are you prepared to deal with that?"

Leo nodded resolutely. "I can handle that. Anything for Mom."

"Thank you," she said, her eyes misting with tears, love for this boy filling her heart.

"I won't show you any favoritism," Cole continued. "And while I want to have a relationship with your mom, I don't want you to feel left out. Sometimes, we'll want to do something with just the two of us. Sometimes, though, we'd like to include you if you won't be too embarrassed being seen in public with us."

Leo flushed. "No, that's okay. I mean, I could go eat with you or something."

"Good. Because your mom loves you more than anything in the world. I know if I'm involved with her, that means I'm going to be involved with you, too. I just wanted you to know up front and be okay with that."

Leo stood. "I'm good with it, Coach. I won't go advertising it. But if someone asks, I'm not ashamed of it, either."

"If you do get a hard time, let me know. I can step in if I need to."

"Yes, sir."

Cole glanced to her, and Nova asked, "How was tonight?"

Leo spent a few minutes talking about the guys he'd gone to dinner with and how much he liked them and the pizza. He then told them about the movie he and Jake had watched.

"I like Jake. He's really a good guy."

"He is," Cole agreed. "I know he's a year older than you are, but he's a nice kid and a fine leader. Not to mention he's got an arm on him and can throw a ball from here into tomorrow."

Leo laughed. "He does. Boy, he can drill some of those passes. We're going up to school tomorrow to work together."

"I like hearing that you're both taking the initiative," Cole praised.

"I know not ever having played before, I've got some catching up to do." Leo yawned. "I need to hit the sack. Goodnight."

Once the teenager left the room, Cole said, "That went better than I thought it would. Most kids would be mortified to know their coach was involved with their mom."

"Leo has always been the man in the family, even as a young boy," Nova said. "He's very protective of me. I am happy that he didn't seem to have a problem with you being around, though."

She smiled. "As long as we don't go heavy on the PDA in front of him, he should be fine."

He stood and pulled her to her feet, his head dipping to brush his lips against hers.

"Goodnight, Nova. I'll call you tomorrow."

She walked him to the door. "Thank you. For being upfront."

"I'll never lie to you, Nova. I promise you that."

Cole kissed her briefly again and then opened the door. His hand cradled her cheek. "Sweet dreams."

She watched him head down the porch and toward his truck. He waved as he got in, and she returned the wave, watching him back out of the driveway and leave.

Closing the door, Nova leaned against it. While part of her thought it was much too soon to get involved with someone else, a larger part thought it would be foolish to push Cole Johnson away for that reason alone.

She wouldn't think about the future. She would take things one day at a time.

And treasure the times she did get to be with Cole.

10

———————

The following Monday, Nova decided to stop by Rolling Scones and see if she might forge a friendship with Jessica Fletcher. If they didn't have enough in common, at least she would have had a face-to-face with Jake Fletcher's mother. Already, Leo and Jake were spending quite a bit of time together. They had worked at the high school both Saturday and Sunday, Leo explaining to her all about running patterns and timing. He'd even asked if Jake could come over on Saturday night, and she had ordered pizza for them before heading out on a date with Cole.

They had driven into Tyler for dinner and then come back to his place, where they'd watched *Rudy*, which Nova had loved. She found the film inspiring, and Cole extended her football knowledge, explaining why certain plays were called during the movie's game sequences. She didn't particular care for the new Notre Dame coach in the last part of the film, but she adored how the crowd chanted Rudy's name and his teammates stepped up to make certain he was able to play. Nova even leaped off the couch when Rudy sacked the quarterback, adding another word to her growing sports vocabulary and seeing how easy it was to get caught up in the emotions of a game.

Cole had walked her to her car, giving her a lingering kiss, the only one of that night. She hadn't minded because they had talked and learned so much about one another. She wanted their relationship to be more than physical, and it was easy to see how Cole Johnson was the total package.

When she left home this morning, she dropped Leo at Bobby Hilton's house. He was a fellow sophomore and football player and the son of the town's librarian. Leo said Bobby also had an interested in graphic novels and art, and they were going to work on a story idea Bobby had.

Nova drove to the town square and easily found Rolling Scones. She parked her car and entered the bakery a little after nine-thirty, finding the place held half a dozen tables. Only one was occupied with a man perusing a newspaper and sipping on a coffee. No one was in line.

A tall blonde with warm brown eyes met her as she stepped to the counter. "May I help you?"

"Are you Jessica?" she asked. "I'm Nova Turner."

The woman gave her a sunny smile. "I am. And I'm delighted you came in." She waved her hand. "Perfect timing. It's a bit slow now. Come to the back and meet Jason."

She followed Jessica and soon met Jason Fletcher, who pumped her hand enthusiastically.

"Jake is so happy to have met Leo," Jason said. "He's a really nice kid, Nova."

"I think the same of Jake. He's so polite and friendly," she responded.

"Take a break, hon. I'll hold down the fort," Jason told his wife.

"Let's go grab something sweet and a drink," Jessica said.

They settled at a table with coffee for Jessica and hot tea for Nova. Both had chosen enormous cinnamon buns.

After one bite, she sighed. "This is the perfect cinnamon bun. The balance of yeast and sweetness is spot on."

Jessica smiled. "We're known for these buns. Jason and I have tinkered with his mom's recipe over the years."

"Have you owned the bakery for long?"

"We met in college. Both business majors. Then Jason's dad died midway through our junior year. His mom managed to keep things afloat until we graduated. Though Jason had thought to be an accountant, we married and came back to Sugar Springs. His mom took us under her wing and tutored us in the baking business. Baking is as much an art as it is a science. After a year, she turned Rolling Scones over to us and moved to San Antonio to live with her sister. She comes back a couple of times a year to visit."

"I was curious about the name of the bakery," Nova said.

Jessica laughed. "Jason's dad was a huge Rolling Stones fan. So is Jason. It was just a play on the band's name. And yes, you can see in the display case that we do bake scones. We've learned a lot over the years. Added and deleted items. Cakes were the big frontier we conquered a few years ago. And we started carrying different kinds of breads in recent years."

"I saw the zucchini bread. I'll definitely be leaving with some of that," she promised.

They spent half an hour talking. Jessica asked questions but didn't press Nova. The back-and-forth conversation was easy and informative, as Jessica told her about many of the merchants on the square.

"You'll have to come to the booster club meeting tomorrow night," Jessica said. "Almost all the parents join, along with different business owners around town. Football is king in Sugar Springs, though basketball and baseball do have a strong following."

"What does being a member involve? Leo is new to playing sports, so I'm new to anything involving it."

"Basically, the booster club supports the needs or wants the coaches have. Things not covered in the school budget, such as banners hung in the gym for titles won. We fundraise. Accept donations. Work concessions at halftime of games. Prepare team meals before the games or pay for those meals for the players. That kind of thing."

"Sounds like it's a really busy group."

"It can get hectic sometimes, but it would be a good way for you to get to meet the other parents," Jessica pointed out. "Especially with you being new in town. I knew your aunt slightly. Bought a painting from her that hangs in our living room. Leo says you're also an artist."

"I am. I haven't painted in quite a while, but I'm thinking of getting back to that. Mostly, I've been working in pottery and jewelry-making the past several years. Leo and I were living in Austin, and there's a strong support for the arts community there."

"Then it would be good for you not only to make friends but connect with parents who might be potential clients. Have you thought about opening a store in town?"

"No. Not at all. In fact, that idea terrifies me, to be honest. And when would I have time to create things if I'm manning a cash register?"

"It's just a thought," Jessica said. "You wouldn't have to run it yourself. You could hire someone to do so. That would free you up to create your art."

"Hmm. It would be nice to have a space to display my work and sell it." Nova brightened. "And maybe I could do classes in pottery making."

Jessica tapped the table. "Or even painting. My sister went to something in Dallas recently. She got a group of girlfriends together. They sipped wine as an instructor walked them through how to copy a painting. She said it was relaxing and fun."

"I've heard of those wine and painting parties. I know sometimes couples do it. Or people go for birthday parties."

"Even holidays," Jessica added. "You could feature Christmas paintings, for example." She whipped out her phone and began typing. "Here. Look at this website."

Nova accepted the phone and quickly perused the site. It offered many different choices of paintings and stated it was BYOB, encouraging people to bring snacks and their own wine to the painting session.

"This is a really interesting idea," she said, her wheels turning.

"You could have a painting room and also a room to display your own artwork," Jessica said enthusiastically. "You wouldn't have to be open seven days a week. You could work from your own home studio and then maybe hold classes a couple of nights a week or on the weekends."

"This is a fantastic idea, Jessica. I'm going to investigate it. Research some websites." She frowned. "Of course, this is a small town. I don't know how viable it would be."

"You'd be surprised. We have about thirty thousand people in Sugar Springs, Nova. I think it's worth pursuing." Jessica paused. "There is one space empty now on the square, directly opposite Rolling Scones. Let's go peek in the window."

"All right," she agreed, eagerness filling her.

They left the bakery and crossed the square, cutting through the green space in the middle where a gazebo stood. Once they reached the other side, she saw the empty windows.

"What was here before?" she asked as they approached.

"It was a paint store," Jessica told her. "The owners retired and moved near Corpus Christi, where they have grandkids. The local Walmart is where everyone has started shopping to get their paint and hardware supplies now."

Nova peered inside, seeing the size of the space, thoughts

exploding in her head. Rain had left her not only the house but all her savings. Without those funds, she would never be able to explore this kind of idea, which intrigued her more and more.

Jessica pointed to a sign in the window. "This is Tamara Heath's info. She's our local realtor. You should give her a call and at least look at the space."

She took a picture of the info with her cell, and they returned to Rolling Scones.

"I better get back to work," Jessica said. "Will you come to the booster club meeting tomorrow night?"

She provided the time and told Nova it would be held at Romano's Pizza, noting that most people came half an hour before the meeting started to grab a pizza and visit.

"Yes, I'll come. And I'll think about the painting parties idea."

"Good." Jessica hugged her, surprising Nova. "It was so good to meet you. I hope we'll become fast friends, like Jake and Leo."

"I'd like that."

Leaving the bakery, Nova was on a natural high. She had never made a friend outside the art world. Even more so, she was excited about the idea Jessica had provided.

Nova drove home and spent the next several hours studying websites of similar places. Many used the name *Painting with a Twist* or a variation of that, although she discovered that particular name was franchised. She made a list of things that appealed to her. She liked that the classes were limited to a dozen participants usually and no more than fifteen. That would give her time to go around and work with each individual present. They all seemed to involve wine. She supposed while a few people who signed up would be serious about the art they created, most people attended for the camaraderie, being with friends and sipping wine and having a good time.

The prices charged were around forty dollars a person. That meant she could earn between five and six hundred dollars a night if the session filled to capacity. Of course, she would have to provide the paints, brushes, and canvases. But she knew of places she could order in bulk, which would make for a substantial savings.

Most of the pictures participants painted involved landscapes. Flowers, mountains, trees, and water all seemed trendy. Jessica had been right about holidays. Christmas seemed to be the most popular time, with classes painting Christmas trees, snowmen, and reindeer frequently listed. Besides canvases, some classes involved painting porch leaners. Immediately, ideas flooded her for this.

She decided to call the realtor and at least look at the available space to see what she would have to work with. Excitement filled her as she dialed the number.

"Tamara Heath, Heath Realty. How may I help you?"

"Hello, my name is Nova Turner. I've recently moved to Sugar Springs and saw a vacant property on the square."

"Yes, Miss Turner. That tenant left a few months ago. Do you have a store you'd like to open?"

"Possibly," she said, playing her cards close to the vest. "Could I make an appointment to see the space?"

"I'm about to leave for a closing, but I could show the property to you at two o'clock this afternoon. Would that suit you?"

"Yes. I can meet you there."

"Great. Looking forward to it, Miss Turner."

Nova hung up and continued scouring websites, learning what she could about this concept of bringing in non-artists to paint and have a little fun. Immediately, she saw the potential in private parties more than simply being open to the general public. With an open session, you never knew if anyone would walk in. Or worse, you'd be full and have to turn someone away, a person who might never return.

The private party idea appealed to her because she could book groups for events such as date nights, bachelorette parties, children's or adult's birthday parties, and even office parties. She could have baby or wedding showers built around a painting event. It could be a scouting field trip. A girls' night out. A Sunday school party. Even a sports team event to help players bond with one another. The possibilities were limitless.

That's when Nova decided she was definitely doing this. It would still give her time during the day to work on her art, especially with Leo gone at school all day. She could schedule a night or two a week and maybe one private party on the weekend. Once people knew she was here and word of mouth grew, she might even possibly expand. It would mean investing in a website domain and building a website, but she thought it would be worth it, especially if she wasn't going to purchase a franchise. The price on the website for a franchise was more than she was comfortable investing. She would use the concept but put her own spin on things. A franchise was too cookie-cutter for her tastes.

Googling, she discovered no class of this type was offered in Tyler. The closest was in Longview, which was to the northeast of Tyler. So she would have a lock on this area. If she could book three parties a week and earn six hundred dollars each time, even with the supplies she issued to customers, she would claim a healthy profit. She hoped the space on the Sugar Springs town square would have room for not only the painting parties but also displaying her own art.

If this idea didn't pan out, she might go the group and individual art lesson route. Although students were introduced to art in the public schools in Texas, she could provide more in-depth training, especially for those who possessed some talent.

Nova forced herself to go throw a pot out in the studio. Her brain was whirling fast and furiously, and she needed to clear her mind. Pottery was her Zen place, and she soon lost herself in molding a new clay pot. While she enjoyed creating pots with bright colors and detailed decorations, which involved using low-fire clays, these pots always needed a strong glaze because they were not good to be used in water.

This time, she chose a high-fire clay and decided muted tans, blues, and grays would make up the design. High-fire clay pots always proved to be sturdy, waterproof, and she had no trouble texturizing them, one of her favorite things to do with a pot. Since glazes could move when fired, she never glazed this kind of pot, not wanted her images to become blurry.

For this pot, she used her potter's wheel, deciding she would make a vase. While she sometimes employed other methods, especially coiling and pinching, she preferred utilizing her years of experience at the wheel. It had taken years of wheel work for Nova to become skilled, but she'd found the potter's wheel good for both small or large objects. The wheel could be unforgiving, though, making it difficult to rework the clay if she made a mistake early on in the process.

She let her mind wander, allowing the pot to take the shape it wanted to. Much as a writer sometimes heard characters speaking, begging about the ways they should be portrayed on the page, she found the clay would whisper to her. Nova always listened and followed these inclinations, allowing whatever lived innately within her to bring the pot to life.

Once she'd finished it, she fired up her kiln. She'd already decided to make this vase a gift to Jessica Fletcher for inspiring her to pursue something out of her comfort zone. Yet Nova enjoyed working with others and knew this idea of incorporating art into the Sugar Springs community would be successful. She couldn't wait to share this with Cole.

Cole...

Other than Leo, Nova had never had anyone to share things with after she'd left Rain's roof. During her childhood, her parents had erected walls between them and her, never caring about what she did. In Austin, she liked several artists and had become friendly with them, but she didn't share art ideas, afraid someone would hijack them. As far as Jagger was concerned, he never expressed an interest in her jewelry or pottery. He always wanted to talk about his own art. She realized now that he most likely had been jealous of her small successes.

Well, her time for being used was up. She was now living for herself. She wanted to be the best mother to Leo she could be.

And she wanted to share everything with Cole Johnson.

Cole was an excellent listener. Most people didn't know how to listen. They might ask you a question but never truly devoted one hundred percent to your answer because they were thinking about other ways to lead the conversation. Cole truly listened. He was attentive in body language. His eyes never left her face. He would nod encouragingly. She'd never had anyone concentrate solely on her. It was a heady feeling.

Of course, she would also talk to Leo about this new venture. She wouldn't burden him with too many details, however. He was starting a new life himself here in Sugar Springs, with a new school and friends and his participation in sports.

Glancing at the clock Rain kept in the studio, she saw she needed to freshen up in order to meet Tamara Heath. Nova pinned up her hair and jumped in for a quick shower. She put on a sleeveless, linen shirt and pair of capris and then headed toward the center of town, parking several doors down from the empty pad site. She saw a thin woman with short, brown hair standing in front and headed toward her.

"Tamara?" she asked. "I'm Nova Turner."

A professional smile appeared as the realtor offered her hand. "So nice to meet you, Nova. Welcome to Sugar Springs."

She explained how she and Leo had recently moved to town, taking over her aunt's house and studio.

"Oh, I knew Rain." Tamara paused, studying Nova. "I can see a bit of you in her. Rain was so talented. Are you an artist as she was?"

"I am. She was a far better painter than I am, but I also make pottery and jewelry."

"Oh? Is that why you want to see this place? We have a few stores along the square that are boutiques."

Not quite ready to share her plans yet with a stranger, Nova said, "I'm thinking about having a definitive space to display and sell my work. That's why I wanted to see this spot. Jessica Fletcher recommended it to me."

"Oh, Jessica's son and mine are friends. My boy is Tim."

"Does Tim also play football?"

Tamara laughed. "Not on your life. Tim is into drama and also competes at speech tournaments. I swear, they're the reason he can argue so well with me. He's either going to be an actor or a hot-shot defensive attorney and sweet talk juries into letting his clients go free."

She laughed. "My son Leo will be a sophomore at the high school."

"Tim is also a sophomore. We'll have to get them together. But for now, come on in and look over the place."

Tamara slipped a key into the lock, and they both entered. She allowed Nova to wander around without talking to her, something she appreciated. She began placing things in her head.

When she'd finished giving it a once-over, Nova said, "Tell me about the space."

The realtor launched into detail, pointing out several features to Nova, including the monthly rent.

"If you have any construction needing to be done or changes to electrical or plumbing, I can recommend people to you."

"Is there a discount if I rent the space for a certain amount of time?"

"Why, yes, that can be arranged." Tamara threw out a few figures.

Though Nova knew spontaneity and business might not mix,

her gut told her this was where she needed to be. It would be in this spot where she would plant her roots in this community.

"I'd like to rent this for two years," she boldly declared.

Tamara beamed. "Then let's go to my office and start on the paperwork, Nova."

11

———————

Cole watched practice, moving from group to group, listening to coaches instruct their student athletes and give feedback. He was impressed by the staff Bubba Reynolds had assembled and hoped he would be able to retain as many of them as he could. Of course, he might change his mind after the season began, but so far, the staff was bright, hardworking, and disciplined.

Even John Peterson.

His defensive coordinator had not given Cole any problems since their talk. While he would never choose to socialize with the man, John did know his stuff and would make an excellent head coach.

Just somewhere other than Sugar Springs.

At least, that's what Cole hoped. If for some reason he had a disastrous season, the school board would cut his contract short and, most likely, tap John, who would be waiting in the wings and no doubt a popular choice to succeed Cole.

He moved to the sidelines and glanced to his quarterbacks now. Jake Fletcher was a terrific athlete and natural leader, but he also thought Bobby Hilton had a good arm on him. Bobby was a sophomore who would be the starting quarterback for the JV team this year and was proving to be an excellent backup to Jake Fletcher. With his team and staff being smaller than what Cole was used to from his previous two positions in larger high schools and districts, he would have a good portion of the JV—if not all that team's players—suit out for varsity games, as well. After all, Jake had been the JV quarterback last year until an injury had him step onto the field and guide the Sugar Springs Knights in their last game of the season and into the playoffs. If Jake went down, Cole wanted Bobby available at a moment's notice.

Fortunately, he sensed no rivalry between the two quarterbacks. Bobby was eager to learn, whether it was from Jake or one of the other offensive coaches. He had a nice touch with the ball and a good understanding of the playbook. While Cole hoped Jake would remain healthy the entire season, if the scores of games got out of hand in favor of the Knights, he wasn't opposed to sending in players such as Bobby Hilton and others on the JV squad to have them gain some experience at the varsity level.

Turning his attention to his receiving corps, he watched them go through some drills and begin working with the two quarterbacks. What had astounded Cole more than anything was just how talented Leo Turner was. For a kid who had never touched a football before, Leo had great hands and quick feet. More than that, he had an innate sense for where the ball would be. While Cole would definitely place Leo on JV to start the season, it wouldn't surprise him if Leo worked his way up, not only to varsity, but to a starting position by mid-season.

Ben Peterson joined him. "I think my brother is shitting bricks right now. Having passed Leo Turner over to my offense."

Cole couldn't help but grin. "The kid does have talent, doesn't he?"

Ben chuckled. "That kid has great football instincts. A nose for the ball. Actually, I wouldn't mind you trying him at defensive back or safety."

"You want him to play two ways?" he asked.

"Not right away. Talented as Leo is, he's still green—and these are early days in practice. Still, you know we have a couple of athletes who play both ways. It helps them gain experience on both sides of the ball. Leo just seems to sniff out things. That's what a good DB or safety needs to possess." Ben paused. "But I'm not giving him up to my brother just yet. John can eat my dust for now."

He laughed. "I'm sure he's giving second thoughts to having pawned Leo off on you and the offense. Of course, Leo looks good now in practice. But a gameday situation is far different. He may have good football instincts, but he'll be going up against kids who've played the sport eight, nine, even ten years. For now, though? Leo might just be our secret weapon since no one has game film of him. I'm looking forward to seeing what he will do in Friday night's scrimmage."

The two men separated, and Cole went to work with the running backs for a while before making his way over to the linebacking corps. The time passed quickly, and the practice ended.

He gathered the team around, something he always wanted to do at the end of each practice session.

"You looked good out there, gentlemen. Keep studying your playbook. Keep eating right and getting enough sleep. With school starting next week, you'll need to factor in homework and projects to your schedule. You know you have to pass every class in order to play. While I'm all about athletics, I came from a family who put academics first. We believed both were equally important—as well as character. We may not win every game, but each one of you will be winners in life. We'll learn from the mistakes we make and move on. Now go hit the showers, and I'll see you tomorrow afternoon at practice. Knights on three. One, two, three!"

"Knights!" the team roared.

Cole met with his staff in the conference room after the

players had left, and they dissected the practice. He gave them his notes of things he had observed, and said, "I want to make certain that every time our athletes leave the field, it's with a good feeling in their guts and their heads. Teenagers have a tendency to beat themselves up over the smallest mistakes. While it's good they learn from their mistakes, we don't want any of them sinking into any kind of depression over it, which could affect their play and schoolwork."

He glanced around the conference table. "Be sure you speak to each player individually in a practice and give him a compliment. I know it's sometimes hard to find one, but it's important to have that personal contact and keep things optimistic and upbeat. We're building more than a football team here, gentlemen. We're building young men and giving them the tools to be the best people they can be in life. On *and* off the playing field."

Cole was pleased to see several coaches nodding in agreement.

"Thanks for today. I know we're heading into long days and nights now, and you've got classrooms to get ready, as well as these players. If you are ever struggling with anything—a player, time management, whatever—talk to me about it. I've been in your shoes, and I know the pressures placed upon teachers and teachers who are also coaches. I want to make certain you're physically and mentally healthy, and you get to spend at least some time with your families. See you tomorrow."

The staff filed out of the conference room, and Cole headed to his office, where he typed up a few notes regarding the practice and ideas he'd had for a few new plays. As he finished, his phone chimed. He saw a text from Nova.

Hope it was a good day of teacher training and practice for you. Leo is inhaling his dinner, and I can tell he will fall into bed soon after.

. . .

HE SMILED, reading her message, liking the fact that she put no demands on him to come over. Still, he needed to see her tonight. Even if just for a few, brief minutes. Nova Turner was quickly becoming as necessary to him as the air he breathed.

He responded to her text.

> Need to finish up here and shower. Could I stop by for five or ten minutes?

COLE SENT the text and waited. Immediately, he received a reply.

A thumbs up emoji. Grinning, he set down the phone and headed for the showers.

Twenty minutes later, he was headed to Nova Turner's house. It didn't take long to reach it, and he pulled into the driveway. He caught sight of her sitting on the porch swing and quickly got out of his car, joining her.

"Hey," he said softly, slipping an arm around her shoulders.

"Hey, yourself."

He sighed. "This is by far the best part of my day today," he told her.

"I know it was a long one. All these days will be for you."

"Mmm-hmm."

She rested her head against his shoulder, and they sat in silence for a few minutes. He soaked up the warmth of her next to him. The subtle scent of jasmine coming from her skin. He took her hand and laced their fingers together.

"I run on about four hours of sleep during football season," he said. "It may be less with me being the head coach now."

"At least you won't have lesson plans to write and papers to grade," she offered.

"You're right. I'll want to keep that in mind when I give my staff assignments. When you're a football coach in season, it's like having two fulltime jobs. You wear your teacher hat and jump through all the hoops regarding that job, then you swap it out for your football cap and all the responsibilities to be seen to in that role. Enough about me. How was your day?"

Nova sat up but continued holding his hand. "Well, it was actually pretty eventful. On the creative side, I made and fired a new pot."

"I want to watch you work sometime," he said. "See what the process involves in making pottery. Or jewelry. You always wear unusual necklaces and earrings. I'd like to see how you go about putting them together."

"Thank you for taking an interest in what I do, especially since you're so busy with what's on your plate. But I have even bigger news."

He sensed the excitement running through her and asked, "Have you decided to go back to painting? I know you mentioned you haven't done much lately but you'd thought about trying it again."

"A different kind of painting." Her eyes lit up, and her tone turned enthusiastic. "I did something today, Cole. Something that a methodical, practical person wouldn't have dreamed of committing to, but I've learned to be spontaneous in my art and trust my intuition. I think the decision I made today—a life decision—could be a whole new start of something for me."

She talked of meeting Jessica Fletcher for coffee and how Jessica had mentioned an empty spot on the square, suggesting Nova might want to display her work there.

"Rain never had that," she said. "She would either have people over to her studio to view paintings, or she would sell them through art shows, trade days, and craft fairs in the area.

Occasionally, she might take up a commission from someone who wanted something specific painted. But she never had a dedicated space in which to sell her art."

"So, have you decided to rent this space?"

"I've already shared all this with Leo as he ate dinner tonight, and now I want to let you know what I'm up to. Have you ever heard of paint and wine parties?"

He laughed. "No, can't say that I have."

She pulled out her cell and brought up a website, asking him to look it over. Quickly, he understood the gist of it as he scrolled through.

"You want to open something like this sip and paint in Sugar Springs?"

"I do. These classes happen usually at night and on the weekends. It would leave me free to create my personal art during the day, and I could display it in this space on the square. At the same time, I could book a party a night or two during the week and maybe one on the weekends."

Quickly, she ran the numbers by him, and he could see how this kind of venture would be profitable if the idea caught on.

"I thought about all the different kinds of circumstances people might want to hold a party." She elaborated on everything from girls' nights out, bridal showers, and birthday parties.

"It could be for all kinds of ages. I've always thought children needed to be exposed to art more than at school. To create art for fun and not necessarily a grade. I might even think about holding after school group lessons. Have a Girl Scout or Boy Scout troop in. That kind of thing."

As Nova continued to talk about the idea, Cole caught her enthusiasm.

"I can see you've given this a great deal of thought."

"I spent all day researching it and creating ideas. Not only for the kinds of private parties I could hold but the different types of paintings. Look at the website again."

She went through it, showing him why landscapes and objects would be so popular and even flipped to a holiday tab. Christmas was, by far, the most popular holiday, but he saw the potential such as couples' nights around Valentine's Day or Halloween paintings for both children and adults.

"The best thing is that Tyler doesn't have any of these franchises, nor do they have anyone using this concept. The closest place is Longview, which is far to the east. If I could start something here, I would really have a corner on the market."

"This would be a lot of fun, and it could grow by word of mouth," he said.

She nodded eagerly. "I thought so, too."

He gazed at her with new eyes. Yes, he had found Nova quite attractive and intelligent. He'd enjoyed the time they'd already spent together. Now, though, he saw in addition to her creative side, she might prove to be a shrewd businesswoman.

Cole cupped her cheek and said, "I am so proud of you. I think it's a fantastic idea with a lot of untapped potential. When do you think you might start?"

"I leased the space today from Tamara Heath, a local realtor. I'm going to have to reconfigure it slightly. I want to add two sinks in the workspace. The only one is in a restroom in the back. I'll need to have a couple of larger ones put in for washing brushes and hands. I also need to think about the design. Most of these places hold classes in a U-shape so the instructor can move around easily. At the open part of the U is where the painting is displayed, the model the students go by. Tamara gave me names and numbers of a plumber, electrician, and even a handyman. I'm meeting with the first two tomorrow. The handyman the following day. I want to have the store painted and spruced up a bit. Put my mark on it. Right now, I'm working on designing a business logo. Trying to come up with the perfect name."

"You'll definitely need a website. That'll be the way to advertise and book parties. If I can suggest something, you might want to contact the tech teacher at the high school. Kids today are so bright, you might find one who could build and run your website for you and not have to worry about that end of things."

"A website will be key in getting the word out. That's a great idea to use a student to help with that."

He leaned in for a kiss, making sure to keep it tame and not start up something. He'd had a long day. Besides, he still needed to think how to approach things with her having a teenager in the household.

Cole broke the kiss. "I would say we both had terrific days, but I'm going to need to go."

She touched her fingers to his cheek and caressed it. "Thank you for coming by. I know I can't expect this every night, but I'm so glad I was able to share with you this new venture. I didn't need your approval, but it's nice to get it, all the same."

"Walk me to my car?" he asked, pulling them both to their feet.

They strolled the short distance to his truck, and then he framed her face with his hands, giving her one last, sweet kiss.

"I won't be able to see you tomorrow night," Cole told her. "We're actually cutting practice short because of the booster club meeting."

Nova smiled. "Yes, I know all about it. Romano's. Seven o'clock." Her eyes twinkled as she added, "I'll be there."

12

Nova didn't know how to dress for the event she was attending. Just thinking that let her know she was back in a small town. Rain hadn't really cared for what others thought and had tried to impress that on Nova when she'd arrived at her aunt's door all those years ago. Then again, Rain was the most bohemian woman Nova had ever encountered. It had been culture shock to come from her fundamentalist parents' household, where no emotions were ever displayed, to Rain's, where emotions ruled the day. While her parents had been secretive and never confided anything, Nova found herself almost knowing too much about Rain's life.

For one thing, her aunt had never lacked for a lover. Rain was discreet, but she was rarely without a man in her life. When Nova had asked if she'd ever gotten serious with anyone, Rain laughed and said she wasn't serious with any of them. She didn't want anyone or anything to ever tie her down. Nova remembered she must have looked crushed at that proclamation because Rain had immediately assured her that attitude did not include Nova and her soon-to-arrive baby. Rain said family mattered—and that they were family and her top priority.

Rain had been good to her word. Nova never felt as if she and Leo were a burden to her aunt. Rain spent quite a bit of time with them both. While she continued seeing different lovers, that never interrupted or interfered with family time. Nova, upon leaving for Austin and its free-spirited ideas, had never quite leaped onto that bandwagon. She did think family was the most important thing, but she couldn't quite bring herself to taking lovers left and right for pure pleasure. Even committing to Jagger had been a huge deal for Nova. Sadly, she realized now that Jagger never truly had committed to her, much less Leo. She was better off without him.

Especially with Cole Johnson in the picture now.

Nova had never been the kind of woman who considered she needed a man to be happy. She truly believed she could have come to Sugar Springs and made a life for herself and Leo without ever having thought of dating, much less being in a relationship. That's why her sudden spontaneity to agree to seeing Cole had surprised her. So had their instant chemistry. Yet she understood what they seemed to have ran deeper than the physical. How deep, she didn't know yet. How long it would last, she couldn't say.

For now, she would enjoy when she could be with him. Take things one day at a time. See if they both wished to take it to a different level, both physically and beyond.

She was interested to see how Cole would be tonight. Their interactions had been almost exclusively one-on-one, with a few times of Leo being thrown briefly into the mix. Their one dinner with the three of them together had proven more successful than all the times put together when Jagger and Leo had been in the same room with her. The moody artist usually ignored her son, while Cole had done everything possible to include Leo in the conversation. The two had even bonded over their knowledge of football and how they would teach her about the game.

That's why she knew tonight would be important. She wanted

to watch Cole in his element, around other coaches and parents. She was curious to witness how he would present himself. His manner. His speech. This would give her a glimpse into his life and how he handled other people. She hadn't voiced it, but it would be a test—if Cole could be the same person with others as he was with her. She had never liked pretension in any form. Cole had been honest and open with her. Would he be the same with others? Or would he need to be more guarded? She was curious what his professional persona would be like.

At the same time, she was a bit worried about tonight's meeting. Not for Cole.

For her.

This would be her first true introduction into life in Sugar Springs. She had filled her tank with gas once they'd gotten to town and shopped at the local grocery store, restocking the fridge and pantry since Rain wasn't much of a cook and survived on green tea, protein shakes, and takeout. She'd also gone to Walmart and stocked up on basic household needs, such as toilet paper and paper towels. Her interactions with the clerks had been brief, though.

Tonight would be different. These would be the parents of Leo's teammates. Rain had told her years ago that some people couldn't help but be gossips and judgmental, and small towns had their fair share of those people. Nova expected to be gossiped about. First, because she was new in town. Some would pump her for information because they were merely curious about her and Leo and wanted the scoop about why she'd moved to East Texas.

Then there would be the group who gossiped for pleasure. Her age alone would make her a target of those people. She would have to think how much she truly wanted to reveal and what she wished to keep to herself. While she had wanted Cole to know her backstory, she didn't feel the need to be an open book to every citizen of Sugar Springs.

At the same time, she would soon be operating a business here, one which she needed to succeed if she were going to be able to send Leo to college. She didn't want her son drowning in debt, taking out thousands of dollars in loans in order to pay for his higher education. While she made a decent living off her art and could pay the everyday bills—especially since she had no mortgage—it didn't leave much for college savings. She was going out on a limb and using a good chunk of what Rain left her in renting the site on the town square.

She supposed she would think of herself as a highwire act. It would be a delicate balance in trying to fit in with the other parents, share a bit of her background, and hope to make connections which might lead to being able to book painting parties down the road.

A thought struck her. At some point, it would come out that she and Cole were seeing one another. That might lead to a torrent of gossip. She hoped she had enough resolve to weather whatever storm brewed among the town's gossips. At least she'd made a friend in Jessica Fletcher and hoped she might have another one in the librarian, Ruth Hilton. Both women would be present tonight and with Leo becoming friendly with these women's sons, she might be thrown together with them more often than not.

Glancing back at her closet, she decided to wear a sundress. The meeting was certain to be casual, but she didn't want to underdress and wear shorts or capris. A casual sundress was a good compromise, especially in the August heat. Today had topped out at just over one hundred and two degrees, and she'd tried not to worry about Leo practicing in this heat.

Nova slipped into the sundress and spritzed on a bit of perfume. She rarely wore makeup but put on a matte lipstick that gave her a more polished look. She exchanged the earrings she wore for a dangling pair that went well with the sundress and also placed the matching necklace she'd crafted around her neck.

As usual, she left her fingers and wrists free of adornment. She never wore any jewelry on them when she worked, not wanting to damage them with clay or paints.

Fluffing her hair a bit, she went to the kitchen to retrieve her car keys and found Leo there, guzzling from a water bottle. He was dripping with sweat and smelled exactly as a teenage boy who'd been at football practice would.

The bottle empty, he lowered it and wiped his mouth with the back of his hand, giving her a lopsided grin. "Hey, Mom. You look pretty."

"I'm going to the booster club meeting soon. I thought I was supposed to pick you up from practice."

He shrugged, refilling the bottle and then downing the entire contents again before he spoke.

"Jake gave me a ride home," he explained. "He said he can do that instead of you picking me up. It's not far out of his way to drop me off."

"You and Jake are becoming good friends."

"Yeah. He's cool. We're going to get together tomorrow morning so I can work on running some routes and catching his passes. Bobby and another receiver are also coming."

"Who's Bobby again?" she asked, trying to keep straight all the new names.

"He's my quarterback on JV. He'll back up Jake on varsity."

She frowned. "Are you sure you have enough energy to do that tomorrow morning and go to practice in the afternoon?"

"Mom." Leo's exasperated tone sounded like any teenager's on a sitcom. "I can come home and rest after. Eat. Maybe even take a nap. We're meeting at six in the morning, so we'll miss some of the heat. Just for a couple of hours. Please?"

Nova ruffled his damp hair. "All right. I just don't want you to push yourself too much."

He grinned. "All I want to do is push myself. I've done it academically. In my art. In the play last year." He paused. "I think I'm a pretty good receiver, Mom. Jake and Bobby think so, too."

"But you haven't been playing that long, honey."

His grin grew cocky. "Some people just have natural talent," he said, pretending to boast.

"Well, some people need to get in the shower before my kitchen begins to stink to high heaven. By the time you're out, I'll have dinner ready for you."

"K."

She had made stew in the slow cooker and sliced several pieces of sourdough bread, slathering them with butter and popping them in the microwave. Several minutes later, Leo joined her again in the kitchen, and Nova heated the bread as she dished up a large bowl of the stew.

"There's more in the slow cooker if you want it. Bread, too."

"This is great, Mom. Can I have a few of the guys over soon and you cook for us?"

A pleased feeling rippled through her. "If you want me to. Just let me know what you want me to make."

"I'll think about it," he said, shoveling a huge bite into his mouth.

"I should be home by eight-thirty. Nine at the latest."

He laughed. "I'll be in bed. I'm beat."

"What time do I need to drive you to school for this extra workout?"

"You don't. I'll jog. It's about a mile and a half. That'll be a good warmup. And Jake'll bring me home. Sleep in."

She kissed his cheek. "See you tomorrow."

Nova drove to the town square, seeing it was crowded. She parked a block off it and walked the short distance to Romano's. When she arrived, she saw a note on the door stating the pizzeria was closed starting at six o'clock for the booster club meeting. Steeling herself, she opened the door and went inside, taking off her sunglasses. She glanced around as her eyes began adjusting to being indoors after the bright sunshine outside.

"Nova!" a voice called.

She spied Jessica waving at her and moved toward the table.

"I saved you a seat," her new friend said. "You know Jason. This is Rilda and Ken O'Riley. Their son Teddy is a junior running back on varsity."

Taking a seat, Nova smiled. "I met Rilda at school when I registered Leo." She offered her hand to the husband. "Nice to meet you, Ken."

"Same," he responded as they shook. "I own the gas station and body shop on Main. I'm also president of the booster club."

"Jessica tells me you'll be needing volunteers tonight for various things. I'm happy to help in any way I can. My son Leo is a sophomore. And a wide receiver," she added, glad she knew what position her son played and actually understood what he did on the field.

"I ordered pizza for the table," Jason told her. "Hope you like sausage and pepperoni with a lot of toppings."

She laughed. "I've never met a slice of pizza that I didn't like. Let me know what I owe you."

"Nothing," Jason said easily.

"I'll get it the next time then," she promised.

"Oh, there's Ruth," Rilda said, waving. "Bobby Hilton's mom," she added for Nova's benefit.

A woman in her mid-forties with auburn hair joined them. Ken introduced Nova.

Ruth's smile was a genuine one, welcoming Nova. "I'm so glad to meet you, Nova. Bobby showed me the artwork he and Leo did on a graphic novel Bobby's been working on all summer." She smiled. "My boy loves art, and he's so glad Leo's come to town, so he has a fellow artist to talk to. Bobby plays quarterback on JV."

"Yes, Leo said they're going up to school early tomorrow morning to get in some extra practice time on their own."

Jessica nodded. "Quarterbacks and their receivers have a special relationship. It's all about the timing between them. Oh, here's the pizza."

A woman set down one on a stand, while another young teenager placed a second and third one on the table.

"You must be Leo's mom," the woman said. "I am Sophia Romano. My husband Eduardo and I own this place. Your son is a very polite young man."

"I know he came in on Friday with friends. He raved about your pizza and said I had to try it."

"You will like my husband's crust better than any you've ever had," Sophia promised. "Can I get you something to drink? You, too, Ruth."

Both women ordered iced tea. Pizza slices were distributed, and Leo was right—a Romano's pizza was the best Nova had ever eaten. The crust was divine, and the toppings were generous.

"I can see I'll be doing takeout from here at least once a week," she joked.

The door opened, and Cole came in, followed by a bevy of other men. Nova guessed them to be his coaching staff. As they passed by, Jessica told her each coach's name and what position he held on the staff.

"You won't remember all of them," Jessica said. "But I'm sure one stands out. That's Coach Johnson. He's new this year. Quite the looker. He'll have a ton of pressure on him, though. This town expects wins. Lots of them."

Nova watched the coaching staff take their seats at a table reserved for them. Pizzas immediately appeared, and the men dived into the meal, their hunger obvious. She wondered if she should say something to Jessica about seeing Cole, but Rilda started telling a story and before Nova knew it, it was time for the meeting to begin.

Cole stood and didn't even have to strike a knife against his water glass to get the crowd's attention. Immediately, the place quieted. She sensed what she only guessed must be urgency in the air. This was his first time being in front of the group that might make or break him. She held her breath a moment, sending him good vibes.

"Thank you for coming tonight. If we haven't met yet, I'm Cole Johnson, the new head football coach and athletic director for Sugar Springs."

Applause followed. She noted it was somewhere between polite and enthusiastic. She supposed the previous head coach had been beloved since the football team had a winning tradition. Cole would be an unknown at this point, and this kind of crowd would want him to prove himself before they threw their total support behind him.

"I'm going to turn things over to Ken O'Riley, a familiar face to you. Ken tells me there's some business to take care of before I get you all to myself."

Chuckles sounded as Ken moved from their table to the front and Cole took his seat.

"Coach Johnson is right," the booster club president said. "You know me. I play by the rules, so I'll call the first meeting of the Sugar Springs Knights Football Booster Club to order."

He then welcomed the parents of the football players, giving a special shoutout to freshmen parents. She supposed hooking and grooming these parents would be important, as they would be the new foundation for the coming years.

What followed was necessary but boring. Officers were introduced, and they gave various reports. She was surprised by the amount in the treasury, wondering why any fundraising would be necessary with that much money in the kitty. Ken did mention that the booster club would be providing two portable water stations and a football passing machine, which would be helpful in receiver and punter training, these being the items Coach Johnson had prioritized as things to help the football team for this year.

Ken took over again. "We'll have sign-up sheets for volunteers for the pre-game meal coordinators and working concession booths. I'm opening the floor now to ideas for fundraisers for the coming year."

Raffles seemed to be important to this group, and they decided on a trip for four to Walt Disney World in Florida as the grand prize, to be awarded at halftime of the final district home game of the season in November.

She couldn't help but raise her hand after this had been decided, and Ken called on her, saying, "This here is Nova Turner. She and her boy Leo just moved to Sugar Springs. She's Rain Turner's niece."

A murmur went through the room as others looked at Nova with interest. She felt the blush stain her cheeks but plunged ahead.

"I think along with selling raffle tickets for the vacation, we could get the crowd attending the games to perk up and buy more tickets if we also raffled off smaller items each week."

"You mean have winners every week?" someone from three tables over called out.

"Yes," she said, nodding in agreement. "This is a large group of supporters. We all could donate small items—goods and services from right here in our community. That way, we could get income from the raffles weekly, building up to the final week of play. For example, I'm an artist. Pottery is one of my specialties. I could design and make a vase. A set of coffee mugs. A bowl to raffle off. Ken has a body shop. He could offer a free rotation of tires or an oil change. Jessica and Jason could give away a coupon for a free birthday cake or a dozen scones from their bakery."

She looked across the room at the club members. "If we had lots of smaller prizes each week, we could sell lots of tickets and have multiple winners. As fans in the stadium bought their weekly raffle ticket, we could also push the larger grand prize raffle and at the same time make others aware of the businesses here in Sugar Springs."

A buzz broke out across the room, and then various people started tossing out ideas of what they could provide or solicit from businesses as prizes.

Ruth nudged Nova. "You certainly know how to make an impression. Even Coach Johnson is smiling approvingly at you."

She looked to Cole. He winked at her, causing her to go hot all over.

Ken got everyone's attention. "See, this is why it's always good to have newcomers to Sugar Springs and our booster club. New ideas like this could help raise a lot of money for us. Shall we vote on this?"

"I move that we hold a small item raffle each week in addition to the larger one," Jessica said.

"I second the motion," Rilda added.

"All in favor?" Ken asked.

Nova saw the hands fly up. Then she spotted one blonde glaring at her. She was in her late forties and still very pretty. For some reason, though, she'd taken a disliking to Nova. That was obvious.

"Motion passes," Ken told them. "Nova, no good deed goes unpunished around here. I'm putting you in charge of this weekly raffle thing. We'll have a sign-up sheet. Nova can decide how many prizes are to be raffled each week and assign the prizes to a week. She'll also need volunteers to sell at the games each week."

"I can do that," she said. "And I suppose I'll learn to keep quiet in the future."

Everyone laughed, and she saw the smiles around the room. Smiles for her. In that moment, she felt her imaginary roots pushing into the ground, taking hold, making her feel accepted.

"What about the homecoming mums?" the blonde woman who'd stared at her asked. "I thought we were going to try and do those this year as a fundraiser."

"I think we'll probably make more doing the weekly mini-raffles, Phyllis," Ken said agreeably. "Making mums would be pretty time-consuming and need a lot of labor. Raffling our goods and services is so much easier. Let's table mums until next year, okay? We can revisit it this time next year."

She watched the woman's reaction. Her lips tightened in a smile, one which didn't quite reach her eyes. "Of course, Ken. We'll do what Nova wants this year."

Phyllis turned and glowered at Nova.

In that moment, she realized she'd just made her first enemy in Sugar Springs.

$$13$$

Cole watched Phyllis Arnold look at Nova and knew Nova was in trouble. He had met several parents such as Phyllis during his years in coaching and dealing with booster club members. Phyllis' son Keith was a senior on the team and because of that, Cole would try to play the boy as much as possible.

The problem was that Keith was a mediocre receiver. The other varsity starter was head and shoulders above Keith Arnold. For that matter, Leo Turner was showing more promise than Keith at this point, and Cole had figured not only would he move Leo up to varsity at some point but that he would bench Keith in favor of Leo if Leo proved to be the real deal. Seeing Phyllis Arnold and being familiar with her type, it would cause an enmity to grow between the two women. Not on Nova's part. She was one of the sweetest-natured women he had ever known. Phyllis could cause a lot of problems for Nova, however.

He needed to protect Nova. While he had thought to keep their relationship under wraps for a while, Cole decided they better be totally in the open, so others such as Phyllis couldn't blame either Cole or Nova for their lack of transparency.

He listened as Ken O'Riley brought his portion of the program to a close and began his introduction of the featured speaker tonight.

"Cole Johnson comes to us after a stellar career playing for the University of Texas Longhorns. He was recognized as an All-American tight end and was thought to have a promising career in the NFL until a serious knee injury brought his playing days to a halt in Austin. However, like the phoenix that rises from the ashes even stronger and more confident, Cole Johnson became a graduate assistant on the Longhorn staff as he completed his master's degree. From there, Coach Johnson moved into high school coaching, successful at two different high schools in Texas, being a part of leading both schools to playoffs multiple times and one team to a state championship."

Ken paused a moment and smiled. "Our beloved Bubba Reynolds met Coach Johnson at coaching clinics and saw this fine man's potential. Coach Johnson was Coach Reynolds' hand-picked successor to lead our Sugar Springs Knights to newer and greater heights. I give you Coach Cole Johnson."

This time, Cole noticed the applause was resounding as he went to stand by the booster club president. Shaking Ken's hand, he said, "Thank you for that glowing introduction, Ken, and your service in leading our booster club this year."

Ken took a seat, and Cole gazed over his audience, the first time he would address a large group of parents in his new role at Sugar Springs High School.

"I didn't prepare a speech because I've been too busy getting to know your sons and my staff. I will speak to you from my heart, though. A booster club is at the center of any athletic program. You parents do more than give your time and money to our program. You are there supporting your sons, no matter how foul the weather. You embody what parents should be."

He paused. "Although I don't have children of my own yet, I feel my staff and I are surrogate parents to your boys because we get to spend so much time with them. We teach them not only how to play the game of football but how to be good, upstanding young men. They are at a very impressionable age in their lives, and we know the influence we as coaches have over them. I'll tell you now—and I have told the team the exact same thing—that I came from a family who valued academics. I will be in close contact with your sons' teachers to make sure they are model students in the classroom, as well as model athletes on the field. I don't want to lose a single player to the no pass, no play rule. If your boy needs tutoring, we'll get it for him. I myself taught science and also love math, so I can help tutor in those two areas.

"I value academics, but playing football taught me how to be a good man because of the role models I had as my coaches. These coaches taught me about respect. Discipline. Loyalty. Friendship. Trust. When we run out onto that field, we do so as a team, representing this community. Yes, my coaches and I will do our utmost to bring out the best in your boy, no matter what position he plays, but I am not interested in superstars. I will never point the finger at one player and blame him for a team loss. It's hard enough to be a teenager these days, much less carry around the pain and burden of having cost your team a game. I don't want to hear any booing from our stands—and this group of parents will lead the way in that. If one of our athletes drops a ball, no booing. If our kicker misses a field goal, no booing."

He took a deep breath. "That goes for our opponents, as well. They are teenagers, just like our boys, teens trying to do their best, playing a game they love which means so much to them and their community, same as ours.

"Does that mean I don't want you to cheer to the high heavens if we sack our opponents' quarterback? Of course not. If the other team goes for it on fourth down and our defense holds? Let our guys know you're behind them one hundred percent. But I want everything to be done in the spirit of good sportsmanship. I want visitors to come to our stadium and be greeted with enthusiasm.

Welcome them to our town. Make them feel happy to have come to the game, knowing they'll be safe sitting in our stands. I want the Sugar Springs Knights—and their parents and fans—to be the models for all the districts around us to emulate."

His words were met with enthusiastic applause.

"I will do my best to see that each of your boys gets in playing time. Some will see more than others. When the score goes up and we're comfortably ahead, starters will be rested, and backups will finish the game. That includes JV players who could use the experience at the varsity level. I'll do my best to have seniors start, but sometimes hard work isn't enough. Sometimes, those seniors may have to sit on the bench a bit and let another, more talented player play more downs. If you ever have a question regarding how your son is being coached, my door is always open. I will be as honest and transparent as I can be, because we are in this together. You. Me. This amazing staff sitting here.

"We've put in long hours. The staff watches game film, and we will grade your son on every single play he's involved in."

Once more, Cole scanned the crowd and told them, "I've told your boys this, and I'll share it with you now. I've said that academics and athletics are equal in my mind, but what matters most of all? Character. I want to help mold the young men of the Sugar Springs Knights football team into be the best people they can be. I want them to exhibit kindness to all. I want them to understand when they give their word, they are to keep that word. Thank you for trusting my staff and me with your boys."

Again, the applause was thunderous. At this point, Cole thought if he were wise and wanted to keep this crowd on his side, he would simply sit.

He had other things in mind, though.

"I have already met several of you after practice and hope by the end of the season that I will come to know all of you in this room. I'm from a small town myself, and that is why I was excited to be able to take on the head coaching position at Sugar Springs

High School. I look forward to becoming a part of this community in all ways, starting with eating more of this fine pizza from Romano's."

The group laughed, and Mrs. Romano called out, "Anytime, Coach! Just call in your order, and we'll deliver it to you. Even if it's on the practice field."

More laughter echoed.

Cole's tone grew serious now, and he said, "My staff and I are members of this community. Some of them, such as Ben Peterson here, have children who go to the local schools. We shop in your stores. Buy your gas. Attend your churches. We'll be out and about in the community. I hope that you'll accept us not simply as football coaches and teachers—but as people. Citizens of Sugar Springs, same as you. At this point, I don't have a family, but I wanted you to know that I am seeing someone in Sugar Springs."

His gaze went to Nova, whose eyes widened in surprise.

"While most of my waking hours are spent living and breathing football, even I have to eat every now and then. I sometimes ask someone to join me when I do so. And that someone is here. You've met her tonight. She had the terrific idea about the weekly raffles. I wanted you to know that I'm seeing Nova Turner."

The room sounded like a swarm of bees as it buzzed at this revelation. He saw Nova's cheeks redden as everyone in the room focused their attention upon her.

"In the spirit of openness, I thought it only fair for people to know about this relationship. I'm not someone who would try to date a woman and hide that fact. I'm an open book and will always be one to you. I will not favor Nova's son over another player simply because we are seeing one another. When Leo Turner takes the field, it's because every coach on this staff has confidence that he is the right player in that moment.

"The same goes for Teddy O'Riley. Just because I've become

friends with Ken and he's serving as president of the football booster club, it doesn't mean that Teddy gets any more playing time at running back than another student athlete. Playing time is based on merit. I will always do what is best for this team. Having said that, I know that some of your sons have tremendous potential. That includes Lyle and Luke Smith. They are two of the best offensive linemen I've ever seen in my coaching career, and I'm going to do everything in my power to see the Smith cousins land athletic scholarships."

Cole studied those in the room. "I want the best for every player on my team. I won't stand up here and promise you a district championship. I won't boast or brag about how deep I expect us to go into the playoffs. My philosophy is to take it one game—one opponent—at a time.

"What I do promise you is that this team will be prepared." He grinned wryly. "Most likely, overprepared. My coaches will have worked with each athlete individually and as a unit. They will have broken down game film and instructed our players just as well as they have been taught in their academic classrooms. Our players will never go into a game where they don't feel comfortable or confident. That's my one guarantee to you. That our student athletes will know what they can and cannot do and what they'll be up against. They'll be prepared so thoroughly that they will know what the player opposite them is thinking. Do I hope that takes us to a district title and beyond? Of course, I do. Every coach dreams of a district championship and making his mark in the playoffs.

"But the Sugar Springs Knights' slogan will be..." He paused dramatically, holding up his index finger. "One game at a time. Now, give me a Knights on three. One, two, three!"

"Knights!" shouted the booster club members, followed by enthusiastic applause.

Cole hoped he would have the support of the majority of the members present tonight. He deliberately didn't look at Phyllis or

Fred Arnold. The mean girls would do what they always did. He hoped their pettiness wouldn't upset or get to Nova. Already, it looked as if she had been making friends, based upon what he'd observed tonight.

He began circulating around the room as Ken O'Riley adjourned the meeting. Fortunately, Cole had excellent recall and was able to use the names of parents he had already met before and after practice, even as he filed away the names of new ones he was now introduced to.

Members began to leave the restaurant, and he nodded to his staff, saying, "Thanks for coming, gentlemen. See you at school tomorrow."

Making his way to Nova, he saw she was talking with Jake Fletcher's parents and a woman he had yet to meet. Cole approached them, offering the woman his hand.

"Cole Johnson, ma'am. We haven't had the pleasure of meeting yet."

"I'm Ruth Hilton, Bobby's mother. I am the Sugar Springs city librarian and also run a tutoring program at the town library. I know your coaches' hours are limited as far as when they can tutor students, and so I have a cadre of parent volunteers who take up the slack at the library."

He grinned shamelessly at her. "Ruth Hilton, you may just be my new favorite person in Sugar Springs."

The librarian's brows arched. "Why, I thought that might be Nova, Coach Johnson," she said coyly.

Cole burst out laughing, and Ruth did, too.

He turned to Nova and said, "Would you mind giving me a ride back to the high school? I rode over with Ben Peterson."

"Sure," she said and began collecting pages in front of her.

They said their goodnights and walked to her dilapidated car, which was just off the square. Cole opened the driver's door for her and then walked around and seated himself in the passenger's seat.

Nova handed him the sheaf of papers and started the car. Glancing down, he saw it was signups from different members and what they would raffle. He noted everything offered from a free bouquet of flowers to a free pair of shoes. It also included a list of names willing to man the raffle tables at home games.

"I'm glad you spoke up at the meeting and shared your weekly raffle idea. From all these signatures, you received a great response."

She glanced to him, and he saw the worry in her face. "Should I be glad you spoke up about us?" She turned her eyes back to the road.

"Are you worried about Phyllis Arnold?" he asked. "I know you were pretty much homeschooled, Nova, but there are always mean girls who gossip about others viciously. Not only in high school. To me, I wanted to let people such as Phyllis know we were seeing each other. I meant what I said. I have to lead an exemplary life because a small town is like living in a glass fishbowl. Everyone sees and knows everything. I believed I should share that we were seeing each other."

He took her right hand from the steering wheel and squeezed her fingers. "Mostly because I want people to know we're in a relationship. If the booster club members had found out one at a time, that gossip would have spread like a wildfire which couldn't be controlled. I needed to be upfront and not only let them know that I was seeing you, but I also wanted them to know I won't favor Leo simply because of our status."

"Ruth told me that Phyllis Arnold's boy plays the same position as Leo does."

"He does. Keith is a senior, and so he'll start. But I'll be honest with you, Nova. Keith is a fair-to-middling player. A good kid with a good work ethic but not much talent. I can see at some point that Keith will need to be replaced." He hesitated. "Most likely by Leo."

"I see," she said quietly.

"It won't happen right away. Leo is as inexperienced as they come. He'll definitely play a lot on JV as a starter, but I will have a good number of the JV players dress out for varsity games. I anticipate Leo eventually seeing some playing time at wide receiver on varsity. I don't want you to worry about Phyllis Arnold or her reaction, though."

He squeezed her hand again. "I will do whatever I can to protect you."

She jerked her hand from his, placing it on the wheel again. "I don't need you protecting me, Cole," she said curtly, pulling into the teacher parking lot at school.

Nova drove him to his truck, the only vehicle sitting in the lot this time of night. She stopped her car but left the engine running, facing straight ahead.

"Nova, I don't want to leave things like this," he said.

She whipped her head toward him. "Shouldn't I have had a say in your grand announcement? Maybe I wasn't ready for the entire town to know my business."

He froze, realizing he had only thought of the situation from his point of view. "You're right," he said quietly. "I should have run it past you before I spoke. I just didn't think you were the kind of woman who would want something like that to remain a secret."

"We haven't known each other long enough for you to know what kind of woman I am, Cole," she snapped.

Anger sizzled through him. He got out of the truck. "I guess I jumped to conclusions about you. I'm sorry I did so." He slammed the door and stared at her, but she was looking straight ahead. "Thanks for the ride."

"You're welcome," she said stiffly and pulled away.

Cole watched her drive off. He didn't like the sick feeling in his gut, but he didn't think he really had anything to apologize for. He stormed to his truck and got in, driving home, the radio blaring so he wouldn't be able to think.

He parked in front of his apartment and went inside, too worked up to do anything except pace.

Had he really read Nova wrong? He was usually a good judge of character. He had thought her different. Special. Though they'd only known each other a short while, he'd believed they had begun to lay the foundation of something special.

Something lasting.

His cell dinged, and he pulled it from his pocket.

It was from Nova.

Can you come outside?

HURRYING TO HIS DOOR, he opened it. No one was there. Cole closed the door and took a few steps forward, glancing around.

Then he spotted Nova standing next to her car. They met halfway, and she flung herself against him, clasping him as a woman drowning. One who needed rescuing.

His arms went about her. His mouth sought hers. The kiss was hard. Punishing. He wanted to hurt her because she had hurt him. His gut told him it was wrong, though, and he gentled the kiss, finally breaking it.

"I'm sorry," she said, tears swimming in her eyes. "I'm so sorry."

"What happened?"

"Phyllis Arnold," she said dully. "She made a point to stop by as she left. She said a few pretty ugly things. I shouldn't have let her get to me."

He brushed his lips against her forehead. "No, you shouldn't. She's a gossip. Every group has a few. She'll have some loyal followers who'll probably be pretty rude to you, too, but the majority of the booster club members—and this town—will treat you with respect."

Nova brushed away the tears that fell down her cheeks. "I let her get to me. I shouldn't have. I knew I'd made her mad with my suggestions regarding the raffle and Ken telling her the club was putting her mum idea on hold."

He swiped his thumbs against her cheeks. "I shouldn't have surprised you with the announcement about us like I did. You were right. I should've run it by you first."

"No, we've agreed to see each other. I knew other people would find out. You did the right thing, stating up front and not trying to hide our relationship. You're under a magnifying glass as it is. I certainly saw that tonight. I know a small town can rake people over the coals. You have to tread a fine line, keeping parents happy and yet doing the job the way you see fit."

Nova sighed. "I don't want to be a liability to you, Cole. I've told you I have very little experience with men. If you want to break things off now, I'll understand."

"Why would I want to do that?" He kissed her softly. "Not when I've found someone kind and smart and beautiful." He wrapped his arms around her. "I'm not letting you go, Nova Turner. You're perfect for me."

"You think so?" she asked, doubt reflected in her eyes.

"I know so," he assured her.

Cole kissed her again, wanting to comfort her and show her how much he cared for her. She responded to his kiss, letting him know how she felt about him.

Nova broke the kiss. "I better get home. I know you have all kinds of football-y things to do."

"Football-y? Is that even a word?" he teased.

She smiled. "It is now."

"Let me walk you to your car."

He took her hand and led her to the vehicle, seeing her safely inside it.

"You know, you could've just come to my apartment."

"I didn't remember which one it was. It was dark when we got back from Tyler the other night." She bit her lip. "And I was paying more attention to you than to which apartment we went in."

He leaned inside the car and kissed her softly. "Well, now you know where it is, I'll have to invite you over and cook dinner for you sometime."

"You cook?"

He laughed. "Not much. You're a great cook, though. Maybe you could come here and cook for us."

"I'd like that."

"Me, too."

Cole was reluctant for her to go but said, "I'll call you tomorrow."

"Okay," she said. "I'm sorry."

He smoothed her hair. "Nothing to be sorry about, babe."

She blew out a breath. "Okay. I'm going now. Talk to you soon."

He watched her drive away and as he did, Cole realized something out of the blue.

He was in love with Nova Turner.

14

———————

Nova headed to the main office of Sugar Springs High School, the first time she had been back since registering Leo after their move to the small town. The last three weeks had been busy ones. She had met with service people, explaining exactly how she would be using the space on the square, even drawing the diagram of where she wanted everything to be located. The plumber had been able to put in two industrial farmhouse sinks, deep and long, on opposite sides of the room where the painting parties would take place. The electrician had done some rewiring, and the space had brighter—yet softer—lights. She had also strung some white party lights for a playful effect.

Furniture had also been ordered, and those tables and chairs would be coming in next week. The handyman was busy this week with painting the entire store and building shelving so that she could display her pottery. He also, along with his son, had designed display cases for her jewelry. Every minute not spent at the store was busy creating pieces for display and coming up with paintings for the partiers to try and emulate. Fortunately, she had been inspired by her new life here in Sugar Springs and had been productive.

Now, she was going to meet with the tech teacher, Brendan Whittaker, about the possibility of the teacher and some of his students creating her website, as well as speaking with the principal regarding the raffles she was heading up.

Entering the office, Rilda O'Riley spotted her and rose from her desk.

"Hey, Nova. Come sign in if you would."

She did so, and the clerk issued Nova a visitor's badge after taking her picture. She peeled the back from it and stuck the pass on her blouse.

"Thanks again for bringing the snacks last night, Rilda."

The office worker smiled. "You can't have a meeting without snacks. I thought everything went really well, creating teams to sell raffle tickets as fans enter the gates, as well as having those volunteers circulate throughout the stands during the first half of the game."

"I think it'll help moving into the stands. I know parents don't want to miss any of the game and hurry through the gates in order to grab a good seat."

"You've got smart ideas, Nova. Don't let anyone say otherwise."

She frowned. "You mean Phyllis Arnold and her crew."

She had learned through her friends that Phyllis was on a rampage, badmouthing Nova—and also Cole. Jessica had told her not to worry about it, saying most booster club members came down firmly on Cole's side and hers. It didn't hurt that Cole's team had won their first two games, both away ones. Winning was the golden ticket in football.

"Let me call Brendan and let him know you're here."

Rilda stepped away and made the call, saying, "I'll send her right up." Signaling to a student sitting in a chair scrolling through her phone, she said, "Take Miss Turner up to Mr. Whittaker's classroom." To Nova, she added, "Come back to the office when you're done, and I'll get you in to see Joe Bob. He's just going to rubberstamp the raffle ticket sales."

"Thanks, Rilda."

The student aide escorted Nova upstairs. She was chatty and asked, "Is Leo your son?"

"Yes, he is. Do you have any classes with him?"

"Two. World history and English. He's really smart. And he played really well in both games. I cheer for the JV. Daddy taught me about football, so I know what to watch for. Leo runs a mean pattern."

Fortunately, after being tutored by her son and Cole, Nova understood the comment. "Yes. He's really been working on his timing with Bobby."

"I think Coach should move Leo up to varsity," the cheerleader added.

"We'll see," she said noncommittally, knowing what a controversy that might bring.

They arrived at their destination and the aide asked, "Do you think you can find your way back to the office?"

"Yes, I can. Thanks for bringing me here."

Nova knocked on the door, and it was answered by a student. She entered a room with about fifteen students. Most worked at computers or were gathered around one, discussing what they saw on the screen with their classmates. The teacher, who looked about her age and was tall with the stereotypical black geek glasses, came and met her.

"Nova Turner."

"Brendan Whittaker." He offered his hand. "Thanks for thinking about using us, Miss Turner."

"Nova, please. And it was Coach Johnson who actually suggested I speak with you about my website."

"What do you know about websites?"

"Nothing. I can find my way around a computer, but I have no idea what creating a website, much less maintaining it, involves."

"Let me walk you through things."

Brendan explained about registering a domain name and finding a service to host it, telling her while some of this could be free, it was usually better to pay for the option.

"Paying a fee helps build credibility," he explained. "Especially since you're trying to create a business and brand. And with a custom domain name, you'll get a custom email address. That adds to your business's authenticity."

"I like the sound of that," she said.

"Let me get a few students over here to walk you through the rest of it."

Soon, they were seated at a table with a team of four students Brendan had selected to work with Nova on this project. They convinced her that writing code from scratch would be too complicated and recommended she use a drag-and-drop website builder.

"So, let me get this straight. Even as a beginner, I could create my entire website using a drag-and-drop editor. No coding needed."

They showed her various website design templates and asked about what her business involved. She described in detail what would occur at the site and how all ages and genders would be potential clients for the private parties. Once they had a grasp of the idea, the students guided Nova in selecting the template design and page layouts. They even walked her through customizing it by selecting font styles and color schemes.

"This really appeals to the artist in me," she declared. "And since I can do them from the editor, it really makes creating things simple."

"You'll want your logo to be prominent," Brendan recommended. "It should be your webpage's header. And all images need to be high res. Clear. No sloppy stock photos."

"We should talk about Google Analytics, Mr. Whittaker," one of the students said, turning and facing her. "It's a website tool that'll let you understand how visitors interact with your website, Miss Turner."

"What about PayPal?" asked another student. Are you going to sell items from your website? Or I guess you'll book the parties you mentioned on it. You've got to have PayPal."

"I'm familiar with PayPal—but not how to place it on a website."

After another quarter-hour, Nova really had a handle on what she wanted and said, "I'll take care of registering my domain name and finding a host for the site. I'd like to build the site with your help, though. As an artist, I have a good eye for how to use space on a page, but you have the expertise."

"Can you come back on Monday?" Brendan asked. "If you have those things taken care of by then, we can build the site in probably less than an hour. My classes meet in ninety-minute blocks that day."

"I can do that," she said enthusiastically, and they arranged the time for her to return. "Thank you for your time today," she told the group of students. "I look forward to working with you."

As the teacher walked her to the door, he said, "This gives them real-world experience. Again, thanks for using us."

"While I think I could run the website because uploading content seems pretty easy, I don't know if I want to take the time to do so. Would I be able to pay a few of your students to do the updates for me?"

"They couldn't accept payment, but I can see they earn an extra half-credit for an internship," he told her. "That would be for this school year. The two I have in mind are both seniors. Once they graduate, you're more than welcome to negotiate payment with them if they want to continue. Or you might find by then you have time to run it yourself."

"Thanks for your time, Brendan. I'll see you Monday."

Nova returned to the front office, where Rilda greeted her and took her down the hallway. Tapping on the door, she said, "Joe Bob, Nova Turner is here to see you."

The principal waved her in. "Hello, Nova. Have a seat." He indicated the ones in front of his desk, and she took one. "What's all this raffle ticket business about? I thought the booster club did a big raffle at the end of each season."

Briefly, she explained how the booster club would have a table set up inside the school gates to sell weekly tickets at home games, as well as circulate in the stands during the first two quarters of the game.

"So, no big prize this year?" the principal; asked, looking disappointed.

"Oh, we still will have a grand prize. A trip for four to Walt Disney World in Florida."

He frowned. "Then what's all this other stuff you're raffling off?"

She walked him through the weekly drawings for various goods and services, saying, "This will help promote the different businesses in the community, and we think it will raise even more funds for the booster club in the long run."

"Sounds good." He smiled. "Since you're here talking to me about it, must've been your idea."

"Guilty as charged," she told him. "But I have a legion of volunteers, different ones each week, who'll man the booth before the six home games and move through the stands until just before halftime. I'm here to see if that works for you and if we can announce our weekly winners over the P.A. at halftime each week."

"Don't see why not. I'm the lucky son of a gun who gets to announce the games. I can definitely make time to say a few winners' names before the band marches out and the drill team does their dance."

"Thank you, Joe Bob. This will mean a lot to the booster club.

Coach Johnson has his eye on several things he'd like us to purchase this year with the funds we raise."

"I hear Coach also has his eye on you."

She felt the blush stain her cheeks. "We are seeing one another."

The principal beamed at her. "Well, good for you. I liked the boy from the first time we talked. Bubba Reynolds was smart to go with an outsider. Coach Johnson knows his stuff. He's doing a fine job so far."

Rising, she said, "I don't want to take up anymore of your time, Joe Bob. Thank you for giving us permission to sell our raffle tickets and agreeing to announce our winners each week. I think the immediacy of hearing the winners' names during half-time will help add to the excitement—and boost ticket sales in the future."

Joe Bob told her how to reach the press box so he would know who the winners were, and Nova left, waving goodbye to Rilda as she exited the office. She hated being this close to Cole without seeing him but didn't want to interrupt his day. Still, she decided to text him on the off-chance she might be able to steal a few minutes with him.

Hi. You busy?

IMMEDIATELY, he fired back.

Babe, I'm ALWAYS busy! But I have a few minutes to talk. I'll call you.

As she read the text, her phone rang. "Hello?"

"Calling one beautiful artist and mom," Cole said huskily. "What are you up to?"

"I'm at school."

"Here? Now?"

"Yes, I took your idea of having students work on my website and just met with Brendan Whittaker and a team from one of his advanced tech classes. I'll be back on Monday so we can firm up some things and get my website activated and full of content."

"Where are you?"

"By the front office."

"Start walking down that long hall. Keep going until you get to the doors heading outside. I'll meet you there."

"Okay."

Nova did as Cole asked, glad she hadn't removed her visitor's badge. When she finally reached the end of the long corridor and pushed open the door, he was approaching.

Taking her hand, he said, "Come see my office."

They cut across a parking lot and entered what he called the fieldhouse. He took her to his office and then showed her the conference room.

Closing the door, he said, "This is where I spend a lot of time with my staff."

"I like your office better. It's got windows. This looks like a cave."

He laughed, capturing her waist and pulling her to him. "It needs to be dark. We watch a lot of game film in here. Same with the classrooms in this building. They're windowless, as well, so we can view film with our athletes."

She placed her palm on his chest. "So, what do you do in this room with your coaches? Make up plays? Talk about your opponents? What's your routine like? I mean, I know during the week you oversee practices and then coach during games. What else do you do as a coach? You really haven't talked about that much. I know you're up here a lot on the weekends."

His thumbs grazed her ribs, causing her body to heat.

"The weekend starts right after the game ends on a Friday night. The coaches accompany the players into the locker room. We check for any injuries that might have occurred. We watch the kids—their body language. Maybe a kid didn't feel like he played enough, or he had a bad play and is beating himself up over it. You learn to watch their body language so you can pick up on those things."

"That's smart," she said. "That way something doesn't fester."

"We also collect their soft goods. Their uniforms, compression shirts, girdle pads. Those have to go in the wash. Student managers help the coaches with that. My biggest job is to download the game video into the computer and send it off. UIL rules state that the video has to be downloaded and shared with our upcoming opponent by eight o'clock the next morning. It's just easier to do it right away so I don't miss the deadline." He chuckled. "And that's just Friday after a game."

Nova caressed his cheek. "That's a long day for you. What about Saturday? I know I drop Leo off, or he gets a ride to school for some players' meeting."

"Coaches arrive at seven. We watch the previous night's game together as a staff and discuss the good, the bad, the ugly—and what we'll communicate to the team overall as a group. Then we discuss what we'll talk about with the various units, such as the receivers or defensive backs. Players are given a grade for every play they participated in."

"Every play?" she asked. "That's a lot of detail."

"It's a learning experience, just like in the classroom, Nova." Softly, he kissed her lips. "Then the players arrive at nine. We put them through about a half-hour workout to get the soreness out after all the hits from the previous night. After that, they watch video with the staff. We make sure we emphasize the good things they did and make any corrections needed. We try to leave them on a positive note. It's important they walk away feeling good about themselves, even after a loss."

"Sounds like coaching includes psychology," she observed.

"It does."

"What comes next, Coach Johnson?" she asked coyly.

He backed her into the large conference table and lifted her, setting her on it. Cole stepped between her legs, his hands still on her waist.

"We stay another ninety minutes or so. Compile data on our next opponent. I've assigned each coach a part of the scouting report which he's responsible for. Call it his homework for the next day. Then if we have a future opponent who might be playing a rare Saturday game, either one of my coordinators or I attend that game to scout them. See how they respond as a unit. The plays they're running. If any weaknesses can be spotted."

He paused. "Next Saturday is one of those cases. I'll still make time to see you, but I'll need to go to that game. Fortunately, it's an afternoon one, so that'll give us Saturday night to be together."

"I'll go with you," Nova volunteered. "I've enjoyed going to Leo's two JV games. I'm sure I'll enjoy our first home game tomorrow night. You can teach me a little more about football, Coach." She pulled him down for a lingering kiss.

"It's a date," he said, his voice low and rough, causing her pulse to jump.

"What about Sundays?" she asked, trying to get herself under control.

"What about them?"

"What do you coaches do? I know you're tied up then, too."

"The staff reports to this room at one o'clock. Each coach presents his part of the scouting report. We look over the data we've gathered. Watch film as a group of what's been sent. Based upon that, we put together our game plan for the upcoming week. We always finalize the offensive plays first, then move to the defense, and finish up with special teams. Based on our game plan, it helps solidify the practice plan for Monday and Tuesday."

"You work so hard," she said. "I'm in awe of the time you put in, Cole. I had no idea how involved coaching was or the hours spent by the staff away from the players."

"It's a lot," he agreed. "But I love it, Nova. I love everything about football. From teaching players in practices to breaking down game film to the actual coaching of the game itself."

"No wonder I only see you for a few stolen hours."

He framed her face in his large hands. "I hate that. I wish it could be more."

She wanted to reassure him and said, "No, I understand. You're like Atlas, holding the world on your shoulders. It's a lot of responsibility. I never want to be a distraction to you."

Giving her a lopsided grin, he said, "Hey, you're the distraction I *need*." He paused. "The one I want."

Cole kissed her, and Nova felt on top of the world. She found her thoughts turning more and more toward him throughout each day. She missed him when they were apart. Constantly, she thought of things she wanted to share with him or ask about.

Startled, she broke the kiss, staring at him. She hadn't wanted it to happen. Hadn't even consider it would happen. But it had sneaked up on her without her realizing it.

She had fallen in love with Cole Johnson.

15

———————

Cole said to his staff, "You've done an excellent job preparing our team ever since the season began. You've put your hearts and souls into all I've asked you to do. I'm proud of you, gentlemen, and what we've accomplished so far. We've been at a slight disadvantage with playing a couple of away games, but we're coming into our first home game undefeated now, and I know we'll be the team to beat in district. We can't let our guard down. I want to emphasize that to the kids, too."

Ray Barker said, "You've done a great job motivating everyone, Coach. Players and staff."

The line coach had become Cole's closest friend on the staff as the past few weeks had unfolded. Ray taught biology, and besides football, he and Cole had talked a lot of science. He'd given Ray copies of his old lesson plans, including tests and projects. Ray had already assigned one of those projects and found it to be a roaring success, thanking Cole for a fresh idea after teaching the same subject at three high schools for the last dozen years.

Cole had even talked about Ray so much that Nova had asked

the coach to dinner. She'd fried chicken and okra and had also served corn on the cob and peach cobbler. After, Ray had teasingly told Cole if things didn't work out for Nova and him, he'd be willing to step in.

"Appreciate hearing that Ray," he said. "A positive attitude goes a long way, whether it's in a teenager or an adult. I've always thought negativity breeds negativity. That's why I try to keep things upbeat and positive." He looked around the conference table. "You've all got your assignments. I'll see you tomorrow."

"What about Randolph?" John Peterson asked, referring to next week's opponent. "You haven't said anything about who's scouting them this afternoon."

Peterson wore a smirk, which Cole was happy to wipe off. "Got it covered, John," he said smoothly. "I know usually coordinators are sent to scout opponents, but I already ask enough of you and Ben as it is. I'm leaving now and will go to the game this afternoon."

"I can go, Coach," Ben offered. "I don't mind."

"Nope," he said. "Go play with your kids, Ben. That's the priority for you today."

"I'll go," John growled. "You don't have to."

He could see he'd gotten under his defensive coordinator's skin. "Go work on your gameplan for this coming week, John. Or get some of those geography papers graded. I've got this covered."

Irritation filled John's face, but Cole didn't acknowledge it. Instead, he said, "I'll see you all tomorrow at one."

Leaving the conference room, he headed for his office and retrieved his phone, texting Nova that he would pick her up in ten minutes.

Sensing someone's presence, he glanced up to find John Peterson hovering at his doorway.

"I'm a great scout," John said stubbornly.

"I'm sure you are, John. You're also a great coach. You're getting things out of our defense that I wouldn't have thought possible just a couple of weeks ago. The players listen to you. They respect you. They learn from you."

"Then why don't you want me to scout today's game?"

Exasperated, he said, "It's not that I don't want you to. It's like I said—I've already asked a lot of my staff. I'm trying to give you a break."

"I want to go," the other coach insisted.

A light bulb went on in Cole's head. The Randolph head football coach had announced before the season began that he would be retiring at year's end. His team had dedicated their season to the longtime coach, and the Raiders would be the first real challenge faced by the Sugar Springs Knights. He wondered if John Peterson might have his eye on the soon to be vacant position.

Instead of calling out John on his motives, Cole was actually relieved. If he didn't have to scout this game, it meant he and Nova could do something else.

Something he'd been thinking about for a while now.

"All right. If you feel like you're caught up on everything else, I appreciate you stepping up and attending the Randolph Raiders game."

He slipped his phone into his pocket and pulled out his keys to lock his office.

John looked puzzled. "That's it?"

"Yes, that's it. You want to do it. I'm happy for you to do it—as long as you don't go around bitching that I'm piling too much work on you."

Peterson snorted. "Nah, I wouldn't do that, Coach."

Sure, you wouldn't.

He left the fieldhouse and went to his truck, a spring in his step. Usually, he stayed after everyone went home on Saturdays, trying to do a thousand little things. Since he hadn't planned on staying today, though, all he could think was he had the gift of several hours with Nova.

Without football.

On the way to Nova's, he thought about what they could do. It was a quarter to one. They'd talked about picking up something to eat on their way to the game. He had an idea and texted Nova he'd be there in about twenty minutes and then called the diner.

"Ida Lou's," a voice said, and he recognized it as the owner of the diner. He'd picked up food from the restaurant several times and found it good.

"Hey, Ida Lou. Cole Johnson here."

"Well, hello, Coach. You sound hungry."

"Actually, I was hoping you might put a quick picnic together for me. I find myself with a free afternoon and thought I'd take Nova to the lake and chill."

"I met her the other day. She came in with Jessica Fletcher. They seem to be thick as thieves."

"Yes, they and their boys have become close friends."

"Leave it to me. I'll throw something together. Nothing fancy. Give me ten minutes."

"See you soon."

Cole drove to the square and parked. Knowing he had a few minutes to kill, he went into Rolling Scones, where he was greeted by Jason Fletcher.

"Hey, Coach. What can I get for you?"

"I'm headed to a picnic, so something sweet and easy to hold. Cookies, maybe?"

"Got you covered." Jason indicated the display case. "I baked those peanut butter with the Hershey's kiss in the middle about an hour ago. The iced sugar cookies are also a local favorite."

"Let me have half a dozen of each."

He knew Nova and he wouldn't eat a dozen cookies between them. A hungry Leo Turner, though, would easily devour whatever they didn't touch.

The baker placed the cookies in the box and rang him up. "Team's looking good."

"Your son is a big part of our success this season," he replied.

"Jake can think quick on his feet. He's a dual threat and can run and pass."

Jason beamed. "Jake has a better arm than I ever did. I was accurate up to twenty-five yards when I quarterbacked, but my kid can put it in the numbers fifty yards down the field."

"I didn't know you played."

"Just high school. I wasn't good enough to even think about college ball. I remember watching you play, though. You were really good."

"Those days are long behind me, Jason." He paid for the cookies. "Keep the change."

Walking a few doors down, he entered the diner. Ida Lou crossed and met him at the hostess stand, handing over a sack.

"I went super-easy, Coach. Roast beef sandwiches. Potato salad." She looked at the box he carried. "I see you already handled dessert. I was going to ask your preference."

"Cookies. No muss, no fuss."

"I'll put it on your tab. You and Nova have fun."

Cole left the square and headed straight for Nova's. His heart beat just a bit faster as he turned onto her street. While he'd enjoyed spending time with his college girlfriend, she had never made his pulse pound or dominated his thoughts the way Nova did. He only hoped he and Nova were on the same page because he wanted to push things between them to the next level.

When he knocked on her door, he got shooting tingles that raced through him.

She answered, wearing a top of light brown with a pair of form-fitting jeans. Her hair was swept into a ponytail, and the only makeup he could see was on her luscious lips. She looked almost as young as her son.

"I wore neutral colors for our spy mission," she revealed, closing the door behind her and locking it. "Didn't want any Raiders fans to know we're on a scouting mission."

"Actually, change of plans," Cole told her. "I'm free this afternoon. John Peterson's covering the game for me."

"John volunteered to do you a favor?" she asked, doubt in her voice.

He shrugged. "John wanted to scout it. I think he had ulterior motives, but I'm fine with a free afternoon."

"Wait. What motives?"

He explained how the Randolph coach was retiring and that he suspected Peterson might be considering applying for the job at season's end.

"If he wants a little FaceTime with those fans, I'm good with it. As long as he brings back a thorough scouting report. He will. John may not like me, but he's a professional. He wouldn't do anything to hurt our players."

"Then what are we doing?"

"We are borrowing your aunt's canoe. We'll also need a blanket. I picked up something for lunch, and we're going to Sugar Springs Lake for a picnic."

The smile which lit up her face stole his breath. "That sounds heavenly. I'll go back inside and grab a blanket. You know where the canoe is."

Soon, they were headed to the lake. They found an area with no one in sight. Nova spread the blanket close to the water, and he set out the sandwiches and containers of potato salad. Ida Lou had thoughtfully included two large iced teas.

Nova's stomach rumbled as they sat on the blanket and unwrapped their sandwiches. "Mmm. Roast beef. It looks wonderful."

"I've found anything that comes from Ida Lou's is good."

"I had lunch there with Jessica a few days ago. It was fantastic."

"What were you two up to?" he asked before biting into his sandwich.

"The furniture came in, and she was helping me arrange it.

She also helped me store the art supplies which I'd ordered from a place in Dallas. The handyman finished up on the painting. The shelves and display cases are put together. I just need to fill them now."

"How's the website coming?"

She swallowed a bite. "It's up and running now."

Nova explained to him all about drag-and-drop and how she could place things on the site or let the team of students do so.

"I'm going to let the students handle it for now. Brendan is giving them some kind of credit for doing so. He said it would also look good on their college apps. It's good to know I won't have to deal with that aspect of the business for several months, other than checking the website for reservations."

"What are you going to call the place?"

She sighed. "That's been hard. I went through all kinds of names. Draw and Drafts. Art for Fun. Painting with Glee. Amusing Art. Cheers to Painting. Sketch and Sip. I decided I didn't want to lean too heavily on the tippling part, though. While I believe a lot of the date nights and girls' nights out will involve plenty of wine, I do want to also include kids and teenagers for birthday parties. It was between Playful Painting and Pals & Art." She paused. "Do you have an opinion?"

"Is this like when a woman asks if you like her dress or hair? I'm afraid I'll pick the wrong one." Hesitating a moment, he said, "I would've gone with Playful Painting."

Nova grinned. "I did. I wanted painting in the title somewhere, and these paint and sip places are all about having fun. I also liked the alliteration." She pulled out her phone and typed something in, handing it to him.

He saw it was her website, with the Playful Painting logo at the top. Smiling, he asked, "Did you design this logo?"

She nodded. "I had fun with it. Do you like the color scheme?"

"I do. I think my girlfriend is pretty darn creative."

He snaked an arm about her waist and leaned in to kiss her. A burst of longing exploded within him. He kept his head and gentled the kiss, then broke it, going back to his sandwich.

"That was a nice timeout," she said, placing her hand on his thigh and taking a bite of her potato salad.

They finished their sandwiches and she reached for the Rolling Scones box, opening it and sighing.

"Chocolate and peanut butter. My favorite combination."

"I didn't know that. And Jason didn't tell me. He just said they'd been freshly-baked this morning."

"You bought a lot of cookies."

"I figured Leo would scarf down whatever we didn't eat."

Nova laughed. "True. I thought he ate a lot before we moved to Sugar Springs, but now that he's playing football? He must be burning calories like crazy. He inhales everything at lightspeed."

Cole bit into a cookie and sighed. "Now, that's a cookie." Curious, he asked, "What's Leo up to today?"

"He was going over to Tim Heath's this afternoon to work on some history project about Ancient Rome. He's always talking about Miss Addison's class. Says she's tough but he's learning a lot."

"What about tonight?" he pressed.

"He's having dinner with some friends. They're doing a sleepover at Bobby's. Don't worry, they're all football players and conscious of needing to get enough sleep. Especially with the big Randolph game coming up this week."

Cole bounded to his feet and grabbed her hands, pulling her up. His mouth came down on hers, the kiss hard and demanding. He felt her fingers tighten on his.

When he broke the kiss, he said, "I don't want to canoe now."

"You don't?"

He brought her hands to his lips, kissing them tenderly. "If you're ready to take the next step, I say we use this gift of time with Leo away."

She sucked in an audible breath as understanding dawned on her face. "And?" she asked, her eyes beginning to dance with mischief.

"And make love as many times as we can before Leo gets home tomorrow."

16

———

Nova had daydreamed over and over what making love with Cole would be like. He'd been such a gentleman to this point, his kisses heated but his hands never touching anyplace she might object to. Hearing now that he was ready to make love let her know his feelings for her were growing, just as hers were for him.

On her part, though, she knew it was love. She'd kept silent about that, not wanting to scare off Cole. She determined not to reveal the true depths of her own feelings unless he voiced his first. But wanting to make love was a huge step. She couldn't help but wonder what had triggered it.

Fortunately, it only took two minutes to dump the trash and take the blanket back to his truck. They had left the canoe in the truck's bed, waiting to bring it to the water after they ate.

Cole helped her into the vehicle, and they drove the short distance to Sugar Springs.

"I think I should call Leo," she said.

He looked at her as if she were crazy. "You aren't going to tell him what we're up to?"

"No," she said, smiling as she shook her head. "But after his project, he's bound to come home and throw things in a duffel bag for tonight. I'll call him and check in with him. Feel him out about his timeline."

Nova called, glad Leo picked up. "Hey, Mom. What do you need?"

"I just wanted to check on you and the project. How are you and Tim coming along?"

"Really well. I wish I could work with Tim on all my projects. So many kids are slackers and sit back and make others do all the work. Tim's super smart and has great ideas."

"Are you still going to sleep over at Bobby's? And you said you have dinner covered?"

"Yeah, I'll leave Tim's in probably another hour or so. I'll come home and chill a while and then grab my stuff."

"Okay. I won't be home. Coach Johnson and I decided to go on a picnic at the lake. I convinced him to bring the canoe along."

"Make him do all the work, Mom," Leo joked. "Guess I'll see you tomorrow."

"What time can I pick you up?"

"I dunno. I'll text you."

"Okay. Have fun," she told her son, hanging up. "Leo will be home in an hour or maybe a little longer. He'll stay until he leaves for Bobby's. Then he's gone for the rest of the night."

Cole took her hand and kissed it, keeping it in his. "Then we'll go to my place now. I needed to anyway. Something I left there."

"Okay."

As they came into town, her heart danced in double-time. She was growing nervous, worried she wouldn't be enough for him. Cole Johnson was a lot of man. What if he found her boring?

"You're quiet."

She startled at his comment. "Sorry. Just... thinking."

He glanced at her, his grin crooked. "Thinking about all the things I'm going to do to you?"

His words caused her face to flame. "Yes," she mumbled, though it hadn't been true until now.

They reached his apartment and pulled into the parking lot. Suddenly, she looked around, worried about who might see her go inside with him. What they would say. What they would think.

Oh, this was a terrible idea.

Cole came and opened the passenger's door. "It'll help if you take off your seatbelt so you can come inside." He hesitated. "Unless you're having second thoughts."

"Not exactly," she began but fell silent.

"Come inside. Let's talk about it. If you want me to take you home after, I will."

He was almost too perfect...

Taking her hand, he led her along the sidewalk to his door. He unlocked and opened it, ushering her inside and pulling her to where his two lawn chairs sat. He had picked up another one so she would have somewhere to sit when she came over. They both took a seat. Her mouth dry, Nova didn't know how to begin.

"Are you worried we won't have chemistry?" he asked. "Because if you are, I can tell you that you're dead wrong." Squeezing her hand, he said, "Nova, I practically explode when I'm near you. And when I kiss you? It's the most incredible feeling in the world. I think we'll be just fine."

He leaned in and kissed her, a brief, sweet kiss.

She tried again. "It's not that. I worry about... that is, what I'm thinking is..." She stopped talking and blew out a long breath. "You are more experienced than I am. I'm afraid I won't live up to your expectations. Yes, I grow fevered when we kiss, but what if I'm not enough for you, Cole? You're this incredibly sexy man, hot and handsome. I'm... well, I'm average."

He looked at her incredulously. "You are as far from average as a woman gets, Nova."

"But I've only been with two men. One a handful of times half my life ago. The other one more recent, but sex with him was sporadic. He was often too stoned or drunk to finish up."

Resting his hands on her shoulders, Cole said, "I don't care what came before. Who or how often or if it was great or mediocre sex. This is us. Now. You and me. I have no doubt we are going to light the sheets on fire."

She laughed. "Oh, you think so?"

"I *know* so, babe. I've been thinking about touching you—being inside you—for a long time now. It's my daily fantasy."

Nova bit her lip. "Reality rarely lives up to what we fantasize about."

His fingers began massaging her shoulders. "That's where you're wrong. You just haven't been with the right partner before. Fantasy is just the tip of the iceberg. Reality is going to be so hot, it just might kill us." He grinned. "But what a way to go out."

She knew he was doing his best to reassure her. "Just tell me if I can do more for you. If I'm doing something wrong or you don't like—"

"I promise I will like everything about making love with you, Nova. Everything."

"Okay," she said, her voice quiet, doubt still filling her.

He cupped her cheeks. "Do you still want to do this? We don't have to. We can just sit here. Talk. Kiss. Go for a walk."

"No," she said firmly. "I *want* to do this, Cole. I've thought a lot about it, too," she admitted.

His thumbs caressed her. "You have? Well, let's stop thinking and start doing."

He stood, helping bring her to her feet. His arms went around her, and he kissed the top of her head. His fingers massaged her nape, helping her to relax. His lips grazed her temple. Nova shuddered. They traveled across her forehead. Down her nose, arriving at her lips.

As his arms enveloped her, Cole brushed his mouth slowly

against hers. Immediately, her body heated, the blood rushing through her. He teased her mouth open, and his tongue swept inside. He didn't rush things. Instead, he took his time exploring her mouth as if he'd never kissed her before. Nova responded, wanting more from him.

Much more.

Her hands roamed his broad back, wanting his shirt gone. She tugged it from where it was tucked in, not breaking the kiss until she pulled it high enough to come between them. Cole quickly got rid of it, his mouth seeking hers again, his bare chest pressing against her aching breasts.

His heat now enveloped her, his cock pressing against her. Excitement filled her. So did yearning. She wanted her bare flesh against his.

Boldly, she broke the kiss and took his hand. "Where's your bedroom?" she asked.

"To the right."

He let her lead him to it. She only dropped his hand to unbutton her blouse. The minute the last button was unfastened, he pushed it from her shoulders, dropping kisses along the slope of her neck and along the shoulder. When he reached her bra strap, he bit into it, dragging it down her shoulder and arm, before returning to do the same with the other one.

Delicious shivers now shot through her as his hands undid the clasp to her bra. He took the straps in his fingers and pulled the bra down and tossed it aside. Bare to the waist now, she moved to him, needing, wanting his heat, his flesh against hers.

Cole held her to him, his lips nuzzling her neck, nipping it playfully, desire continuing to ripple through her. He cupped her breasts, the pads of his thumbs brushing against her nipples, making them pebble in need.

"Do you think they want my attention?" he asked huskily, continuing to brush against them.

"Yes," she panted, experiencing sensations she'd never dreamed of.

Cole swept her from her feet and took her to the bed, placing her gently upon it, saying, "I finally had this bed delivered last week—anticipating this very moment with you."

She hadn't realized he hadn't had a bed and wondered if he had slept on the floor.

"I want to give all of you my full attention," he said, moving to lie next to her and turning her to face him.

His mouth covered one breast as his hand kneaded the other. His tongue and teeth worked their magic, and soon Nova writhed on the bed. She pushed her fingers into his hair, gliding through its silky texture as he continued sucking, laving, grazing her nipple with his teeth, driving her out of her mind.

He moved his lips to the other breast. "Don't want to neglect this one," he said, a bit of his West Texas drawl slipping out. "Looks like it needs more convincing than the other one."

He continued to devour the breast, licking, sucking, gently biting until her body was flush with fever and something built inside her. Neither Ace nor Jagger had taken a tenth of this time with her, but Cole was all about foreplay.

She wanted to touch him and allowed her hands to roam his back, rubbing up and down, feeling the sleek muscles. As he sucked hard on her breast, her fingers found his nipples and grazed them. He groaned, and she rotated her thumbs in circles around them, hearing his moan, feeling powerful and feminine and different than ever before. Playfully, she tweaked the nipples, and he gasped.

His mouth found hers again. Hard, demanding kisses enveloped her, almost swallowing her whole. Cole took and took and took, his mouth possessing her as much as his hands did. His fingers found the button on her jeans and undid it, lowering the zipper, then pulling them down her hips and legs before discarding them. He slipped his fingers inside her panties, running them along the top, edging them down her hips and along her legs before they, too were gone.

Cole looked down at her, and Nova saw satisfaction in her eyes. She had worried what he would think of her body.

"I like your tattoo," he said, bending to the right side of her belly where the feather tattoo had been inked in light blue and a soft purple and pink. "This is amazing. It looks like a real feather is just resting here."

He moved his lips to it, his tongue outlining the feather, causing her core to throb until she ached.

"Why a feather?" he asked, raising his head, his index finger tracing the outline.

"It's a dove's feather," she explained. "Doves symbolize peace and pure love. I got it after I gave birth to Leo. He brought such love into my life and anchored me. At the same time, I felt freer than I ever had when I'd lived with my parents, and I wanted to soar through the skies and revel in my new freedom."

"Did you design it?"

"I did. Rain took me to a friend of hers in Dallas about three months after Leo was born. I guess being young, my body bounced back more quickly than most postpartum women. Leo nursed from me while the tattoo artist made a stencil of my design on a thermal imager. It transferred the design in about three seconds. He did the line work, and then Rain burped Leo and held him while the artist did the coloring and shading."

Cole framed her face in his hands. "It's beautiful, Nova. Just like you are."

She'd always thought beyond her hair that she was average-looking, but she saw in his eyes that he believed she *was* beautiful. Suddenly, she believed it herself, causing her confidence to soar.

Looking into his eyes, Nova said, "I love you," just as Cole said, "I love you" at the same time.

They looked at one another and then burst out laughing. He kissed her, his fingers pushing into her hair, massaging her scalp.

Breaking the kiss, he said, "I've wanted to tell you that. I was waiting for the right moment. Now... just felt right."

"I love you," she repeated, amazed that this incredible man felt the same about her as she did about him. "I haven't been in love before, Cole. With Ace, it was all about rebelling against my parents and a hot guy wanting to kiss me. Then he was gone. Jagger? I just fell into being with him. I thought it was love, but I see now how self-centered he was. He used me. He didn't like Leo. He was a selfish man and an even more selfish lover."

Cole frowned. "He didn't take care of you?"

She sniffed. "Jagger only wanted me to take care of him. I've spent more time kissing you than I ever did him. He barely touched me when we had sex. He just wanted me to do for him."

"Bloody bastard," he muttered under his breath. Then his scowl faded. "I'm here for you, Nova. I love you. I love Leo. I want to make you feel special. Alive. I want you to call my name and know I'll be here for you."

He kissed her tenderly. "I want you to know just how extraordinary you are."

Pushing from the bed, he stripped off his shorts and boxer-briefs. Oh, if she'd thought the top half of him was well-formed, the bottom gave the top a run for the money. Everywhere, he was sleek muscles, and all she wanted to do was touch them. Touch him.

Especially his cock, which was standing at full attention.

She held out her arms to him, and he rejoined her on the bed, his body hovering over hers. Slowly, he ran a finger along the seam of her sex.

"You are wet for me, babe."

She supposed that was a good thing because she was feeling awfully good right now.

His fingers danced along her core, teasing it, causing it to pound violently. Slowly, he pushed a finger inside her, causing her to gasp. He stroked her, another finger joining the first, moving within her, causing her hips to rise and meet him.

Whimpering, she grabbed his elbows, wanting him to come closer. "No," he said. "I want you to come. I want to watch you come. Look at me, Nova," he commanded, his fingers moving more quickly now, the caresses long and deep.

Her gaze met his, her body moving of its own accord now, shaking, the pressure building inside her. His intimate touch broke something within her, and she let herself go.

"Ride it, babe. Ride it out," he encouraged, as she peaked and cried his name, her body shuddering violently.

Nova clutched at him, frantic, the wave cresting and then ebbing. Suddenly, she felt weak as a newborn kitten, her hands falling from him back to the bed. She was spent.

Cole pushed on the mattress and leaned to the nightstand, opening it and withdrawing a condom.

"I have an implant," she said, touching her arm and turning it over. "It's here."

Jagger had said condoms took away sexual pleasure from him. Nova had tried birth control pills and found they made her feel sluggish and bloated. She had opted for the implant, which was highly effective and the size of a matchstick. It could also be removed easily and lasted for several years.

"You sure?" he asked. "I don't mind."

This man was too good for her. But she loved him and was ready to begin this next chapter.

"You don't need it. We don't need it."

Cole tossed the condom back in the drawer and closed it, moving to the bed and kissing her as he hovered over her. As the kiss grew more passionate, he pushed inside her easily and began to move. Soon, Nova caught his rhythm and excitement. She clung to him as they rocked and danced. Then the warmth exploded inside her again, all the light and fever coming to a head. A second orgasm rippled through her body, and she wrapped her arms about his neck, hearing his own groans of pleasure.

He collapsed atop her, driving her into the mattress, his forehead resting against hers.

"You, Nova Turner, are simply amazing," Cole declared, taking her along with him as he rolled onto his back.

She now rested atop him and stacked her hands beneath her chin, looking at him. "You are ten levels higher than amazing." She thought a moment. "I'll go with spectacular for now."

He stroked her hair. "Nova, it's never been like this for me. Yes, I've had sex, and it was good. But this? It was different in every way. Because I'm invested in you. In us."

Tears misted her eyes. "I know. I feel the same."

"I love you," he said. "Gosh, that feels good, finally saying it aloud to you."

She smiled. "I love you, Cole. I didn't know love could be like this. I wish I had met you... before."

His strong arms held her close. "Neither of us was ready for the other back them. We're adults now. We're on interesting career paths. Me, with this first head job. You, starting your private painting parties. We needed the time to find who we are before we could find each other." He sighed. "I'm beat, Nova. I don't know if I can keep my eyes open."

"Then don't."

She moved from on top of him and pressed against his side. Her head rested on his shoulder. His arm went around her.

"Let's just be together," she said. "And when we wake?" She giggled. "I'm ready to go again."

"Ah, you'll be the death of me, woman," he said.

Within seconds, his breathing evened out, and she knew he was asleep. Nova savored being next to Cole.

Next to the man she loved.

17

———

Nova drove to Sugar Springs High School's stadium, eager to watch her first varsity home game in person. She had attended all of the previous JV games, where Leo had started each one, catching several passes and even scoring a touchdown in last night's victory. She was amazed by Leo's athletic ability and tried to recall if Ace had ever mentioned playing any kind of sport. She couldn't. It had been too long ago, and she and Ace had not wasted time talking about much of anything. The sexual attraction between them had been too great, and Ace was only too willing to take advantage of a rebellious, naive teenager.

So far, she hadn't been involved in the pregame dinner, which the booster parents put on each week. Tonight's meal was being catered by Ida Lou's Diner. Nova liked the feisty, sassy diner owner. In fact, she liked many of the tenants on the town square.

She had gone around to each business on the square this week, her mission twofold. One was to introduce herself as a new merchant on the square and explain what Playful Painting was. Several of those merchants had agreed to put a flyer advertising Playful Painting in their store's window, and Dahlia Jones, who owned a clothing boutique, promised she would book her girl-friends for a party as soon as Nova opened. She told Dahlia Playful Painting would be open for business starting next week and gave her the website, so Dahlia could book her party. These first few clients would be critical to her new business' success. Dahlia was very friendly, and Nova thought with Dahlia being a business owner, she would be more conscious about leaving a review.

The second thing she had done was explain to all of the merchants on the square about the weekly raffles for the home games. All of them proved to be enthusiastic and willing to donate items, in addition to the ones she had already collected from various booster club members. Tonight, she had donations from the sports bar, the florist, and Phyllis Arnold's hair salon which would be up for grabs.

That latter donation had surprised Nova. At first, she almost skipped going into the salon but didn't want to give Phyllis any kind of ammunition to use against her. Cole had used the term *mean girl*, and Nova asked Leo about it, as well. Her son had pulled up a movie for Nova to stream, one of the same name, and she was exposed to Cady and the Plastics. She realized mean girls existed at every level and were simply a part of life which had to be dealt with.

Phyllis had been cool to Nova during their interaction, but she contributed a cut and blow dry to this week's raffle. The woman might not have liked Nova or her idea, but it was obvious Phyllis was a businesswoman who knew the value of the free advertising she would receive by participating in the booster club's raffle. She had declined, however, to put up one of Nova's Playful Painting flyers. It didn't matter. Enough of the businesses on the square were supporting her. She would hit up other busi-nesses in town this coming week for more raffle prizes.

The parking lot to the stadium was filling quickly even though it was more than an hour before gametime. Nova took the cash box and two glass fishbowls the booster club treasurer had provided her. Inside the metal box were not only tickets for tonight's raffle, but a different colored roll of tickets for the grand prize awarded at the end of the season. She went through the admission gates and found both sets of Smiths setting up card tables and chairs and taping up banners Betty Smith had painted. Betty and Bob were parents to Luke, while Steve and Sue Smith were parents to Lyle.

Bob told Nova, "I thought it would be easier to keep the different raffles separate since we're charging more for the Disney than the weekly one."

"Good idea," she praised. "I only have the one cashbox, though. We'll have to pool all the money inside it."

Steve said, "I can remedy that. There are usually several in the concession booth. I'll see if they'll loan us one this time, and then we can let the treasurer know we need a second one."

True to his word, Steve returned with another cashbox, and Nova gave him the tickets for the grand prize. The treasurer had also given her some petty cash to use as change, and she divided that between the two boxes.

"Remember that you'll also circulate through the stands during all the first quarter and half of the second," she said. "I'll stay under the stands and man this area since we're close to the concession stand, and someone might want to buy a ticket while they're getting refreshments. I hope you'll be able to follow the game and watch your sons play."

Sue laughed. "There's enough time between plays where we can easily hawk tickets. You know what might be good for next week? One of those aprons servers at a restaurant tie around their waists. We could keep tickets and money there instead of trying to hang onto everything and shove stuff into our pockets."

"Good idea," Nova said. "I'll be sure I talk to the treasurer about that and another lockbox."

Fans started streaming into the stadium at that point, and she did her best to direct them to the two tables. She explained to others as they came that they could buy a raffle ticket for the grand prize or for this week's raffle.

One fan asked, "We have a raffle this week?"

Nova nodded enthusiastically. "Yes. Our merchants in Sugar Springs are helping to support our football team by donating items for each home game. If you buy a raffle ticket this week, you have a chance to win a fifty-dollar flower bouquet. You might win fifty dollars in food and drinks at our local sports bar. Or you could win a cut and blow dry from Salon on the Square."

The woman's eyes lit up. "Those are terrific prizes. I'm ready to buy a ton of tickets."

Smiling, she directed the woman to the card tables and watched as the Smiths did a brisk business.

Just before kickoff, Nova heard the playing of *The Star-Spangled Banner* begin and went to relieve her volunteers.

"You sure you can handle all this by yourself?" Bob asked.

"Yes, most fans will be up in the stands watching the game. I think the big rush is over."

Betty said, "I think we did more sales tonight than we used to do for a season. Great idea, Nova."

"Thank you," she said humbly. "We want to do what we can to raise funds for the football team."

The Smiths took some of the rolls of raffle tickets, and as they left, Sue Smith leaned down to where Nova had just seated herself and said, "I know you're seeing Coach Johnson. My boy and nephew think very highly of him. It's been nice getting to know you as well, Nova. I hope the two of you will remain a couple."

Her cheeks tinged with a blush, and she said, "Thank you. Coach Johnson is a very fine man."

The band finished playing the school song, and Nova saw beneath the stands was now deserted. It gave her time to think back on this past week.

And Cole.

After he had awakened from his much-needed nap, he'd made love to her again, leisurely exploring every inch of her body. The man definitely believed in foreplay, and Nova realized how much she had been shortchanged by her previous two lovers in that area.

They had gone to Playful Painting after that, Cole wanting to see how everything looked with the furniture and cases in place. He was full of compliments as she showed him the setup, including her artwork on display. He had even told her he wanted to book a party for his coaches and their wives a few weeks away when they had their open week, which he explained was when they didn't play an opponent. Cole thought it would be something the wives would enjoy being included in, and Nova said she would reserve that Saturday night for his group.

The Smiths returned with the money from their raffle sales, and they placed the tickets into the different fishbowls.

"I don't think any of us should be the one to draw the winner," Nova told them. She glanced around and saw three students standing in line at the concession stand.

Walking up to them, she asked, "Would one of you be willing to draw the raffle winners for this week's booster club drawing?"

A tall, handsome young man grinned. "I'd be happy to do so, Miss Turner. I'm Freddie Otts. I play basketball for the Knights. I met your son when you were registering him for classes."

"Oh, I remember seeing you in the gym. And I'm happy to have you select our winners in a random drawing."

He and the two teens who accompanied him came back to the table with her, and Freddie said, "My mom and dad own the sports bar in town. Mom told me about your painting store. It sounds like a lot of fun. Is it something teenagers might do?"

"Of course, Freddie. It would be fun for a birthday party or just to hang out with your friends. You book a party, and my place holds up to sixteen people. I encourage you to bring your own snacks and drinks to add to the fun."

"Sounds awesome, Miss Turner. What's your website?"

She told him, and Bob held out the fishbowl, telling Freddie to turn his head away and stick his hand in. Soon, they had their three winners, and Nova thanked Freddie, telling him she hoped she would see him soon.

Steve and Bob offered to hang onto the cash boxes for her and hand them over to the treasurer after the game. Sue said they could leave the tables and chairs for now and collect them at the end of the evening.

"You need to be able to go and watch some of the game," Betty encouraged. "I know Leo's not playing now, but you never know."

Nova snapped pictures of the winning tickets and took the tickets up to the press box, handing them to Joe Bob Milton. She had already jotted down which ticket would receive each prize, and he said he would announce the winning numbers after the visiting Randolph Raiders had performed their portion of half-time and before the Sugar Springs band and drill team took the field.

"My wife already texted me that she bought twenty tickets," the principal said.

She laughed. "Then I hope Mrs. Milton is a winner tonight."

Leaving the press box, she headed down the stairs to the bleachers. Jessica waved at her, and she went to join her and Jason.

"I saved a seat for you," her friend said. "I knew you'd be able to watch the game by halftime."

"How has Jake done tonight?" Nova asked as she glanced at the scoreboard, seeing the Knights were ahead 14-10.

"He's thrown one touchdown pass and gone five for seven. No interceptions," Jessica said proudly.

She was pleased she knew enough about football now so that she could interpret what her friend had just told her.

The Raiders pushed down the field and were inside the ten yard line with less than ninety seconds to go before the half ended. Cole had told her how important going into the locker room with momentum was after the first half ended, and she hoped the Knights defense would hold.

Fortunately, it did on all three attempts to reach the end zone. When the Raiders lined up in field goal formation, she held her breath, knowing being this close almost guaranteed points going on the scoreboard. Much to her surprise, though, the Raiders ran what Leo had told her was a fake. The center snapped the ball to the holder, and the kicker pretended to kick as the holder ran to his right. The entire stands leaped to their feet, Raiders fans cheering on the holder, while the home crowd shouted for the defense to stop the player.

When the Knights knocked the running Raider out of bounds at the two yard line, the home stands erupted. Nova could feel them vibrating beneath her as the crowd jumped up and down. The Knights took possession, with Jake taking a knee as the clock ran out. Joe Bob announced it was halftime. She located Cole as he ran off the field with his team and staff, seeing the joy on his face.

The Randolph Raiders performed their portion of halftime and then as planned, Joe Bob announced the three winning numbers of tonight's raffle, reminding the fans there would be a weekly raffle at home games and a drawing for the grand prize to Walt Disney World at the last home game. He told the winners to find Nova Turner and show her their ticket to claim their prize, telling her to stand up. She did, waving both hands in the air, and soon three different people made their way to her.

She checked their tickets to insure they were the correct winners and then opened her purse, pulling out the gift certificates she had designed. She filled out the name of each winner on the certificate and signed it, having already had Ken as the booster club president sign in advance. She handed the certificates over.

"Thank you for supporting our Sugar Springs Knights," she told all three winners.

"Great idea," one of the men said. "We'll be sure to buy these tickets every home game."

She settled back to watch the rest of the band's performance, followed by the Sugar Springs drill team. She was impressed with how in sync the girls were in their dance.

The third quarter started, and she got into the game, cheering on Cole's varsity team. Nova felt terrible when Keith Arnold dropped two passes in a row. Once the offense left the field, she saw Cole call Keith over, putting his hands on the boy's shoulders and talking to him. Keith nodded. Nova couldn't think about how dejected the teenager must be.

When the Knights' offense took the field again, Jake tossed a quick pass to Keith. This time, the receiver caught it and ran for a first down and then some. She clapped enthusiastically, knowing this had to help Keith's self-esteem.

Several plays later, Keith caught another pass and was hit hard. He came down and even from a distance, Nova could see Keith landed off-balance. The clock was stopped as the team's trainer hurried onto the field to check on Keith, along with another man.

"That's Rex Carpenter," Jessica whispered. "He's the local doctor. His wife Sandy serves as his RN. Dr. C attends home football and basketball games, in case he's needed for a medical emergency."

The two men got Keith to his feet and helped him limp off the field as the crowd gave the senior wide receiver a standing ovation.

She glanced to Cole, who motioned for Leo to go in, surprising Nova. Her son had been standing on the sidelines, his helmet cradled under his arm. Leo now slipped it on and jogged onto the field.

Jessica nudged her. "I know Jake will get the ball to Leo. They've been practicing pass routes like crazy."

Jake led his team down the field, four running plays in a row. They were barely inside their opponent's twenty yard line when the quarterback went back to pass. Nova watched the ball float through the air in Leo's direction and held her breath. Leo caught the ball and turned, making a quick move to his left, then right, and then cutting past the defender on him. He raced into the endzone, putting his team up by eleven points.

Jessica threw her arms around Nova, and the two women hopped up and down.

"They make a great team," Jason said, smiling broadly.

Nova watched as the Raiders scored again, making it 21-17, but Jake once more led his team down the field, throwing two completions to Leo at critical times. With seven seconds to go in the game, Jake handed off to Teddy O'Riley, and the running back powered through the mob of players and into the endzone as time expired on the clock.

The home fans went wild with the victory against a tough opponent.

Leo began looking into the crowd, and she waved, standing on the bleachers so he might see her better. He caught sight of her and took off his helmet, waving it in the air in victory, a huge smile on his face.

Cole came up and gave Leo a hug before moving on to another player to congratulate. She watched her boyfriend and was filled with a sense of pride for him. Cole had said this was the first real challenge his team had faced this season. They had done so, her son being a key part of the win.

Before Nova climbed down, her eyes skimmed the crowd—and locked on Phyllis Arnold. The hairdresser glared at Nova, and she stepped down, her elation falling flat. Still, she thought she should go over to the next section and say something to Phyllis.

"I'll be right back," she told Jessica, moving through the crowd until she reached Phyllis and Fred.

"I'm so sorry Keith was injured. I hope he'll be okay and can play next week."

"Do you?" Phyllis asked, not bothering to disguise her bitterness. "Your boy wouldn't have been out there if mine hadn't gotten hurt. I'm sure you think Leo will be the starter now. Well, that's not going to happen. Keith is a senior. He's a wonderful receiver. Leo is new to football. He can't hold a candle to my Keith."

Phyllis pushed past Nova and rushed down the stairs.

Fred said, "Forgive her. She's always been close to Keith. Probably too close. She couldn't have any more children after he was born. She's a good mom, but she smothers him sometimes."

"I am sorry Keith was injured," she said sincerely.

"I know you are, Nova," Fred said wearily. "But you'll never convince my wife of that. Good evening." He followed Phyllis down the stairs.

She should be elated now, Leo getting to play in his first varsity game and Cole securing his first district win. She couldn't let anyone see how Phyllis had gotten to her and put on a smile, returning to the Fletchers.

"Do you want to come to Romano's with us?" Jason asked. "A group is going to meet up there now."

"No, go ahead," she said. "I need to hit the sack. I've got things to do this weekend to prepare for Playful Painting's opening."

Jessica hugged her. "I'll talk to you tomorrow."

Nova went to her car and drove home. She knew Cole was busy after a game but sent him a quick congratulatory text, not expecting to hear from him. She got ready for bed and waited up for Leo, who got home an hour after she did, his hair still wet from his after-game shower. She listened as he talked her through several plays in the game, his enthusiasm bubbling over.

"I'm sorry Keith got hurt," Leo finally said, winding down and looking as if he were ready to crash. "But Jake and I have put in a lot of hours together away from the practice field. I knew I would be ready. And I was, Mom."

She hugged her son tightly. "I'm so proud of you, Leo. It was a big deal for you to get into the game tonight, much less score a touchdown."

"Thanks for moving us here," he said. "I love playing football, and I have lots of friends. I like most of my teachers. Sugar Springs is a great place to be, Mom."

Nova hugged Leo again. "I know it is. I'm glad we're both happy we came here."

Leo went to bed, while Nova moved about the house restlessly. She picked up a sketchpad, doodling a few new jewelry designs.

Then her phone dinged with a text from Cole.

Are you still up?

HER HEART BEAT FASTER and she replied she was.

A light tap sounded on the door, and she ran to open it. Cole stood there, and Nova flung herself into his arms.

18

———————

Cole had seen the text from Nova and waited to reply to it. He'd finished up with his coaching staff and then downloaded the required video of tonight's game to next week's opponent. He locked his office and went to his truck, intending to go home, and found himself driving to Nova's instead. He doubted she was still up. Even as he walked to her porch and texted her, he wasn't expecting a response. But when she immediately replied, he quickly tapped on her door. Suddenly, she was in his arms.

And everything was right in his world.

He walked her backward, guiding her into the house, closing the front door. Turning her, he pushed her against the door, his body pinning her to it, his kiss demanding and deep. If a thousand years passed, he would never get enough of Nova. His hunger for her caused everything else to fade away. There was only Nova. Him. Their bodies against one another, the heat and desire building.

Breaking the kiss, he hoarsely asked, "Leo?"

"He's home. In bed," she said breathlessly. "Probably asleep by now. He was crashing fast."

Even though Nova's bedroom was on the opposite side of the house from Leo's, Cole wasn't willing to chance the teenager overhearing them. Grabbing Nova's hand, he pulled her through the house and out the kitchen door, headed toward her art studio. She had a motion detector security light in the back yard, which made it easier to find their way.

Opening the door, he yanked Nova inside, closing it. Knowing they had complete privacy now, he wrapped his arms about her tightly, bodies and mouths fusing together. Each kiss was deeper, longer, more demanding than the one before. His need for her was all-consuming, driving every thought from his mind.

He broke the kiss, gazing around the workshop, seeing the large worktable only a few feet away. He backed her toward it, grateful it was clear of any pieces of her art. When she couldn't move any farther, he lifted her onto it and leaned her back until she lay atop it, her legs dangling from the table. He hovered over her, his body covering hers, his fingers lacing through hers, bringing her hands to rest beside her ears.

Cole kissed her thoroughly, relishing the taste of her mint toothpaste and the curves of her hips and breasts. Still, he hungered for more.

Releasing her hands, he broke the kiss, trailing his lips down her throat, to the valley between her breasts. He found the hem of her short nightgown and worked it up so that he could devour her breasts. He sucked and licked them, feeling them swell as he kneaded them, enjoying the small sounds Nova made as he did so.

But he needed even more of her, and his mouth went lower, grazing her belly. He swirled his tongue around her belly button and dragged it lower still. His hands reached for her ankles, lifting them so her feet were placed flat against the table. Then he took her knees, opening her to him. Heat shot through him when he found her bare beneath the gown, and his tongue plunged inside her.

Nova was already wet, her sweet juices flowing as he lapped at her. Her sighs turned to whimpers. She pushed her fingers into his hair and tightened her grip as his tongue moved in and out of her. She began to writhe, her breath hitching, the whimpers louder. He found her nub and swirled his tongue around it, teasing it as she moved her hips faster. He let his tongue and teeth do the talking for him, showing her the depths of his desire for her.

Then she came, hard, fast, and he quickly pulled out from her, his mouth covering hers and swallowing her noises. She moved beneath him, panting, crying, trembling, the orgasm rocking her.

She stilled, her body going limp. He looked at her, seeing she was sated.

And still he needed more of her.

He pushed up, her mewl of protest not lasting long as she saw him quickly pushing down his pants and boxer-briefs. He was rock-hard now. No time to strip because he was about to explode. He grabbed her waist and slid her body upward until all of it rested on the table. Then he climbed up and thrust into her, again and again, consumed by desire that demanded he possess every last bit of her. His blood sang her name over and over until the orgasm flooded him, igniting until he felt his entire body afire.

Nova trembled beneath him, clinging to him, murmuring his name again and again, as he collapsed atop her, spent. Yet he searched for her mouth, his lips finding hers, kissing her again and again, the wild need for her like a siren's song.

Finally, he was too weary to even do that. He broke the kiss, his mouth resting against her neck, her pulse beating beneath his lips.

"That... was... earth-shattering," Nova said, her breathing ragged.

He realized he must be crushing her and turned on his side, half on and half off her.

"No kidding," he managed to say, his own breathing coming in gasps, his heart still pounding violently.

They lay there several minutes, coming back to earth. He brushed his lips against her throat and then licked the pulse point.

"You are incredible, Nova Turner."

"Me? You did all the work. I feel spoiled rotten, Cole."

He grinned at her. "If I could move a finger, I'd caress you with it. But I don't think I can. I am drained. But in the best way possible."

They fell silent again, and he relished the warmth of her body against his, her jasmine scent, faint.

Finally, he disengaged from her, pushing up on his elbow, climbing from the table and pulling his clothes back into place. She watched him, a satisfied smile turning up the corners of her mouth.

He took her hands and helped her from the table, her nightgown falling mid-thigh again.

Wrapping his arms about her, he said, "You didn't tell me you didn't sleep in underwear."

"You never asked," she said coyly, a faint smile playing on her lips.

His hands slid to her ass and cupped it. "I like that. You being ready for me."

"I like you," she said, tugging on his hair so that his lips met hers again.

Cole made certain to keep the kiss sweet and tame because he had absolutely nothing left in his tank to give tonight.

Nova broke the kiss. "You need to go home and get some sleep after your big victory."

"The one on the field—or in your studio?" he flirted.

"Both," she said, laughing, kissing him again.

She broke away from him. "It was a great win tonight."

"Even sweeter because Leo contributed to it," he told her. "I was so proud of him. He's come farther in a shorter time than any athlete I've ever worked with. He played a huge role tonight. I can't see him riding the bench anymore, Nova. I need to replace Keith Arnold with Leo."

"But Keith is a senior."

"I know. But Leo really stepped up for us tonight. Besides, Dr. Carpenter diagnosed Keith with a high ankle sprain."

She frowned. "What does that mean? How long will he be out?"

"A high ankle sprain is actually above the ankle itself. It's a sprain in the upper ligaments of an ankle. Those ligaments are the ones that stabilize you as you walk or run."

"That sounds serious," she said, worrying her bottom lip.

"It can be. Keith had pain and swelling. He could put his weight on his foot and ankle, but he still experienced pain above his ankle. Dr. Carpenter said the good thing was that Keith didn't fracture his fibula, which can happen sometimes with a high ankle sprain. After the game, he took Keith back to his office, along with his parents, and did a CT scan. No other ligament damage showed up."

Cole smoothed her hair. "I talked to Dr. Carpenter, and he said, for now, Keith is alternating ice on and off his ankle. He'll wrap a compression bandage around it tomorrow and keep it elevated, as well as take ibuprofen to reduce inflammation and pain. Dr. Carpenter will stop by in the morning and decide if Keith needs to wear a boot or use crutches. Carpenter and our trainer will work with Keith on a physical therapy program to strengthen the area and prevent this type of injury again."

"It sounds complicated. When can Keith play again?"

"We'll know more in the next forty-eight hours. Healing usually is at least six weeks, though, depending on soft tissue damage."

"Six weeks is pretty much the rest of the season," she pointed out.

"Yes, that's when district will be wrapping up. Hopefully, our season will be extended, and we'll go to the playoffs."

"But it sounds like this is it for Keith."

He nodded in agreement. "Probably so. Injuries are a part of football. Fortunately, we have a player of Leo's quality to step in for Keith."

She bit her lip again. Cole smoothed the lip with his thumb. "Nothing you can do. And don't go borrowing trouble and worrying about Leo being injured."

"You're starting to know me too well," she said. "I've tried to ignore the injury aspect of playing."

"We condition our players. We do everything we can to avoid injuries, Nova."

Sighing, she said, "I know. But he's my baby. I don't care if he's six inches taller than I am and still growing like a weed."

Cole brushed his lips against hers. "I know. It'll always be like that."

"Phyllis Arnold is going to blame me for this."

"What?"

"Never mind," she said quickly.

"No, tell me what you mean," he urged.

"She doesn't like me. She hasn't since that first booster club meeting when Ken O'Riley tabled her mum fundraising plan. With Leo stepping in for Keith now, it won't be good. I even tried to express how sorry I was about Keith's injury tonight, but she brushed off my concern."

"Keith is hurt. She'll understand he has to be replaced," he said.

But the look on Nova's face told another story. She shook her head. "You need to go home. You're going to be exhausted tomorrow. You shouldn't have come by tonight."

"I'm glad I did," he said, caressing her cheek. "Seeing you

energized me, Nova. I needed to be with you." He kissed her softly. "I love you."

"I love you, too," she said.

She took his hand and led him from the studio back into the house and to the front door.

"Can I see you tomorrow?" he asked. "After we finish up? Actually, I think I'll stop by and see Keith first. Could we have dinner?"

"I'd like that," she said. "I could roast a chicken."

"You spoil me."

"Not as much as you spoil me."

"Okay. I'll text when I leave the Arnolds."

Cole went to his truck and drove home. His weariness was now catching up to him. Still, he wouldn't have traded the last hour for anything. Any time spent with Nova was special.

He fell into bed, exhausted, and rose with his alarm, shaving off a quarter-hour from his usual run so he could get to school earlier and make a call to Aunt Ju before the coaching meeting began at seven. She served breakfast on the ranch at five every morning. Since it was six-thirty, she would be finished cleaning up by now.

He touched her name on his cell, and she answered on the second ring.

"I saw you won last night," she said. "Randolph was a good early season challenge for you."

"They had a tough defense," he told her. "But the quarterback I've told you about has a sixth sense where to get the ball. He's only a junior. If he can stay healthy, I think we'll go deep into the playoffs."

"What else is up? You still seeing Nova?"

Cole had told his aunt about meeting Nova and her son and how they'd begun dating.

"Whenever I can," he admitted. "Aunt Ju, she's... special."

Laughter sounded on the other end. "Oh, honey, I knew that from the first time you mentioned her."

"I love her."

"That's wonderful, Cole. It's about time you found a good woman."

"I want you to meet her. And Leo." He hesitated. "Aunt Ju. I think—no, I know—Nova's the one. I would marry her tomorrow if I could."

"Have you told her that?"

"I've told her I love her. She feels the same. I'm taking things slowly, though. She's been burned twice. Badly."

He hadn't shared Nova's entire backstory with his aunt, only saying she was very young when she had Leo and that Leo's father wasn't in the picture.

"I'd love for you to meet her."

"You know I don't get days off, Cole. I cook for this brood three squares a day, seven days a week."

"Have you ever thought about quitting? Retiring, I mean."

She didn't respond right away, and he let the silence play out, almost hearing her think over the line.

"I have," she said quietly. "I've saved a ton of money over the years. You winning an athletic scholarship sure helped. I don't have to pay any rent. I eat what I cook for the boys on the ranch. All my bills are paid for. The utilities. The water. Other than my car and health insurance, I've saved a pretty penny."

Cole thought a moment. "Aunt Ju, you're only fifty-one now. Have you ever thought about going back to college? You left because of me. You gave up on that dream. What if you went back now?"

"Oh, Cole..." Her voice faded, and he heard her sniffing, knowing she was crying.

"You're still young. You could move here. Maybe not Sugar Springs—unless you wanted to—but you could move to Tyler. It's close by, and they have a terrific university there. You could apply for the spring semester."

She hiccupped, a dead giveaway that she had been crying. "Probably none of my credits would transfer. It's been so long."

"So what? You could start from scratch. Major in whatever you want to. And we could see each other often."

"I wouldn't want to infringe upon your time with Nova. I know how much coaching takes up."

"You're family, Aunt Ju. I would love it if you came to East Texas. Would you think about it?"

"I will," she said, and he heard determination in her voice. "I think I'm ready for a change."

"Good. That's all I ask. Just consider it. Talk tomorrow?" he asked.

"Yes. That sounds good, Cole."

"I'll call in the morning. Before I have to go in for my weekly Sunday afternoon meeting."

He didn't have to tell her about his routine. Long ago, he'd shared the demanding schedule he followed during football season, and Aunt Ju was aware of it more than most.

"Love you," she said.

"Love you," he echoed, feeling good about nudging her as he hung up. Aunt Ju had given up her entire world to raise him. It was time she did something for herself.

He would love having her here, coming to his games, meeting Nova. He knew the two women would hit it off.

Feeling energized, he left his office and entered the conference room, finding every seat filled except his own.

"Good morning, gentlemen. We had a terrific game last night, and I'm ready to build upon that foundation. Ben, get us started."

As his offensive coordinator began to speak, Cole felt all the pieces were falling into place for him.

19

Nova saw the last of the birthday party guests out the door and began cleaning up from the afternoon session. It had been the birthday for a girl turning thirteen and half a dozen of her friends. The birthday girl had chosen a blue jay sitting on a branch in a tree as the group painting, and Nova had been impressed with what the newly-mined teenager had produced. The teen's mother had pulled Nova aside and asked if she might consider giving her daughter painting lessons. She had told the parent she would have to think about it.

Playful Painting had really taken off in the month since it had opened. She had hosted everything from baby showers to girls' night out to a Sunday school private party. She had slotted parties for Tuesday and Thursday nights during the week, Thursdays being open now since Leo no longer played on the JV squad on Thursday nights. Nova had kept the weekends to a session on Saturday afternoon from two until four and another one on Saturday night. She had wanted to keep those evenings open for Cole, but he encouraged her to book sessions while lightning was striking, and the concept was taking off. Since the parties ran two hours long, she had decided to schedule the

Saturday night ones from six until eight. That way, after cleanup, she could be home no later than eight-thirty—and in Cole's arms.

It surprised her how deeply her feelings ran for him and how easy and right everything was between them. She liked that she was busy and not sitting around waiting for him. Her days were filled with producing art, and she regularly sold items she had on display when groups came in for their painting parties. Jessica had convinced her to put her jewelry on the Playful Painting website, and now customers could order it directly from there.

Nova was glad she had turned the website over to the two students because she wouldn't have had time to update it regularly. It was enough to check the site daily to see what parties had been booked and what jewelry sales requests had been submitted. She was constantly being stopped at football games or when she was out running errands, people asking her to add more party times to the website's calendar. Right now, she was booked solidly for the rest of October and all of November. She hadn't opened up the December calendar yet, but she decided when she did, she would need to offer several more sessions because people were already clamoring to book holiday parties with her. She had spent this past week coming up with several paintings for the Christmas season for clients to try and copy.

Nova finished with the cleanup and made sure new brushes and blank canvases were laid out for tonight's party, one she had been looking forward to. It would be Cole's coaching staff, along with their wives or plus-ones. Since it was an open week and the Knights did not play, he had actually come to the extra party she had booked last night, wanting to see what the process was like before he participated in a group painting session with his staff. Cole had been enthusiastic and had fun going around, looking at the partiers' canvases.

Everything ready to go for this evening's party, Nova locked the door to her shop and drove home for a brief respite. When she arrived, Leo was there with Teddy, Jake, and Tim. They were playing video games as they munched on popcorn.

The boys greeted her, and she asked if they needed any more snacks. Leo said no and told her they would be going to a football game tonight between two of their upcoming rivals. She asked him when he thought he might be home, and Teddy spoke up, saying everyone was coming back to his house to sleep over.

Nova smiled at the boys, excited she and Cole would have the house to themselves this evening.

She went and showered, putting on fresh clothes and spritzing herself with a perfume Cole told her he liked. He was a very good boyfriend, always complimenting her and doing small things for her that made her feel special. After last night's party session, he had even gotten Leo to watch a movie with the two of them, this time a basketball movie called *Hoosiers*. Cole called the film a classic, and Nova could see why. While it was a movie centered around sports in a small town, it was so much more than that. She knew even less about basketball than she had football and enjoyed sitting between Cole and Leo as they explained the finer points of the movie's basketball sequences to her. Nova decided she liked basketball almost as much as she did football and told Cole she would like to attend some of the Sugar Springs games once basketball season began.

He had told her it was important to him as the district's athletic director to support other sports beyond the one he coached and hoped she might accompany him to other sporting events, such as volleyball, baseball, or soccer games.

She heard Leo holler "Bye," and she went to the window, seeing him climb into a car with his friends. Her son continued to blossom in Sugar Springs. He had made good friends and was pulling top grades. Leo's counselor had called Nova and told her it wasn't too early to begin speaking to Leo about colleges he might want to attend and scholarship opportunities. The counselor said with Leo's grades, he could easily qualify for an academic scholarship and explained to Nova how the class valedictorian in Texas was able to claim free tuition at any public university in Texas.

Obviously, she would have to fill in with paying for a dorm room and meal plan, but she had shared this information with Leo, explaining to him the opportunities available if he kept up his grades. They decided once football season ended, they would make an appointment with his counselor and talk more in-depth about his career plans after high school. Leo said at this point, he had no idea what he might wish to major in because his interests were broad and extended to several different areas.

While she was still at the window, she saw Cole pull into her driveway, and her heart sped up as it always did anytime she caught sight of him.

Nova went to the door to greet him, and Cole came in, handing her a bouquet of fresh flowers.

"What are these for?" she asked, pulling him down to give him a thank-you kiss.

"No special reason."

She smiled. "Then that's the best kind of reason."

"Are you ready for my coaching staff and their wives tonight?"

"I laid out everything for the party before I came home. Jessica brought over a couple of boxes of cookies. We talked about how we might start selling items from Rolling Scones during painting parties. Most people remember the wine when they come, but oftentimes they forget to bring snacks. Jessica said cookies would be easy to hold while painting, and it would be good advertising for their bakery. I may use your party as the test case and see if people are willing to pay for cookies."

"How was the birthday party today? A lot of giggling girls?"

Nova laughed. "A few got the giggles but for the most part, they were a fun group who happened to be serious about their art. One mom even asked me if I might be available to give private art lessons to her daughter."

"Have you considered doing something like that?"

She shrugged. "I had given it a thought at one point, but I'm already so busy that I'm not sure I want to take on anything else at this point. From a financial standpoint, my time is better spent creating my own art and then doing group parties."

"Speaking of taking things on, I have some news for you."

She looked at him in anticipation. "Has Aunt Ju made a decision?"

Cole nodded. "She's decided she's coming to East Texas for good."

Nova threw her arms around him, hugging him tightly. "I know you've wanted her to make the move. Has she decided whether or not she's going to enroll at UT-Tyler?"

"She has put in her application and wants to start in January with the spring semester."

"When will she get here?"

He grinned. "She's on her way now. She loaded her car with the little she owns and took off a few hours ago. The house we lived in on the ranch came furnished from bed linens to kitchen items to furniture. Beyond her clothes and books? She didn't have much to pack."

"Has she decided if she's going to get a place in Tyler or stay in Sugar Springs?"

"She wants to see the area first before she makes any decisions on where to live."

Impulsively, Nova said, "Aunt Ju should stay with Leo and me for a few days. At least until she makes up her mind. She can't stay with you in your one-bedroom apartment."

"That's generous of you, Nova, but I can't ask you to do that."

"You didn't ask, silly. I volunteered."

She went to the kitchen, Cole following, and put the flowers in one of her favorite vases.

"I suppose I could call her and see what she wants to do when she gets here."

"FaceTime her," Nova suggested. "Let me talk to her."

He pulled out his phone, and she heard the ringing and then a woman answering. "Hello, Cole. Checking to see where I am on the road? I'm about to stop in Abilene for the night. In fact, hold on. I'm pulling into a motel parking lot now."

Aunt Ju cut the motor and lifted her phone from the cup holder. Nova could see her much better now and studied the woman who had raised Cole. She could see they had the same hair and eye color. When she smiled, Nova also saw that Cole had inherited that, as well.

"Why, hello. You must be Nova. I'm Julia Johnson, but you can call me Aunt Ju. Cole has talked my ear off about you, honey."

She laughed. "He's told me quite a bit about you, too. I'm thrilled that you're coming to live in our neck of the woods."

"I'll have to figure out where I want to live. Either in Sugar Springs or closer to Tyler and the university. One thing I know is that I'm not cut out for dorm life with girls thirty-plus years my junior."

"I encouraged Cole to call you just now because I'd like to offer my house for you to stay in until you're ready to decide something more permanent."

"Oh, I can't put out you and Leo."

"You wouldn't be. The house Rain left me has plenty of room. Leo is at school and football practice all day, while I'm out back in my studio. You'd have the house to yourself a good portion of the time."

"Are you sure you don't mind? I don't want to infringe upon your privacy."

"You wouldn't be. It would give you time to make an informed decision without being rushed."

"Well, if you're offering, then I'm accepting. I only have one stipulation."

"What's that?" Nova asked.

"Let me do all the cooking for you. Cole tells me you're a great cook yourself, but I'd like to earn my keep while I'm staying there."

"That would be terrific. It would free up some time for me. I have to warn you, though, that Leo eats enough for three people these days."

Aunt Ju chuckled. "Honey, I've been serving hungry cowboys for decades now, not to mention feeding Cole himself. One teenager won't be a challenge."

"Then Cole can text you my address."

"I'll give you a heads up when I'm about an hour away. It looks like now after I stop in Dallas for a quick visit with an old friend, I should get there tomorrow afternoon around three."

"I look forward to seeing you in person, Aunt Ju," Nova said sincerely. "You raised a pretty wonderful guy."

The older woman smiled. "I think we helped raise each other. Okay, I'm going inside to check in and find somewhere to eat. Driving makes me hungry. See you two tomorrow."

"Bye," Cole and Nova said together, then Cole ended the call and texted Nova's address to his aunt.

"It's really kind of you to offer for Aunt Ju to stay with you and Leo."

"I've looked forward to meeting her ever since you mentioned her. With her doing the cooking while she's here, it will be a tremendous help to me." She glanced at the clock on the microwave. "We need to head to the square. And just so you know, we'll have the house to ourselves tonight."

He pulled her to him for a very satisfying kiss. "I like the sound of that."

They drove to the square, and Nova unlocked the door, turning on the lights. Soon, the place began to fill with coaches and their wives. The only other single men on the staff besides Cole were John Peterson and Cole's good friend Ray Barker. While John arrived alone, looking sullen and ill at ease, she noticed Ray came in with a tall blonde who was drop-dead gorgeous.

She watched Cole move in the couple's direction, shaking Ray's hand. But then he hugged the woman—and even kissed her cheek. A shot of jealousy zipped through Nova.

Who was this woman?

As Cole stepped away, Nova went up and greeted Ray, and he introduced his date. She was a couple of inches under six feet and had emerald eyes and flawless skin. Beside her, Nova felt insignificant and extremely ordinary.

"Nova Turner, I'd like you to meet Brynn Mattson. She's the school district's psychologist."

The women shook hands, and Nova put on a smile. "Nice to meet you, Brynn."

"I've seen you at the football games," Brynn said. "I never miss one. Leo has been shining these last few weeks."

Relaxing a little, she said, "Yes, he's really come into his own as far as football is concerned. I worry a little bit about when Keith Arnold returns to the team. Cole has already let Leo know that a starter doesn't lose his starting spot because of an injury."

"Do you think Leo will have a problem with that?" Brynn asked.

"I don't think a problem. Cole has said that while Keith will start, Leo will definitely see playing action. It's just a mom worry. That's all."

"If you think he's having a hard time making an adjustment, give me a call." Brynn passed her card to Nova. "I can have him in for an individual session or two. He may tell me things he might not necessarily share with you. I already know Leo since I've met with the team several times now. Cole has really seen the value of incorporating psychology into sports."

"Thank you," she said, slipping the card into her pocket, wondering why Cole had never mentioned Brynn Mattson to her. Trying to focus on her son, she added, "Leo has a sunny nature, but this is something new for him. Playing football. Replacing an injured player."

"It'll be a learning process for him. For all boys his age, really. I'm happy to help in any way I can." Brynn looked around the room. "I'm excited to see what we're going to paint."

Continuing in her effort to be friendly, Nova said, "Come in and have a seat. Let's get you something to drink."

She noted that several coaches had brought six-packs of beer, while the wives seemed to be partial to wine.

"I've got glasses for the wine drinkers," she called out. "Bring your bottles over, and we'll get them opened and glasses poured."

She had invested in wine glasses and corkscrews since those who brought bottles of wine to their parties rarely remembered to bring those other items. Once everyone had arrived, she had the group take a seat, telling them, "Playful Painting is all about fun. Having a good time. It doesn't matter your skill level, age, or gender. Some of you will find you have a knack for art that you didn't know existed. Others?" she smiled. "Let's just say that you'll enjoy the company and your adult beverage."

Everyone laughed, and Nova indicated the canvas. "This is the painting we'll be copying this evening. I'd spoken with Mrs. Peterson, and this is the one the wives all agreed upon. You coaches simply need to go along with their decision."

Ben said, "I'm well trained. Laurie tells me what to do—and I do it." He picked up a brush. "Let's paint!"

Nova started by showing them from the finished painting what they would start with, and then she moved to the blank canvas next to it, telling them which brush to use and what color to choose. She walked them through the painting step-by-step, stopping at various times and walking around the room, giving advice, helping show how to hold a brush and how to mix paints together for different shades.

As she circulated, she saw the group was enjoying themselves immensely. The coaches ragged on each other, while the wives were talkative and guzzled their fair share of wine as they painted. Her gaze met Cole's, and he winked at her. Nova moved to him and looked at his canvas.

"Not bad so far, Coach," she said.

"The painting is fun, but just look around, Nova. These couples don't have a lot of time together during football season. I'm seeing joy on a lot of faces. This was a good activity to bring them to, not only to cement us as a staff but also to give them time with their loved ones."

"I get to see this reaction every time I hold a party. Whether people have any artistic talent or not, they really enjoy hanging out with their friends and creating something."

He snagged her waist and pulled her onto his lap, earning a few whistles from his coaches.

"I'm happy you hit upon this business. You've got such a positive nature. You bring sunshine into a lot of people's lives, Nova Turner."

He tugged her down for a kiss, and she could hear the catcalls and laughter. It didn't matter. She was full of happiness in this moment. She had found a man she loved, one who loved her. A man who was thoughtful and kind and fun to be around. She'd found a home in this community. Both she and Leo were making friends. Nova glowed inside, happiness spilling from her.

She pushed off Cole's lap and told him, "Work a little more on the movement in the water, Coach."

Ray, seated next to Cole, burst out laughing. "And you just thought you'd be teacher's pet."

"I'm getting the munchies," Ben Peterson said. "We should've thought to bring snacks, honey."

That reminded Nova of the cookies Jessica had brought over, and she said, "I do have cookies from Rolling Scones for sale if anyone's hungry for something sweet."

She retrieved the box and opened it, showing it to Ben. He

bent close and inhaled the sugared sweetness. "Hell, I'll buy the whole box, Nova. I've got a weakness for Jason's cookies."

His wife emptied her wine glasses and said, "He doesn't need the entire box. Pass it around, Nova, and any other boxes you might have. Ben, you can have two cookies—but you're paying for them all."

John Peterson laughed. "That's the reason I don't get married," he told his brother. "I don't need anyone telling me what I can and can't do."

Ben bit into a cookie and sighed. "You better play nice, bro, or you don't get any of these."

Everyone laughed heartily, and Nova returned to the front, demonstrating the next step in the painting as the boxes of cookies were passed around.

Forty-five minutes later, everyone had completed their pictures. They took turns going around and looking at one another's efforts, and Laurie Peterson's was voted best painting by the group.

Nova told them they would need to leave their canvases so that they could dry properly and said times for picking them up were listed on the Playful Painting website. Two wives bought some of her pottery, and Brynn bought a pair of earrings. As everyone collected their things to leave, Nova received hugs and handshakes.

Once the last coach was out the door, Cole pulled her into his arms.

"I'd say that was a very successful party. I think everyone will remember tonight fondly. Worth every penny." He kissed the tip of her nose. "What do you say we get this cleaned up and see if we can go back to your place and make a few more good memories?"

Nova looped her arms about his neck and kissed him thoroughly. "I think that's a really, really good idea, Coach Johnson."

20

———————

Leo arrived home mid-morning. Cole had just left a few minutes earlier, and Nova was sitting at the kitchen table sipping a cup of herbal tea.

"Are you hungry?" she asked when he plopped into a chair across from her.

"Starving!" he proclaimed. "Teddy's mom is really nice, but she doesn't know how to cook. I mean, anything. Teddy says they eat a lot of takeout, and breakfast this morning was just a bowl of cereal."

"I made breakfast for Coach Johnson. We had pancakes. Sound good?"

He grinned. "You are speaking my language, Mamacita. Especially if you'll fry up some bacon with it. Or sausage."

She rose and retrieved the leftover pancake batter from where she had stored it in the fridge and pulled out a rasher of bacon, as well. She fried the bacon and made Leo a tall stack of pancakes, using all of the remaining batter in the bowl.

Placing his plate in front of him, he sipped on the large milk he had poured himself.

She sat again and said, "I have something I want to talk with you about. I've invited someone to stay with us for a little while. It's Coach Johnson's aunt."

"Is she coming to see him coach our upcoming game?" Leo asked, pouring maple syrup over his pancakes as he munched on a piece of bacon.

"No, she's actually moving to this area. She is the one who raised him from a baby, and she's lived in West Texas all these years."

Leo frowned. "Why did his aunt raise him?"

She treaded a fine line here, not wanting to give her son too much of Cole's personal story since it really was his to tell.

"Coach Johnson's mother was very young when she had him, and so she let her sister raise him."

Leo chewed thoughtfully and then asked, "Did his aunt have a family of her own?"

"No, she never married. She dropped out of college to raise her nephew."

He reached over and took her hand, squeezing it. "Thanks for sticking around and raising me, Mom. I know you had Rain's help, but it couldn't have been easy because you were just a kid yourself. Like, my age now. I can't imagine having a kid and doing all you did for me."

Nova blinked away the tears which formed in her eyes. "Thank you, Leo. I loved you from the moment I knew you were growing inside me. I would never have left you. But it was also very overwhelming, so I would never judge Coach Johnson's birth mother for the decision she made."

She brightened. "Anyway, Aunt Ju—Julia Johnson—is coming to stay with us for a bit. She's going to fulfill her dreams and return to college. She'll be starting in January at UT-Tyler. In the meantime, she wants to become familiar with this area. See if she would prefer living in Tyler and be close to her classes or move here to Sugar Springs and commute. I offered for her to stay with you and me until she finds a place to live. I'm sorry I didn't run that by you. I hope you won't mind."

Her son gazed at her steadily. "You're really serious about Coach Johnson, aren't you, Mom?"

She wondered how much she should reveal to Leo. "Yes, we are very serious about one another. We have decided to see each other exclusively. That's a big step."

"If you decide to get married, that would be cool with me." Leo went back to his pancakes.

She felt flustered as she said, "We haven't come close to talking about marriage, Leo. But yes, I like him a great deal."

"Mom, I know you love him. You don't have to hide that from me. I see how you look at him. I see how he looks at *you*. You two are meant to be. And I'm more than fine with it."

Nova cleared her throat. "I'm glad that we have your blessing in case things progress, but I don't see marriage in our future anytime soon. I will tell you that I do love Coach Johnson, but he has a lot on his plate right now. A coach has to continually prove himself to his school's fans every year, game to game. The first year, obviously, holds the most pressure."

"Well, we're undefeated, Mom. I know we're going to the play-offs. It'll just depend upon how far we go." He paused. "I won't be starting on Friday night. Keith should be back by then."

"Does that bother you?" she asked, concerned.

Leo chewed thoughtfully and then swallowed. "Not really. I know Coach will give me some playing time even if I don't start. And Keith and I are good. He's actually helped me in practice. Talked to me about different things. Given me some pretty good tips on how to avoid defenders and hold onto the ball."

"I did meet Miss Mattson at last night's Playful Painting party," she began. "If you ever need to talk about something bothering you—and you don't want to talk to me—Miss Mattson would be a good person to discuss things with."

He laughed, spearing the last of his pancakes on his fork. "I don't need a shrink, Mom. I'm fine with Keith starting. I'm just a sophomore. And I'll get in my playing time. With him being a senior and graduating, my goal is to start both my junior and senior years. So don't worry about me. Having Coach's aunt here will be fine, too." He grinned. "I'll just look at her as extended family for now."

Cole texted Nova several hours later, telling her that Aunt Ju was on schedule and would arrive in Sugar Springs about three o'clock. He added that he would be at Nova's house by then to introduce them in person. Normally, he would be tied up on a Sunday afternoon with his staff, working on the next week's game plan and practice session for the coming week. Since the Knights had had an open week, however, the prep work had been done in advance and their regular Sunday meeting would be brief.

When he arrived at her house at a quarter till three, she told him, "I talked things over with Leo when he got home from Teddy's this morning. He's fine about having Aunt Ju stay with us indefinitely."

Cole slipped his arms around her and drew Nova in for a long, slow, delicious kiss.

"You might have to come to my place a little more often so we can have some privacy. I hope that's okay."

"I don't mind," she said, thinking she would walk through fire to be with this man.

They went to wait on the porch swing. While Nova hadn't brought up Brynn Mattson last night, she decided she needed to say something about her to Cole.

"How do you think last night went?"

He smiled. "Really well. It was good to see the guys away from football, having fun. Brynn said fun activities such as last night's painting are good team building activities."

Glad he had brought up the psychologist's name first, she said, "You hadn't mentioned her before."

"I hadn't? Well, she's been really helpful. I worked with the school's psychologist at my last high school, but Brynn is even better. She's done a few sessions with the team as a whole. Helped them center their minds. Players can become anxious or lose focus during a game. They might be flagged with a penalty and lose their temper. Or they might freeze up. Choke as the pressure builds. Brynn's given the team some techniques on how to cope in those situations. She's also worked with some of the players on visualization."

Nova frowned. "What's that?"

"Basically, people think in pictures," he explained. "Some athletes tend to dwell on the bad things that have happened. A dropped pass. A missed block that led to a touchdown. An injury. Brynn's helped the team with guided visualization, where they see themselves doing something successfully. Making a catch. Kicking the field goal. Intercepting that ball. They key in on the image and think about it, over and over. It builds confidence."

"I'm surprised you haven't mentioned Brynn. Leo hasn't either."

He shrugged. "It's just one of the many facets of the game. Brynn's been helpful. Plus, she really likes sports and understands football. That's a huge plus."

Nova tried not to feel hurt that Cole hadn't discussed this aspect of his coaching with her. She reminded herself that Brynn had given her no reason to be jealous. The psychologist had been very open and friendly to Nova.

"How long has she been seeing Ray?"

"Last night was their first date." Cole laughed. "I haven't asked Ray if there'll be a second one."

A dusty SUV pulled up in front of the house, and she pushed aside thoughts of Brynn Mattson. They rose and went down the sidewalk to greet Aunt Ju.

In person, her resemblance to Cole was even more noticeable. Nova watched the two of them hug, and then Julia Johnson turned to her.

"Oh, Nova, I'm so glad to see you in person."

She embraced her hostess and though Nova was glad the woman would be staying with her, a wave of sadness washed through her, thinking of how Rain was gone and never coming back.

Aunt Ju released her and said, "Let's get my things inside. I don't have much. Just books and clothes." She grinned. "And the books are far more precious to me."

"I've got the guestroom ready for you," Nova said. "Let me show it to you now. We can put Cole to work bringing in your things."

She took the older woman inside the house and to the room where she would be staying.

"The bathroom you'll use is across the hall. You'll be sharing it with Leo, but he's actually fairly neat for a teenage boy."

"I can't wait to meet him, too."

"He's here. In his room. Let me introduce you two now."

Nova went and knocked on her son's door, and he hollered, "Come in."

He stood as they entered and went to their guest. Thrusting out his hand, he said, "I'm Leo Turner. Happy to meet you, Miss Johnson."

As she shook his hand, she said, "None of this Miss Johnson foolishness. I'm Aunt Ju. Short for Julia. My little sister couldn't say Julia. She could just get out the Ju part. I've pretty much gone by Ju ever since." Her eyes flicked to the drawing on his bed. "What are you working on?"

Leo retrieved his sketchbook and began a lengthy explanation about the graphic novel he was working on with his friend Tim. Nova noticed Aunt Ju truly listening to the convoluted storyline, which warmed Nova's heart.

"I draw a bit, and I love science fiction and thrillers. I've never read graphic novels before. Do you have any you might recommend to me?"

Enthusiastically, Leo started naming several and then asked for Aunt Ju's cell number, promising he would text her a list to get her started.

"We'll leave you to your art, Leo," Aunt Ju said. "I need to go back and supervise Cole. I want to thank you and your mom for letting me stay with you until I can make permanent plans."

Leo smiled. "Stay as long as you like, Aunt Ju. We're happy to have you here. Coach is already like family. You can be, too."

Nova led their guest back to her bedroom, where Cole was placing clothes on hangars on the bed.

"I know you'll want to organize these the way you like, which is why I didn't hang them in the closet for you."

Nova saw a suitcase standing in the corner, along with a box.

"Just a couple of more trips, and I'll have everything inside," Cole told them, leaving the room.

"Would you like something to drink, Aunt Ju?" she asked. "I know you've had a long drive these last two days."

"A cup of tea would hit the spot if you have it. Or iced tea."

"I have both," Nova said. "I'm not a coffee drinker like your nephew. I prefer herbal teas and drink several cups a day."

They went to the kitchen, and Nova put on the tea kettle.

Cole joined them and said, "Got the last two boxes in, but I need to run up to school for a while. Football stuff. But if I'm invited, I can be back in time for dinner."

"What time do you usually eat?" Aunt Ju asked Nova.

"It depends upon the day. Five-thirty or six if I don't have a party booked for that evening."

"Then be back here at five-thirty, Cole," Aunt Ju told her nephew.

Over tea, the two women talked, sharing more about themselves.

Nova said, "Cole has told me that you dropped out of college in order to take care of him."

"It was not a hard decision. He was the most adorable, bright-eyed baby I'd ever seen. Not that I'd been around many babies, but I loved children and thought I would major either in education or nursing and become a pediatric nurse. It broke my heart to have to give up on earning my college degree, but I received so much by getting to raise Cole."

"Did you ever hear from your sister? Cole's birth mom?"

"No, she never made contact. He accepted that at a young age, and it was just the two of us for all those years. He wanted to call me Mom, but I told him I was his aunt."

"He thinks the world of you," Nova said.

"I love that boy with all my heart." Aunt Ju paused. "I think you love him, too."

Tears welled in her eyes. "I do. I have never been in love before meeting Cole."

The older woman took Nova's hand and squeezed it. "You didn't love Leo's father?"

"I didn't know anything about love at that age. My parents were strict disciplinarians and belonged to a fundamentalist church. They barely acknowledged me, and I certainly didn't feel any love from them. When I met Ace—Leo's father—it was exciting. Forbidden. I had never even been kissed."

Aunt Ju squeezed Nova's hand again. "So, he was older?"

She nodded. "He was nineteen to my fifteen and working as a carny. The carnival came to town for a week. We... were together a few times. Then he moved on. I didn't know at first that I was pregnant. I hadn't even thought about that possibility, that what we did might make a baby. That's how naive I was. When I finally figured out that I was expecting, I texted his number multiple times."

She wiped the falling tears from her cheeks and said, "I learned that he had been killed in a motorcycle accident."

Aunt Ju leaned over and hugged Nova tightly. "I'm so sorry, dear. You must have felt so alone."

"I really did. My parents disowned me. My father drove me to downtown Dallas and dropped me off, telling me never to come home again."

Aunt Ju gasped. "Oh, Nova. I cannot imagine being in your position, much less at such a tender age."

"It forced me to grow up fast. My aunt lived in this house. She was an artist. A bohemian type, whom the rest of the family had disowned. I had met her a few times, and we'd stayed in touch, which my parents didn't know about. I didn't know what else to do, so I called Rain. She came and got me. Rain brought me here to Sugar Springs and took care of me. Encouraged me in my art. Taught me all she knew. Was with me every step of the pregnancy and birth and enjoyed helping me raise Leo for the first five years."

Nova hiccupped, her tears flowing freely now. "I miss her so much."

"She's watching over you, honey," Aunt Ju declared. "And if you'll let me, I would like to be a surrogate aunt to you." She paused. "Cole tells me that he is very serious about you. That he loves you."

"I do love him, Aunt Ju. I don't know what our future holds, though. He's college-educated, holding two degrees, while I earned my GED. Cole is on a promising career track. I've used the small inheritance I received from Rain and started a business which I can only hope will get off the ground. We're very different people."

Aunt Ju said, "Yes, my nephew may hold two college degrees, but he's smart enough to know what he wants—and that's you, Nova. I feel you are kindred spirits. You both conquered overwhelming odds to become the people you are today. You don't have to rush into anything. Cole isn't going anywhere. Give your relationship time to blossom."

"I will," she promised, still having some doubts that she wasn't a good enough match for the man she loved.

They finished a second cup of tea, and Aunt Ju asked, "Would you mind me going through your fridge and pantry? I need to see what I'm cooking for dinner tonight."

"No, you should go and unpack. I can handle dinner tonight."

"Pish-posh. It will take me all of ten minutes to hang my clothes in the closet and put a few things in drawers. Why don't we cook dinner together?"

As they prepared the meal, Aunt Ju talked about life on the ranch and Cole's growing up years. Nova learned about all the sports he had played and the academic honors he had achieved.

"Not only is Cole remarkable," she said, "but you are, too, Aunt Ju. You made all that possible for him. Without your love and steadfast support, he wouldn't have made so much of himself as an adult. You gave him empathy and an excellent work ethic. Cole's become a wonderful man."

"Don't sell yourself short, Nova," the older woman warned. "You have made a success of your own life, thanks to your aunt Rain's support. I've been on Playful Painting's website. I've seen how quickly the business is growing, and I've also admired the jewelry you've made and posted there. I can't wait to see your store and your studio."

"We can look at both after dinner," Nova said. "If you're interested in sitting in on a party, several of the booster club women are booked for this coming Tuesday night from six to eight. There's room if you'd like to attend that session."

"I would be delighted to do so, honey."

A warm feeling ran through her as she looked at Julia Johnson. Her aunt had often called Nova by the same term of endearment. Rain might be gone, but Nova hoped Aunt Ju might help fill a hole in Nova's life.

21

Nova went to Playful Painting and set up for this morning's session at ten. Everything was going smoothly, and sometimes she had to pinch herself to believe how her life had changed for the better since leaving Austin for Sugar Springs.

Leo's grades were outstanding, and he had continued to get a lot of playing time even after Keith Arnold returned from his high ankle sprain. Her son had been a huge component in the success of the Sugar Springs Knights football team, which had gone undefeated and won the district title. They had advanced in two rounds of the playoffs, coasting to an easy victory in the first round and having a bigger challenge in the second, but pulling off a victory in the final two minutes of last night's game.

The day before the game, Nova had accompanied Cole and Leo to Jason and Jessica Fletcher's house for Thanksgiving. Aunt Ju had joined them for the celebration. She had rented an apartment in Tyler two weeks ago, saying that while she liked Sugar Springs, she wanted to be closer to campus and also enjoy the amenities of a much larger city. Already, Aunt Ju had gone to a play on campus, two guest lectures, and would be attending an upcoming Christmas concert by the university's chorale. She had also made a friend in her apartment complex and was eagerly diving into her new life.

As Nova set out the painting supplies for the upcoming children's birthday party, she almost regretted having scheduled two more parties today. One would take place at four o'clock and was for sorority pledges from UT-Tyler. The other party at seven tonight was a holiday date night for couples. She was booked now through the end of the year, having added extra sessions for the Christmas season.

Unfortunately, that meant she wouldn't be able to see Cole until much later tonight. He was having his usual Saturday meetings with coaches and players, and then he had said he would be working all afternoon in his office on the upcoming game's plan. He was scouting a playoff game tonight, along with Ben and John, since the Knights would play the winner of this particular game next weekend. Nova knew she should be grateful for Cole's success, even though sometimes she was a little jealous, thinking of football as his mistress.

She had put aside her misgivings about Brynn Mattson. Nova had talked to Leo about the psychologist, and her son praised Brynn and the work she had done with the football team and him as an individual.

Her cell rang, and she pulled it from her pocket, not recognizing the number.

"Hello?"

"Is this Nova Turner?"

"Yes, it is," she said cautiously, wondering who this caller was and how he had gotten her number.

"My name is Bill Fine, Nova, and I run Fine Jewelry in Tyler. My wife came to one of your painting parties a week ago with some girlfriends. Her name is Nancy."

A mental image of a plump, friendly woman came to her.

"Oh, yes. Nancy was part of a party last week. They had a lot of fun. I remember she bought a pair of earrings."

"She did. She also showed me the Playful Painting website and the jewelry listed on it. You do very nice work, Nova."

"Since you're a jeweler, that is a high compliment," she said, laughing.

"I would be interested in talking with you about carrying some of your jewelry in my store here in Tyler. I think it would be terrific to spotlight an area artist. Would you be interested in an arrangement like that?"

Excitement filled her. "Yes, Bill, I certainly would."

He went into an explanation of how he would devote a small section of his store to her pieces. He would handle all sales and asked if they could split the profits, with him taking thirty percent of the sale for his portion.

"Make it twenty-five percent, and I think we have a deal," she told him.

"An artist who is also a good businesswoman. You drive a strong bargain, Nova, but I'll accept those terms. Would you have any time to meet with me today? I'd like to get your pieces in my store as soon as possible. I could show you around the store and where your items would be displayed. If you have any completed jewelry you could bring along, we could go ahead and get started."

While she was excited about this opportunity, Nova proceeded with caution.

"I'm sure you're a man of your word, Bill, but I do think it would be smart if we wrote up a legally binding contract with the specifics. I would like to come by the store this afternoon between painting parties if that's okay with you. We'll need to see about having an attorney draw up an agreement if we decide to proceed. I've met one in Sugar Springs that we could use."

"Then come on in this afternoon, and we'll talk. If you're comfortable after we meet, then by all means, contact this attorney and set up a meeting with him so we can hammer out the details."

"I have a painting party, which lasts until noon, and then I'll have some cleanup to do. I can drive into Tyler after that."

"I'll be here all day," he said. "Between Thanksgiving and Christmas is when I do some of my best business. You could be a part of that, too."

Nova thanked him and hung up, thrilled at this unexpected opportunity. While she had sold some of her pieces on display at Playful Painting, having her work in an established jewelry store in a much larger city could result in brisk sales.

She went to the chamber of commerce website, having joined it a few weeks ago and attended their latest luncheon, where she had met Walker Cox. His father had been an attorney in Sugar Springs for several decades and had recently retired. Walker had taken over the practice, and she had sat next to him at the chamber luncheon, liking him quite a bit.

Finding his number, she dialed it, knowing he wouldn't be there on a Saturday. She left a message for him, briefly outlining the situation and asking that his receptionist contact her so she and Bill Fine could make an appointment with him since she believed seeing Bill's store was merely a formality.

The birthday party began shortly after and went well. The girls invited were painting a Christmas tree with presents under it, and they ate birthday cake as they painted. As she circulated, helping guide them, several told her that they would make their painting a Christmas present for their parents. The birthday girl's mother thanked Nova once the party ended, telling her that she would be back with her own friends—and wine—soon.

After cleaning up, she went ahead and set out things for the four o'clock party. She could drive into Tyler now since she had a gap of a few hours and didn't think she'd be at Bill's store too long. Gathering up a few pieces from her jewelry display case, she thought she would show the jeweler more examples of her work. She could leave these with him and collect more items from home to place out for the two remaining parties today. She had a feeling the sorority girls might like her pieces.

The drive into Tyler didn't take long. She listened to a radio station playing Christmas music, singing along the entire way. Nova located Fine Jewelry and parked. As she approached the store, she saw a familiar truck parked in front of it.

It was Cole's truck.

What on earth would he be doing in Tyler, much less at a jewelry store?

She decided she must be mistaken until she noticed the decal in the back window for the Sugar Springs Knights and the bumper sticker for the Dallas Cowboys. It was definitely Cole's vehicle.

Cole had told her he would be in his office all afternoon before heading to the playoff game with his two coordinators. Why would he lie about something like that? She reached the front of the store, which was all glass, and looked in. Several people were browsing inside, but her eyes went straight to Cole. He threw back his head in laughter and then touched the shoulder of the woman standing next to him.

It was Brynn Mattson.

Nausea filled Nova. She couldn't comprehend what she was seeing. Then Cole reached for Brynn's hand and inspected it. Nova could only assume he was looking at a ring on her finger. Brynn nodded enthusiastically and then slipped off the ring, handing it to the man behind the counter.

Cole threw his arm around Brynn, hugging her, as Nova's gut twisted painfully. She turned, fleeing to her car, opening the door and slipping behind the wheel. Her breath came in short spurts as she burst into tears, her sobs coming hard and fast.

Cole was cheating on her. With Brynn Mattson. No wonder he hadn't mentioned the psychologist to her. Everything she had believed about him—about them—crumbled in an instant. Even though Jagger had cheated on her with multiple partners, this was a thousand times worse.

Because she loved Cole.

How could he have looked her in the eye and told her he loved her when he was seeing another woman?

She cursed aloud, calling him every vile name she could think of. Then she began beating up herself for being such a fool. She never should have become involved so quickly with him. Nova felt utterly destroyed, the perpetual happiness she had felt, fading.

Angrily, she wiped away her tears and started the car. She couldn't go in to see Bill Fine looking as she did, much less run into Cole and Brynn.

Dejected, Nova drove back to Sugar Springs, feeling as if her life were over. No, she couldn't collapse and be an emotional wreck. She had Leo to think about. Her business to run. Her art to create.

But her life would be so empty without Cole in it.

Returning to Playful Painting because she didn't want to see Leo at this point, Nova composed herself and dialed Bill Fine's number.

He answered, and she explained a sudden emergency had come up at the store, lying about a pipe bursting and needing repair.

"Perhaps I could come in another day?" she asked, surprised to hear how calm her voice sounded.

"I know tomorrow is Sunday," he said, "but I'm open from one until six if you can make it then."

"I have a painting party from two until four," she told him. "I could be in Tyler at five or a little after."

"No rush, Nova," the jeweler said cheerfully. "If you want to make it closer to six, that's fine with me. I can close the store, and we can talk uninterrupted while you see my setup."

"Thank you for understanding, Bill. I'll see you tomorrow."

Somehow, she made it through the next two parties, closing the shop a little after nine and cleaning up. She drove home, finding Leo and Jake watching TV.

"Are you sleeping over, Jake?" she asked.

"If it's okay with you, Miss Turner."

"You're always welcome here," she told the teenager, glad Leo had made such a good friend in the quarterback.

Nova drew herself a hot bath, liberally sprinkling in bath salts, and submersed herself. Out of habit, she had rested her phone on the edge of the bathtub. It didn't surprise her when a text came in because Cole had told her he would text her when he left the game.

Leaving now. Hope it's not too late to come by.

How could he blithely text her after buying another woman jewelry today? Rage bubbled up, and she responded to his text.

Don't come.

Moments later, her cell rang, and she saw his name pop up on the caller ID. Answering it, she said, "I said don't come."

"Are you all right, Nova? Tired after three parties today? I could give you a backrub," he said playfully.

"I don't want a backrub from you," she said flatly. "I don't want to see you again, Cole."

"What?" he asked, clearly confused by her abruptness. "What's going on, Nova? Talk to me."

"You know exactly what is going on," she said evenly, determined not to lose her temper. "If you were man enough, you would admit it."

"I have no idea what you're talking about. When we started this relationship, we said we would be honest with one another."

"We did, didn't we?" she asked sarcastically.

He was silent and then finally said, "I told you if there were a problem—if you were unhappy—that you needed to tell me so we could try to work things out between us. I love you, Nova. I want to fix this."

His words stabbed her in the heart. She didn't want to get into his lies. His cheating. She was done with Cole Johnson. Period.

"I've decided we are just too different, Cole. There is no fixing anything. I would appreciate if you didn't call or text me again."

Nova hung up, setting down the phone. Immediately, it rang. She didn't need to look to see who it was. After several rings, she supposed her voicemail came on.

Then her cell dinged with a text message. She refused to look at it even though her phone blew up with message after message.

She rose from the water, wrapping herself in a large bath towel. She got into her pajamas and robe and went to the living room. The TV was now off, and the boys were gone. She supposed they were already in Leo's room. Tightening the robe's belt, Nova turned off all the lights and sat in the dark, knowing Cole would show up.

Half an hour later, she heard his truck in the driveway and went and unlocked the front door. Opening it, she did something she had never done since she had returned to Sugar Springs.

She placed the latch on the screen door.

Nova needed a barrier between them.

Cole stormed from the truck and raced up her porch steps. She could only see him in silhouette since she hadn't turned on the porch light.

"Nova," he said, desperation in his voice. "Talk to me. We can fix this."

Steeling herself, she said, "That's the key word—we. The thing is, Cole, I don't want to fix it. I'm done. Let it go. Let *me* go."

"Not without a fight," he said, pulling on the screen door and finding it locked.

Nova tried another tact. "If you truly love me, Cole, then respect my decision to end things. We had some good times, but I'm asking you to walk away."

With that, she quietly shut the door, leaning against, her forehead resting on it as tears streamed down her cheeks.

In the stillness, she heard him say, "I love you, Nova. I always will."

Then the sound of his boots going down the steps echoed in the night. His truck started. Cole drove away.

He was now gone from her life.

22

———

Nova placed Leo's breakfast plate in front of him. Sullenly, he pushed the food around on his plate. They had barely spoken since she had told him that she and Cole had ended things between them.

"Eat, Leo," she said, taking a seat across from him. "You need a good breakfast in you. I know the parents providing tonight's pre-game meal have been asked to bring sandwiches and fruit. The coaching staff doesn't want anything heavy on your stomachs. So, eat up now."

"You mean Coach Johnson doesn't want us to be sluggish," he muttered, but he did stab a sausage link and eat it.

"Yes, he and your other coaches. They've been through this before. They know what's best for you."

Leo stared at her. "Why, Mom?"

"Why what?" she asked, picking up her mug of tea and blowing on it so she wouldn't have to meet his gaze.

"Why did you break up with Coach Johnson? He's been grumpy in practice all week."

She set down her mug. "It's not really your concern, Leo. It's between Coach Johnson and me. No one else."

"I thought you trusted me. You've always said we could talk about anything." He looked at her, oozing teenage defiance. "Well, this is something I want to talk about."

"And I don't," she said firmly. Softening her tone, Nova added, "I can't now. Just like Coach Johnson, I'm hurting. I'll talk with you about it someday."

He shook his head in disgust. "You're just putting me off."

"No, I'm keeping something private to myself."

Leo frowned. "You look miserable, Mom. Coach does, too. Why don't you just talk to him? I'm sure you can work out whatever it is."

"I really don't want to work things out with him, Leo," she stated, her tone firm again, hoping he would take the hint and drop the subject.

"You can't seem to make anything work with a guy."

His words cut her to the quick. She drew in a sharp breath. "That was a low blow, Leo. Apologize. Now."

He looked surly. "You always said an apology needs to be sincere. Well, mine wouldn't be."

Leo pushed away from the table and snatched his backpack off the table. He rushed out the door, slamming it behind him. Nova started to go after him and then placed her head in her hands, tears flooding her eyes.

She was miserable. Utterly miserable. Yet she knew she had to push through it. She wasn't about to go crawling back to Cole. Not after his betrayal.

He had continued to flood her with a barrage of texts and calls for a few days. She hadn't read any of the texts, deleting them the moment they came in. Nor had she listened to any of the numerous voicemails he'd left.

Then suddenly, he'd gone silent. She didn't know if he finally was respecting her wish to be left alone or if he'd seen she wouldn't respond to his messages and had finally given up. Good riddance. It would give him more time with Brynn Mattson.

Leo hadn't mentioned the psychologist this past week, for which Nova was grateful. She didn't know how she would respond if she saw the woman in person. It was likely she would, however, at the quarterfinals playoff game tonight. The entire town of Sugar Springs seemed to be turning out, following the Knights as they made a deep run into the playoffs. If Leo weren't playing, she would definitely stay home. She had to go, however, to support her son. She would avoid looking at Cole. She doubted he would look for her. He would be focused on the game.

Nova worked all morning and for a couple of hours that afternoon on her jewelry. She had been able to meet with Bill Fine as planned, and the two of them had spent an hour with Walker Cox on Tuesday morning. Walker had drawn up a document spelling out the details of the arrangement between Nova and Bill. She packed the jewelry she would now deliver to Bill and drove into Tyler, arriving at half-past three.

Carrying in the bag, Bill greeted her, introducing her to one of his clerks. Nova took out the many bracelets, necklaces, rings, and a few brooches, handing him a record of the delivery. She also had kept a copy of what she was turning over, as well as snapping a picture of each item with her cell phone for her records.

"Thanks for getting all this to me in time for the weekend shopping, Nova," Bill said. "I'll keep you posted as to sales."

"Let me know what seems to be most popular, and I'll work on that this coming week. If you need to be restocked, I can come again next Friday with a new delivery."

Her drive back to Tyler was uneventful. She kept the radio off, in no mood to sing along with the joyful Christmas carols dominating the radio airwaves.

She spent half an hour once she reached home assembling sandwiches and placing them in plastic baggies before driving to the high school. She got out of her car and walked in with Betty Smith.

"How are the offers going?" she asked, her usual question to the woman each time they met.

Betty smiled broadly. "Luke is up to eleven scholarship offers. Lyle has eight. Coach Johnson believes since both boys have a solid B-average, they'll be able to take their pick of the school they wish to attend."

"Do they want to stay together?" Nova asked. "I know you've said they're close."

"They'd like to. Even if part of me wishes they would go to separate schools and forge their own identities, they've been running around together ever since they were in diapers. It might be good if they did attend the same school and have one another to lean on. We'll have to see."

"Any particular school in the running?"

"Luke would love to be a Texas Aggie. Lyle hasn't received an offer from A&M, though. We'll have to wait and see."

They entered the school and took their bags of sandwiches to the cafeteria, where other parents were setting up things. Within minutes, the players and coaches had arrived. Nova caught sight of Cole and averted her eyes, busying herself with placing sandwiches in rows.

The players filed through first, collecting their meals, getting bottles of water at the end of the line. The coaches came through next. She braced herself, knowing she would see Cole at any minute.

When he came through, she mustered a smile, handing him two sandwiches and a plate.

"Here you go, Coach," she said, feeling her heart being torn from her chest as she looked at him. He was—and always would be—the most handsome man she had ever seen. "Good luck tonight."

"Thank you," he said brusquely, continuing through the line, never looking her in the face.

Betty, who stood next to her, touched Nova's sleeve. "Is something wrong?"

Knowing the news would get out now, she said, "We're no longer seeing each other."

Betty patted Nova's back. "I'm sorry to hear that," she said quietly.

Thank goodness Betty didn't press Nova further.

"It looks like everyone has what they need," she said. "I'm going to take off."

Nova returned to her car and sat for a few minutes, trying to stem the flood of tears. She knew it would take time to heal. But she didn't know just how difficult this healing process would be. Yes, she'd lost Ace years ago, but she'd never really had him. Their brief fling had ended when the carnival left town, and she hadn't truly expected to ever see him again. She had been saddened to hear the news of his death, but by then, it had been hard for her to even recall what he looked like.

Ending her relationship with Jagger had been unpleasant, but she could see now how uninvested they both had been in their time together. She had been more angry than sad at his betrayal, and she had realized he hadn't been that good for her to begin with.

Cole was different. He had been a new beginning for her in a new place. She had fallen fast and hard for him. Other than devoting so much time to his job, Nova had thought him a perfect match for her. Little did she know how duplicitous he was. His friendly demeanor hid the true man he was.

There was nothing she could do about it now. Fortunately, she had found out the kind of man he was before she'd become even more enmeshed with him. Leo, too. She wished she could share with her son why she had dumped Cole Johnson's ass, but she didn't want Leo becoming disrespectful toward his coach. Her son was mad for football and would certainly continue to play for Cole throughout high school. She refused to drive any kind of wedge between them. Once Leo graduated, she might discuss the reason she ended her relationship with Cole. That was far down the line, though.

Her phone rang, and she saw it was Jessica.

"Nova, are you all right?"

She swallowed. "I'm fine, Jessica."

"I just heard you and Cole broke up."

Well, that hadn't taken long.

"Yes," she said carefully. "Things just didn't work out between us. It happens. He wasn't the man that I thought he was."

"Oh, I thought you were perfect for one another." Jessica paused. "But it's good to know now, right? I hope you don't mind Leo continuing to play football for him."

"Oh, I wouldn't keep Leo from playing. He loves it too much."

"Would you like to ride to the game with Jason and me?"

She sighed. "That would be wonderful. I hadn't even mapped the directions yet."

"It's almost an hour away. Would you like us to pick you up?"

"I'm about to leave school now. I was helping distribute sandwiches for this evening."

Jessica laughed. "Yes, Jake was telling me that Coach Johnson didn't want them filled to the gills with pizza or chicken fried steak or anything else heavy." She hesitated. "Did you see Cole there?"

"I did," she said. "Gave him a sandwich and wished him good luck tonight."

"That's nice. At least you're still on speaking terms."

Barely—but Jessica didn't need to know that.

"I'll head over your way now," she said. "No, I need to stop at home for my stadium seat."

"I've got an extra one of those. Hand warmers, too. And a blanket. Jason never seems to need one. I swear he's got ice in his veins. You and I can snuggle beneath the stadium blanket."

She drove straight to the Fletcher's house. When Jessica asked if she'd already eaten, Nova lied and said she had. She didn't think she could swallow anything.

Not after having seen Cole.

They got in the car. No one brought up Cole. Instead, Jason talked about some new cookies Rolling Scones was trying out for the Christmas season. They talked about her new jewelry deal with Fine Jewelry. The town's Christmas tree lighting tomorrow night. How Sarah Meinholdt, the high school's speech and drama teacher, was resigning at the end of the semester to pursue a film career. Apparently, a movie had been shot in Sugar Springs just before Nova and Leo arrived in town. The screenplay had been written by another teacher, who had upped and married Tanner Haddock, the big movie star. Nova admitted she had barely heard of Tanner, causing Jessica to shriek.

"Oh, girl, I've got to get you to watch one of his movies. Tanner Haddock is hot, hot, hot!"

"She would leave me for him," Jason said good-naturedly. "Fortunately, he's married now to Paige Laramie, so the chances of that happening are slim to none."

Jessica leaned over and kissed her husband's cheek. "I would never leave you, Lover Boy."

Nova closed her eyes, their playful banter almost too much for her.

At the stadium, they found good seats on the visitors' side, and she and Jessica hunkered down beneath the blanket. Jason volunteered to get them hot chocolate, and they sipped on that as the starting lineup was announced.

The game was close. This far into the playoffs every team was a good one. At halftime, the Knights were down, 21-17.

"Let's hit the restroom," Jessica suggested when halftime was almost over. "We'll have missed the stampede to the ladies' room by now."

They unearthed themselves from the blanket, the brisk wind

hitting them, so they hurried beneath the stands. Sure enough, the line to the women's restroom was non-existent.

Before they entered separate stalls, Jessica said, "I'm going to get all three of us more hot chocolate. Meet you back up top."

When Nova exited the stall and went to wash her hands, her heart lurched, seeing Phyllis Arnold standing there. Nova moved to the sink, not wanting to engage in conversation with the woman.

"I heard you and Coach Johnson broke up."

She didn't say anything, just turned on the water and lathered her hands.

"You weren't good enough for him anyway," Phyllis said snootily. "I've looked you up online. People are talking about you behind your back, Nova Turner. The teen mother with the GED. You think you could have kept a man like Cole Johnson? He's so far out of your league. That was just wishful thinking on your part. A man like Coach Johnson needs a woman with an unblemished reputation."

When Nova began drying her hands with a paper towel, Phyllis pressed harder. "You didn't think he'd want to take on a teenager, did you? Cole Johnson doesn't want to raise some other man's bastard."

Gritting her teeth, Nova tossed the paper towel in the trash can and said, "Excuse me?"

Phyllis huffed. "No one is going to excuse you, Nova. You may have a few friends, but practically everyone in Sugar Springs is raking you over the coals. You're pure white trash, girl. And so is your son."

She didn't care what this woman thought, but her words about Leo stung. "Leave my son out of this, Phyllis," she said, her tone deadly.

"Or what? He's probably going to get some poor girl pregnant and be a teen father himself. I hope he'll stick around. Your baby daddy sure didn't."

Phyllis turned and flounced off. Nova closed her eyes and counted to ten, hoping her blood pressure would return to normal. When she opened her eyes, she saw Sue Smith coming out of a stall.

"Don't mind Phyllis, Nova," the booster club mom said, patting Nova's arm. "She's all talk. She's just mad that Coach Johnson has been starting Leo over Keith in the playoffs. And well he should. Leo can run circles around defensive backs out there."

Nova nodded shakily, returning to her seat in the bleachers. All the joy of the game had gone out of her. She knew she should ignore Phyllis' cruelty, but it was hard to do so.

Suddenly, Jessica hugged her. "I can't believe we won! In the last second! Leo saved the day."

Glancing at the score, she saw the clock had run out. The game was over, and the Knights had won. She had missed it.

Smiling brightly, she said, "I'm so proud of Leo."

"You should be," Jason said. "He and Jake were all that kept us in this game tonight. I'm glad Coach Johnson started Leo in Keith Arnold's place. He better keep doing so."

She looked to the field and saw Leo mobbed by his teammates, joy written across his face. Then she felt someone's gaze on her and turned to her left.

Cole was staring up at her. Their gazes locked, and then he turned away, slapping another player on the back.

Nova promised herself that she would survive this breakup. She had to.

For herself—and for Leo.

23

Cole stood on the sidelines of the high school stadium as the cheerleaders led the crowd in a rousing cheer.

It was Thursday night, the night before the Knights played in the state semi-finals, and Joe Bob Milton had given in to the student body request of a nighttime pep rally. Both sides of the stands were filled, as a good majority of the town seemed to have turned out.

Except for Nova.

Just the thought of her absence caused him to sink in spirit. Here he was, the first-year head coach of an undefeated football team, just two games away from claiming a state championship.

And he was absolutely miserable.

He still didn't know what he had done to turn Nova against him so quickly. One minute, they were happy and in love. The next, she never wanted to see him again. No warning. No explanation.

The only small bit of hope he clung to was that she had never said she stopped loving him. Even that night on her porch, the screen door acting as a barrier between them, he saw reluctance in her eyes. As if she were breaking up with him and didn't want to do it. As if she still loved him.

But for life of him, Cole couldn't figure out what terrible sin he had committed to cause her to turn on him so rapidly and shut him out of her life.

He'd tried to push all thoughts of her aside, finding it near impossible. Especially with Leo Turner being a constant presence in his life. The teenager had grown as a receiver more than any player Cole could remember coaching. Leo was a natural at football. He was so good that once they reached the playoffs, he'd benched Keith Arnold and started Leo in the senior's place. Keith, kind soul that he was, had taken the news with a smile, telling Cole that he would be happy to do whatever was best for the team. Because of Keith's positive attitude, he tried to make certain the boy played a few minutes in each game.

The cheer ended, and the band played a peppy number, the crowd clapping and singing along. He knew he was up next—and he had no idea what he might say.

The head cheerleader, who ran the pep rally with precision, had the fans give another rousing cheer for the band before she announced him.

"Tonight, we're going to hear from the man who has led our Sugar Springs Knights to victory after victory. Let's give it up for Coach Johnson!"

The crowd erupted, chanting his name as he made his way toward the microphone. Taking it from the cheerleader, he waved for the crowd to quiet down, but they only cheered harder. Cole glanced over at his team, standing on the sidelines, egging the fans on.

"Make them stop or you're running laps after the pep rally," he teased.

Immediately, the football players convinced the town's residents and students to settle down.

Cole cleared his throat and brought the microphone close to his mouth.

"We have the best players. The best fans. The best student body in all of Texas. The love and support in the air tonight for this team and its coaches is tangible. We feel it in our hearts. Our souls. Our guts."

He paused, glancing across the crowd, wishing Nova were here to share in this moment with him.

"I can't—I won't—promise you a victory tomorrow night. All I can say is we're prepared. We will play our hearts out. For you. For ourselves. For every Knight who has ever walked the halls of this school or played on this field. We've had a beautiful season so far. We need you to cheer loud and long tomorrow night. That's your part. We'll do our part. Knights on three. One, two, three!"

"Knights!" the crowd roared, the sound so great it reverberated in his ears.

Cole handed the microphone back to the cheerleader and strode toward the sidelines. Several of his staff patted him on the back, as did some of the players.

Leo was not one of them.

They had not spoken in practice all week. Cole had spent time with each position group, watching them practice, giving advice, and correcting mistakes when necessary. Whenever he'd been with the receiving corps, he'd liked what he'd seen. He'd nodded approvingly and even said, 'Good play,' to Leo, but nothing personal had passed between them. He understood that the boy had made the decision to come down on the side of his mom, as he should.

Still, it hurt Cole. He'd grown close to the teenager, outside of practice, and he hated that what they'd begun to build between them was now forever lost.

The band struck up the school song, and he stood stoically, singing along, as he asked his players to do the same. Some teens

—and even college players—thought themselves too cool to do so, but Cole had always emphasized to the students whom he coached that they were playing for their school and needed to be respectful and participate in the singing of the school song.

After the solemn song finished, the band broke out in the fight song. Fans clapped and sang along as his players and staff moved among themselves, shaking hands, slapping backs, gearing up for tomorrow night's showdown.

Though he wanted to slip away, part of being a head coach was acting as the face of the program, and so Cole hung around, pressing the flesh as a politician might, and chatting up everyone from players' parents to town officials.

He finally was able to extricate himself and as he left the field, he saw Leo accompanying Teddy, heading to the parking lot. Teddy had been flying high this week. He'd turned seventeen, and Ken and Rilda had bought their son a new Yamaha scooter. Personally, Cole thought it had been a distraction and felt Teddy hadn't been as focused in practice this week as he should have been, but he trusted that the running back would have his head in the game come tomorrow. He had told Teddy that he better not see him driving the scooter without a helmet, and the boy assured him that was a given.

Going back to his office, Cole sat in front of his computer. He had nothing left to do. The gameplan was solid. His team was prepped. What crippled him now was an agonizing loneliness. Nova should be sharing in all of this with him.

He cursed, pushing to his feet. For whatever reason, she had parted ways with him. He would have to move on. Focus on tomorrow's game.

Locking his office, he went to the parking lot and drove his truck home. On the way, he called Aunt Ju. He'd seen her at the pep rally but hadn't had a chance to talk with her.

"Hey, Cole. I'm almost home. Thank you for inviting me to the pep rally. It was like old times, hearing the band play and the cheerleaders lead the crowd in cheers." She paused. "Are you doing okay?"

He had spoken to her earlier this week, telling her that he and Nova and broken up. He didn't give any details, mainly because he didn't have any, and his aunt hadn't pressed him for those.

"Sure. I've got my team in the playoffs. What more could a first-year coach want?"

"Have you spoken to Nova?"

"No. And I won't. She wanted to break all contact. I have to respect that, Aunt Ju."

"Cole, it's one thing to respect her wishes. It's another thing to fight for her. If she's who you want to spend the rest of your life with, that is."

Pain washed through him. "It doesn't matter what I want. If she's not all in, then there's nothing to save."

"I'll be in the stands tomorrow night," she promised. "If I see Nova there, is it all right with you if I at least say hello to her?"

"Sure," he said, wishing Aunt Ju could pump Nova for more information that would help him understand this out of the blue breakup. But he would never ask for her to do something like that.

"Then I wish you good luck, Cole."

"Thanks."

He hung up and went inside his apartment. Plopping into one of his lawn chairs, he raked his fingers through his hair. Tears stung his eyes.

At the moment when he should feel his happiest, all Cole felt was a raging loneliness and regret for what might have been.

NOVA SET ASIDE HER SKETCHPAD. She regretted not going to tonight's pep rally. She should have put aside her personal feelings and gone for Leo's sake. She hadn't done so because she didn't want to face all the people who would ask her about her breakup with Cole.

She stood, deciding to make herself a cup of tea. As she put on the kettle to boil, her phone rang. Pulling it from her pocket, she saw it was Leo calling. That in itself was unusual. He almost always texted her. She had even teased him about knowing that a phone could be used to make calls to people.

Nova answered, surprised when she heard a voice ask, "Is this Mrs. Turner?"

"This is Miss Turner," she said crisply. "Why do you have my son's cell?"

"I'm using it to call from the hospital in Tyler. Leo was brought in several minutes ago, and this was the number listed in case of emergency."

Numbly, Nova listened as the voice told her that Leo had been in an accident with another boy.

She asked for the name and address of the hospital and received it, saying she would be there right away. Grabbing her keys and purse, she rushed out the door, not bothering to even put on her coat. Her car's heater had been on the fritz lately, and she'd hoped to have it repaired soon. She drove through the dark night with chattering teeth, reaching the hospital and rushing inside the emergency room to the desk.

"My son was brought in," she said frantically. "Leo Turner. He was in an accident."

The receptionist's fingers clicked the computer keys and smiled reassuringly at Nova.

"Yes, Mrs. Turner. Leo is still in the ER, but he's about to be assigned a room. Dr. Raybon would like to talk to you before you see your son. Please have a seat over there in our lounge area, and I'll page him. It shouldn't take too long."

Nova moved like a sleepwalker to the chairs indicated and perched on the edge of one, wondering if Leo would live or die. His injuries must be serious for him to have been brought to

Tyler. Yet the receptionist said he was being given a room. Surely, that was a good sign, that he had a room and wasn't in surgery. She blinked back tears, determined to stay strong for her son's sake.

A doctor appeared in front of her, his white coat bearing the script *Dr. Raybon* above the pocket. She sprang to her feet.

"How is he? Leo. I'm his mother."

In a calm, assuring tone, the physician said, "Let's have a seat, Mrs. Turner. I'm Dr. Raybon. I can tell you all about Leo's condition."

She stumbled back into the chair, her heart in her throat. "He's everything I have. Please, tell me he's going to be all right."

The doctor said, "Leo and a friend of his were in a motor scooter accident."

"Motor scooter?" she cried in horror.

He took the seat beside her, placing a hand on her forearm. "Yes. From what I gather, the other boy was giving Leo a ride home. Leo suffered a broken elbow and wrist, both on his right side. He told me he's left-handed, so he won't have to learn to write with his non-dominant hand while his bones heal.

"The more serious injury was to his head. Leo wasn't wearing a helmet. Apparently, his friend only had the one."

Tears flooded her eyes now, streaming down her cheeks. "His father... died in a motorcycle accident."

This was her worst nightmare.

"Please, don't worry, Mrs. Turner. We did a CAT scan just to make certain that Leo had no serious head injuries—and he didn't. He does have a nasty lump on his forehead and a concussion. We're going to keep him overnight for observation."

"A concussion?" she asked wildly. "What does that mean?"

Dr. Raybon explained what a concussion was and some of the symptoms Leo had displayed.

"Your son has a headache and nausea, which are two of the most common signs of concussion. His vision was blurry when he was brought in, but that's cleared up now. So has the ringing in his ears. Right now, it's the nausea and drowsiness which are the two biggest symptoms. We'll have to see if the concussion has affected his memory, balance, or coordination. Some of the lingering signs include confusion, as if you're in a fog, or dizziness. That's what we'll be watching Leo for over the next several hours."

"That sounds serious," she said, swallowing the lump in her throat.

"Most concussions are sports-related. Leo told me he plays football. Wide receiver. I'm surprised he hasn't had a concussion before now. I'll be sure you receive a pamphlet about concussions. Once we discharge him, some of the symptoms for you to watch for are your son having trouble concentrating and sensitivity to light or noise. He might be slightly irritable—more than how a teenager normally is when talking to his parents—or he could have trouble sleeping. I'll need you to watch for any of these signs, and we may need to get him additional treatment after he leaves the hospital."

"We don't even have a doctor," she said, still dazed by all the information. "Leo had a physical so that he could play football this year. I know a doctor in Sugar Springs is at each game."

"Yes, that would be Rex Carpenter. I know Dr. Carpenter fairly well. I can call ahead and let him know about Leo's injuries. If you need to bring Leo in, Dr. Carpenter will see him," the physician assured Nova.

"When can I see Leo?" she asked anxiously.

"He's been transferred upstairs while we've been talking. We can get the room number from our receptionist. Your boy is going to be fine, Mrs. Turner. He's young and healthy." Dr. Raybon paused. "I have called the police, however, and they will want to speak with Leo. They've already interviewed his friend."

"Why?" Nova asked, confused why the police would need to talk to Leo.

"Both boys claimed that they were deliberately hit."

Shock reverberated through her. "Hit? Like a car struck them on purpose?"

"Exactly," the doctor said. "Leo was mumbling something about it, but with his head injury, I didn't give it much credence. Many victims of a concussion—especially with sports injuries—don't always remember exactly how they received their concussion. Sometimes, they can even forget events for the twenty-four hours or so leading up to their concussion. But then when I treated the other young man, who was wearing his helmet, he also mentioned a car going out of its way and deliberately striking them. That's when I decided to bring in the police. They have spoken to the other young man and his parents. I advised them to wait and visit with Leo in the morning."

Dr. Raybon stood. "Let's go get Leo's room number so you can see him."

He led her back to the receptionist, who with a few taps on her keyboard, came up with Leo's room number. Nova started to leave the emergency room when she heard her name called.

Turning, she saw Rilda O'Riley hurrying toward her. The school office worker threw her arms around Nova.

"Oh, Nova, I'm so sorry about this."

She realized Teddy O'Riley must have been the driver of the motor scooter. "What happened? How is Teddy?"

"He's going to be fine. He broke his left leg, though. His football season is over and done."

She couldn't believe Rilda was thinking of football at a time like this and just shook her head, keeping silent.

Rilda continued. "Ken and I got Teddy a motor scooter for his birthday this week. He's been a careful driver when he's borrowed our cars, but he's begged for this Yamaha motor scooter for months now. We only got him the one helmet, telling him not to give any friends a ride." She smiled ruefully. "Obviously, he didn't listen to us about that."

"What is this about someone deliberately running into the boys?" she asked.

"The Tyler police just left. Teddy told them that a car crossed the line for no reason and hit them. It was dark. He couldn't tell the make or model of the car, much less who might be driving it. It was hard enough to knock them both off the scooter, though. A woman was walking her dog and called 911. The police said they're going to hand things over to the Sugar Springs police. They'll be the ones to interview the woman to see if she might have seen anything or if she can identify the car."

Rilda took Nova's hands and said, "I hope you'll forgive Teddy. He's a good boy at heart. I hope you'll allow Leo to continue being friends with him. They're so close."

Knowing she was not one to judge, having the huge, youthful indiscretion of becoming pregnant in her past, Nova said, "I don't blame Teddy. I hope you will punish him for going against your wishes, though. I plan to do the same with Leo. I've told him never to get on a motorcycle. Ever. The fact he did so, especially without a helmet, makes me livid. I'm just thankful they're both all right. I need to go now, Rilda. I haven't seen Leo yet. He's been admitted to a room. The doctor says besides broken bones, Leo has a concussion. They want to observe him overnight."

"Oh, I'm so sorry, Nova. We're about to take Teddy home now. Ken left to bring the car around. Would you like me to stay with you?"

"No, you go home and be with your boy. Teddy needs you now."

She looked up and saw Teddy sitting in a wheelchair, being pushed by a nurse. His leg was propped up because of the cast on it. The teenager looked at her sheepishly.

"Miss Turner, I'm sorry about everything. Is Leo okay?"

"I think he will be. I'm sorry for your injury, Teddy."

He shrugged. "It was a dumb thing to give Leo a ride. Now,

I've caused both of us not to be able to play in the game tomorrow night. I've let the team down."

Nova bent, placing her hand on Teddy's forearm. "You might have disobeyed your parents in giving Leo a ride, but someone else is responsible for this accident, Teddy. Don't be too hard on yourself."

She rose and excused herself, heading to the bank of elevators nearby. She went to the third floor and as she existed the elevator, looked for the signs to guide her to Leo's room.

As she passed the nurse's station, one of them stood. "Are you Mrs. Turner?"

"I'm Miss Turner," she confirmed.

The nurse came around from behind the desk. "I'm Amy. I'm Leo's nurse tonight. Let me take you to his room, ma'am."

Amy led them down the hallway, telling Nova that she would be checking on Leo several times during the night, waking him if he were asleep and asking him a few questions because of the concussion.

They reached the hospital room, and Amy said cheerfully, "Look, Leo, your mom is here."

Nova moved to the bed, her throat thick with emotion. Her son sported a cast on his right arm and had a huge knot on his forehead. She sat on the bed and took his hand in hers.

"Hi, Mom," Leo said weakly. "I screwed up. You always told me not to get on a motorcycle." He paused. "But in my defense, it was a motor scooter."

She couldn't help but smile. "Same thing." She leaned over to kiss his cheek. "How do you feel?"

"Terrible. Amy says my headache will get better." A funny look crossed his face. "I'm going to be sick."

Quickly, the nurse grabbed a small plastic tub sitting on a tray by the bed and placed it under Leo's mouth as he vomited.

"Good save, Amy," Leo told the nurse, who handed him a tissue to wipe his mouth.

"I'll leave you two here," Amy said. "Ring if you need me."

Nova and Leo sat in silence until he said "I really let my team down. Teddy, too."

"Don't think about that now," she said.

"I can't help *but* think about it, Mom. Coach Johnson is going to be so disappointed in us. He's always talking to us about making good decisions. Getting on Teddy's motor scooter was a lousy one. Especially without a helmet. I know I'm lucky. It could've been a lot worse. I researched and wrote a report about traumatic brain injuries last year. I'm grateful things aren't a lot worse now."

Tears poured down her cheeks, and Leo squeezed her hand. "I'm sorry I screwed up, Mom. Don't cry."

"I was so afraid I was going to lose you," she said, her voice wavering. "I've never told you this before, but your father died in a motorcycle accident."

"He did? You've never really said anything much about him. I didn't want to ask."

"It happened right after I learned that I was expecting you." She hesitated and then said, "He wasn't wearing a helmet either."

Tears welled in her son's eyes now. "I'm so sorry, Mom. I didn't know. No wonder you've always been so strict. "Do you think Dad would've married you if he hadn't have died?"

Nova could lie and appease her son, but she had always been honest with him. "No, Leo. We only knew each other briefly, and then he... moved on. Even if he had known about you, I don't think he would have been interested in being a father."

"Is that why you broke up with Coach Johnson? Was he not interested in being a dad to me?"

Guilt flooded her. "Oh, no, Leo. Our split had nothing to do with you. If anything, Coach Johnson loves you."

"I thought it was kinda weird when he would include me in stuff. But I liked it. I like him."

Not wanting to color her son's impression of Cole, Nova said,

"I know you like him, honey. He's a very good coach, and he cares for you a lot. Don't let what happened between the two of us affect your relationship with him."

Leo yawned. "I'm tired, Mom. I need to rest my eyes."

She kissed his brow. "Go to sleep, sweetie. I'll be here every time you wake up."

Nova pulled up a chair to the bed and held her son's hand, grateful that her boy hadn't been taken from her.

24

When Cole's phone rang, he'd already run five miles, showered, and been at his desk for an hour, combing through tonight's gameplan, watching film on the Knights' opponent.

He saw Ken O'Riley's name on the Caller ID and answered, "Good morning, Ken. It's barely six o'clock. You're up early."

"Coach, I have some bad news."

Immediately, Cole tensed. "What? Spill it, Ken."

"Teddy and Leo Turner were in an accident last night coming home from the pep rally."

His gut twisted. "Are they hurt seriously?"

"They were taken to Tyler by ambulance. Teddy broke a leg. Leo broke something and has a concussion since he wasn't wearing a helmet." Ken cursed softly. "Sorry. We'd told Teddy not to give anyone a ride, especially because of the helmet situation, but he did so anyway. I just wanted to let you know because I know with both boys being out, that'll really affect your gameplan."

His heart sank, knowing two of their key offensive weapons

would be out of commission. Still, he was glad the injuries weren't serious.

"Are they still in the hospital?"

"We brought Teddy home last night. He's pretty broken up about letting you and the team down. Rilda talked with Nova, and she said they were keeping Leo overnight as a precaution because of his concussion."

"I see. I'll definitely stop by and see Teddy tomorrow," Cole promised. "Thanks for the heads up, Ken."

"Coach, one other thing. Teddy told us someone intentionally hit them. They were on the new motor scooter we got Teddy for his birthday, so they were pretty much sitting ducks."

Anger flowed through him. "Have you spoken with the police?"

"Yes," Ken assured him. "Once the ER doc heard their story, he called the police in Tyler. A detective came and talked with Teddy. We were in the room and heard everything. Teddy couldn't tell them much, just the fact that someone hurt them on purpose. Since the jurisdiction was Sugar Springs, the detective said he would speak to Roscoe Hamilton and hand the case over to his department."

"Keep me posted, Ken," he said. "And tell Teddy we're thinking about him."

"Rilda is keeping him home from school today, but I know my boy. He'll be at the game tonight," Ken shared.

"Then he's welcomed down on the sidelines," Cole said. "It would do Teddy and the team good to see him there."

He hung up, in a quandary. He had a lot on his plate now, losing his star running back and top receiver. Quickly, Cole sent a group text for his coaches to hustle to the conference room for an emergency meeting. He spent the next ten minutes revamping the gameplan, printing copies for his staff, and then headed to the conference room.

Everyone was present, obviously worried by his text.

"We have a situation we need to deal with," he revealed, passing out copies of the revised gameplan. "Things have been streamlined some because Teddy O'Riley and Leo Turner won't be playing tonight."

"Are they suspended?" Ray asked. "Have they done something crazy stupid?"

"No to the suspension. Yes to crazy stupid."

Briefly, Cole shared his phone call with Ken O'Riley, even mentioning the car that apparently struck the boys for no reason, causing their injuries.

"That's horrible," Ben said.

"Look over the adjustments I've made for tonight," he told his staff. "We'll also need to meet with the team. I want them to know what we know because rumors will be flying."

The coaches discussed Cole's new plan and the plays they thought would work best against tonight's opponent. He appreciated their input, and they continued making alterations before they went to speak to the team. The players were waiting in the large lecture hall in the fieldhouse, expecting to break out in position meetings.

Cole addressed the room. "Something happened last night. Teddy and Leo were in an accident. Both were injured."

Murmurs filled the room, and he motioned for quiet.

"Some broken bones and a concussion are involved, so we obviously will be down two players when we take the field tonight." He paused. "I know this is hard to hear. Teddy and Leo have contributed quite a bit to the success of our season this year. Going into a semifinals game without them will mean a lot of adjustments—physically and mentally."

He scanned the lecture hall, seeing the worry and concern on his players' faces.

"We are still a top team. We earned our spot in this game. We will go out and play our butts off, gentlemen. I expect no less than your best on the field tonight. Teddy will probably join us

on the sidelines for moral support. I don't want any finger pointing. He's been through a rough time and needs our support."

"What about Leo, Coach?" asked Jake worriedly.

"Leo has a concussion. He's in Tyler now, at a hospital. Some
of you have had concussions before. I know I have. He'll need a
lot of quiet. Rest. But I know he'll be there with us in spirit. Let's
break up into position meetings now. Your coaches have our new
gameplan with the alterations we've made. Knights on three.
One, two, three!"

The response was weak, letting him know how concerned the
team was about the two missing players—and how worried they
must be about the game itself tonight.

Cole watched the coaches and athletes leave the lecture hall.
Jake Fletcher remained behind.

"I tried texting Leo this morning. He didn't answer. Is he
really going to be okay, Coach?"

Placing his hand on the quarterback's shoulder, he said, "He
will be, Jake. I'm sure once he feels up to it, he'll text back. And
you can go see him when he's up to having visitors."

Jake left the room, leaving Cole alone. He stared at the empty
space and thought of how alone Nova must feel now. Despite
what she had told him, Cole knew he needed to go to her, if only
for Leo's sake.

He found Ben Peterson and motioned for him to step into the
hall, saying, "I'm going to Tyler now, Ben. I don't know if I'll be
back or not in time for the game. If I'm not, you're acting head
coach tonight."

"Is that wise, Cole?" Ben asked.

He smiled ruefully, "Wise or not, it's something I've got to do.
I'll let Joe Bob know if you're in charge."

"Wait on it, Cole," Ben advised. "Even if you don't ride the bus
with us to the game, you could always meet us there."

He nodded. "I'm slipping out now."

Protocol probably said he should sign out in the main office, but Cole had already told Ben where he was headed. Right now, the important thing was to get to Nova. To Leo.

"At least I haven't thrown up in a few hours," Leo said, looking on the bright side as he dipped his spoon into the yogurt.

Amy came in. "I'm about to go off-shift. Anything I can get you before I leave?"

"No. Thank you, Amy," Nova said. "I appreciate all you've done for Leo."

"Yeah. All that waking me up every two hours. Asking me my name. Who's the president. What school I go to."

The nurse smiled. "You answered all my questions and passed with flying colors, Leo. I'm glad the nausea is subsiding and you're feeling better."

"Better," he agreed. "But I'm still beat."

"You'll be fatigued for a few days," Amy said. "And then you'll feel like going to school and getting all the pretty girls to sign your cast."

Nova laughed, along with Leo. "He hasn't mentioned any specific girls to me, Amy. Maybe I'll do a daily cast check and get the lowdown on everyone who signs it."

Leo finished his breakfast as the new on-duty nurse came in and introduced herself, explaining that Amy had updated her on Leo.

"The doctor should come see you around mid-morning or later," the new nurse said. "Once he's viewed your chart and spoken with you, I'm sure you'll be discharged."

"Ah, sleeping in my own bed. No one shaking me awake. Sounds like heaven," Leo said, yawning.

"Finish your eggs and yogurt, and then you should probably nap again," the nurse advised. "Sleep is restorative. It'll help give you the energy you need to heal."

Once the nurse left and Leo finished his breakfast, Nova removed the tray. She glanced at her son, who'd already fallen fast asleep. Taking her seat again, Nova closed her eyes, as well. She hadn't gotten much sleep during the night, concerned for Leo. He seemed much better this morning, though, and she hoped she could get a little rest herself.

Then she caught a familiar scent.

Cole's cologne.

Quickly opening her eyes, she saw him standing next to her and pushed to her feet.

"Hi. I hope you don't mind that I stopped by to see Leo." Cole glanced to the sleeping teenager, and then his gaze returned to her. "How is he?"

She crossed her arms protectively in front of her. "His headache isn't raging so much this morning. More like a dull throb. The nausea seems to have left him. He's complained a little about the cast. How it's hard to get used to as he moves around."

"He needs a lot of rest over the next few days. I've had a concussion before. Don't let him try to do too much too soon."

"Thanks for the warning," she said softly, taking her seat again.

Without asking, Cole pulled up the other chair in the room, sitting close to her. Her pulse began pounding. Her lips itched to kiss him. She tried to summon up the anger she had felt toward him, but she was just so tired.

Then Nova realized today was the big playoff game.

"You should be at school, Cole. Preparing your team. Especially with Leo and Teddy out tonight. I'm sure that changes whatever plays you planned."

He looked at her, and she swore he could see down into her soul as he said, "How can I be there when the two people I love are here?"

She startled at his words, hurt by them, wanting to lash out and yet desperate to take comfort from him.

"They might fire you."

He shrugged. "It doesn't matter. I know what's important."

Anger rippled through her. "It should matter. It's your life. Your career."

Cole took her hand, causing her heart to speed up. "There's no life without you and Leo, Nova. You should know that."

His words left her speechless. He settled back into his chair, his hand still holding hers. They sat quietly until a doctor appeared and said he needed to wake Leo.

When the teenager opened his eyes, he saw Cole and beamed. "Hey, Coach."

"Hey, Leo. How are you feeling? The doctor is here to check on you."

Nova saw Leo look to her hand joined with Cole's. She pulled away, clasping her hands together in her lap.

The physician asked Leo several questions and seemed satisfied with his replies. He examined him, nodding with satisfaction. Turning to Nova, he said, "Everything looks good, Mrs. Turner. Have you received the material regarding concussions? Do you have any questions?"

"I've read through it. It's pretty self-explanatory."

"If you have any questions, call your PCP. I see from Leo's chart you're in Sugar Springs. It lists Dr. Carpenter as his primary."

"We haven't actually seen him. Dr. Raybon, the ER doctor on call last night, suggested I list Dr. Carpenter. We just moved to Sugar Springs, but Dr. Raybon said Dr. Carpenter would be willing to see my son if necessary."

Cole spoke up. "Dr. Carpenter is our team physician. I'll apprise him of Leo's condition. I'm sure he'd be happy to do any follow-up visits that are needed."

"Then I think Leo can be discharged. I'll let the nurse know and submit the paperwork. It'll take an hour. Sometimes, two. Nothing we can do about that," the doctor apologized.

After the doctor left the room, Nova listened to Leo and Cole talking about tonight's game and the alterations in the gameplan. Cole said that Teddy would be coming to tonight's game, and they would all think of Leo as they played.

"I'm sorry I did something foolish, Coach. Mom always told me never get on a motorcycle. I didn't know that's how my dad died. But I'm really sorry."

"The cast will come off sooner than you think," Cole said. "When your arm starts itching, you know the healing is progressing. Don't worry about anything, Leo. You'll be out of that cast long before spring training starts."

"I know you're disappointed in me. Mom is."

"I wish you and Teddy would have used better judgment, but it's water under the bridge." Cole stood. "I'm glad you're all right, Leo. I'm going to head back to school since you're going home."

"Thanks for coming by, Coach."

Nova walked Cole to the door. "Thank you for coming. He's already in better spirits seeing you."

"If you need anything, Nova, please call."

Her mouth hardened. "Thank you. But I won't."

Cole's face fell. "I understand." He hesitated and met her gaze. "Actually, I don't. But I respect that you have ended things between us."

He walked away, and Nova believed it would be the last time they ever spoke alone. She blinked rapidly, refusing to give into the tears that threatened to fall.

When she stepped into the hospital room again, Leo's eyes were once more closed. He was snoring quietly. She might as well let him sleep since the doctor had said it might be a while before the discharge papers came through.

Half an hour later, Nova glanced up when a light tap sounded on the door. Not wanting to wake Leo, she went and opened it. Fury filled her when she saw Brynn Mattson standing there.

She stepped outside, closing the door behind her as Brynn

said, "I wanted to come and check to see how Leo is handling not being able to play in tonight's game."

"You are the last person I want to see," she said frankly, hurt and anger mixing within her.

The psychologist looked startled. "What's wrong, Nova?"

"Other than my son almost dying on a motorcycle like his father did? Well, I'd say my ex-boyfriend's new girlfriend coming and pretending to be concerned about my boy is pretty wrong."

"What are you talking about?" Brynn asked, clearly confused. "Clue me in, Nova. I heard you and Cole broke up, but I am definitely not your replacement. How could I be when Cole is head over heels in love with you?"

Now, Nova was the one who was bewildered. "But... I saw the two of you in Fine's Jewelry Store in Tyler. You were laughing. You had a ring on your finger."

Brynn's eyes widened. "You saw us? Oh, Nova, you misread the entire situation. We were there for *you*. Cole wanted to pick out an engagement ring for you. He was going to give it to you for Christmas. He asked his aunt for help, but she said she's never worn any kind of jewelry and wouldn't have a clue what you might like."

Brynn shook her head and then said emphatically, "Cole and I are *friends*, Nova. Just friends. I'm seeing Ray now. I accompanied Cole to the jewelers as a favor. Ray was even in the store. He and I went to a movie after Cole selected the engagement ring he wanted for you."

She hadn't spotted Ray. All she had seen was Cole and Brynn together, having the time of their lives. One man had cheated on her. She had assumed Cole was doing the same. She hadn't given him a chance to explain anything because hurt had consumed her. Instead, she had severed all ties with him, trying to protect her already broken heart. God only knew how much she had hurt him.

And yet Cole had still come today. Told her that he loved her.

And Leo.

Tears brimming in her eyes, she looked at Brynn. "I have made a terrible mistake. I misinterpreted everything. I've totally fucked things up."

"Everyone makes mistakes, Nova," Brynn assured her. "Some small. Some big. Some massive." Brynn paused. "I'd say yours is definitely massive."

Despite everything, Nova laughed weakly, seeing Brynn was teasing her.

"The important thing is to own up to your mistake," the psychologist continued. "Cole is one of the kindest men I've ever met. I'm sure he still loves you. Do you love him?"

She nodded. "More than anything."

"Then you fix it," Brynn said. "Make things right."

Nova would do whatever it took. Grovel. Beg. Plead. Cajole.

She had to let Cole know what was in her heart.

25

The nurse finally returned, telling Nova that Leo was about to be discharged. She was able to help him get into his jeans, but the emergency room staff had cut off his jacket and shirt, making them unwearable. The nurse provided him with a scrub top to wear home.

Nova signed the discharge papers, and the nurse helped Leo into the wheelchair she had brought.

"Why do I have to ride in a wheelchair?" her son asked. "I'm feeling lots better. I'm not sick at my stomach at all. I only have a little bit of a headache."

"All patients are taken by wheelchair from their room to their waiting transportation," the nurse told him. She looked to Nova. "In fact, Mrs. Turner, if you'd like to go downstairs and have your car waiting at the front entrance, Leo and I will take our time getting there."

"Of course," she said, hurrying from the hospital room.

She decided to take the stairs instead of waiting for an elevator and left the hospital, shivering since she had forgotten her own jacket. She remembered a blanket in the back seat of her car and as she pulled up to the entrance of the hospital, Nova got out of the car and retrieved it. She moved to the passenger's side and opened the door just as the doors opened and the nurse pushed Leo to the curb.

Both of them helped him to stand, and Nova wrapped the blanket around him. She thanked the nurse and then eased Leo into the car, fastening his seatbelt, shutting his door, and returning to the driver's side of the car.

On the way home, she decided to address the mistake she had made about Cole with Leo.

Without going into details, she said, "Leo, I have made a major mistake."

He quickly asked, "Are you taking Coach back?"

She glanced at him and saw the hope on his face and nodded.

"That's great news, Mom."

"I jumped to a conclusion, and I didn't give Coach Johnson a chance to correct my false impression or address my concerns about it. I reacted instead of responding."

"I know stuff like that is private, Mom. I won't ask you to tell me what happened. The good thing is, you and Coach will be back together."

She cautioned him, saying, "*I* want to renew and continue our relationship, Leo. That doesn't mean that Coach Johnson necessarily wants to do the same. All I can do is apologize and own up to my mistake and see if he's willing to give me another chance. It's not a given."

"It'll be fine," Leo assured her. "You put the ball in Coach's court, and he'll know what to do."

Nova wasn't as certain as her son seemed. Yes, Cole had told her that he still loved her, but she knew she had wounded him deeply. She understood now that, more than anything, love involved trust. She had made a snap judgement and been terribly cruel, not giving Cole an opportunity to explain things. He might still have feelings for her, but she had broken the trust between them. He might not want to continue as they had before.

And she had to prepare herself for that possibility.

They arrived in Sugar Springs, and she got Leo settled in his room. He began charging his phone and started texting with his friends. Nova told him he could do so for half an hour, and then he needed to get some rest.

For her part, she checked her own phone for the first time since the hospital had notified her Leo had been brought in. She had silenced it, wanting to focus strictly on her son. It was full of texts and voice messages, all asking about Leo and telling her to reach out if she needed anything. Her throat grew thick with emotion, knowing so many people cared about her and her son. Even if things didn't work out with Cole, Nova realized Sugar Springs had definitely become home to them, despite what Phyllis Arnold had told her.

Quickly, she responded to the texts she had received, letting people know that Leo was on the mend, and they were now home. Immediately, she was flooded with offers, people saying they would bring in meals for them. Rilda messaged her and said she would have members of the booster club create a signup sheet so that Nova wouldn't have to worry about cooking for the next two weeks.

She called Rilda and thanked her profusely, asking how Teddy was today. Her friend reassured her that this would be the only day Teddy would miss school and that he would be on the sidelines at tonight's game, representing both him and Leo.

Nova prepared a sandwich and soup for Leo and sat on the bed talking to him as he ate it.

"Mom, Teddy's going to the game tonight. Do you think I could, too?"

"No, sweetheart. The doctor's instructions say you need to stay in bed and get a lot of rest for the next forty-eight hours. If you're doing well, however, you can go to school on Monday if you feel like it."

"Oh, I will, Mom. I have lots of people who want to sign my

cast." He grinned sheepishly. "Including Tammy. She's a girl in my world history class."

"You like Tammy?"

He nodded. "She's already asked if she can come see me. She said she would bake brownies for me. I told her that would be great and that I would check with you about when she could come visit."

"As long as you stay in bed, I don't see why Tammy can't drop by tomorrow. Or any of your friends. The thing is, Leo, you do need to get rest. Your brain is still healing from the concussion. So, we'll need to limit how long people can stay."

They worked out a schedule so that Leo could have visitors tomorrow morning for an hour and again tomorrow afternoon for the same length of time.

"Do you think Tammy could come a little early?" he asked. "Just so we could talk without a lot of people around?"

"That's fine with me. Text your friends and let them know the schedule. Be sure to let Tammy know when she is welcome to come. After that, phone off, buddy, so you can get some rest."

"Will do, Mom," Leo said.

She took the tray with his empty dishes and went to the door, pausing a moment to look back at him. His thumbs were flying across his cell's keyboard, a grin on his face, and she was grateful once more that he hadn't been injured more seriously.

As Leo rested, Nova wondered how and when she should approach Cole. She didn't want to interrupt his day, knowing he should be preparing for tonight's game. He must have been thrown for a loop with Teddy and Leo unable to play, and she didn't want to be a further distraction to him.

Still, she felt as if she needed to make a big gesture to let Cole know how wrong she had been and how much she truly loved him. She finally decided on a plan and called Brynn Mattson.

Brynn answered on the second ring. "Brynn Mattson, school psychologist."

Gathering her courage, Nova said, "Hi, Brynn, it's Nova."

Warmly, Brynn said, "Nova, I'm so glad to hear from you. Did you and Leo get home safely?"

"We did. Listen, I have no right to ask this after I was so ugly to you—"

"Stop right there, Nova. I liked you from the moment I met you at Playful Painting. I don't hold anything against you. I'm hoping that we can become friends, especially since our two guys are so close to one another."

"I have a favor to ask of you then, Brynn."

"Anything, Nova. I know you want to make things right with Cole."

"I haven't contacted him since you and I spoke at the hospital. I don't want him to lose focus on tonight's game. I know you attend all the games, but would you please stay with Leo this evening instead so that I might be able to go? I know Ray will be disappointed."

"Ray will understand. I haven't told him what we talked about because I knew that you would want to talk to Cole first. I'd be happy to stay with Leo tonight."

"Thank you so much, Brynn. It means the world to me. I can't leave Leo unattended. He's doing really well, but he needs someone to keep an eye on him for the next forty-eight hours."

"Is he eating?"

"He's regaining his appetite," Nova said. "Why?"

"I'll stop at Romano's and pick up a pizza for our dinner. Just let me know what toppings he likes."

She chuckled. "What toppings does he *not* like might be a better question. Just get whatever you like, and Leo will be fine eating that."

They confirmed the time Brynn would be there, and Nova hung up. She went out to her studio and found poster board. On it, she painted a huge red heart in the middle, placing *I* and *you* above and below it.

Placing the poster board on her work bench to dry, she returned to the house. She went to the bathroom and glanced in the mirror, seeing she looked a mess. Before Leo awoke, she jumped into the shower, dressing and blow-drying her hair and applying perfume and lipstick.

When Leo awoke, he said he was hungry. Nova fixed him a snack. She told him that she was going to go to the game tonight and would try to speak with Cole afterward, telling Leo he wouldn't be by himself.

"Miss Mattson from school will come stay with you. She came to see you at the hospital this morning, but you were asleep. She was concerned about how you were doing after the accident."

"I'll probably keep beating myself up for being so stupid, but I know what I did was wrong and not to do it again. I like Miss Mattson. Did you know she is seeing Coach Barker?"

"Yes, she told me about that. If Coach Johnson and I get back together, maybe the four of us can go on a double-date."

Leo reached for her hand, squeezing her fingers. "It's gonna be okay, Mom. You and Coach. Just tell him you're sorry. He's a good guy. He'll understand."

"I hope so," she said fervently, not wanting to think what her life would be like without Cole in it.

Nova left Leo streaming a Netflix movie on his tablet and called Aunt Ju. She answered on the first ring.

"Why, hello, Nova. We haven't talked in a while. I've just been so busy. I hope we can sit together at the game tonight and catch up, despite what's gone on between you and Cole."

"Do you have a moment to talk?"

She explained how Leo and Teddy had been injured and that she had just brought Leo home from the hospital today.

"Oh, honey, I know how scared you must have been. Cole had a concussion in high school. I remember sitting in the stands, my heart in my throat, as he lay motionless on the field. He never remembered the hit. In fact, he didn't recall the several days leading up to that game."

"So far, Leo's memory seems to be fine," she shared. "But about Cole and me. Our breakup was my doing. I saw something that totally gave me the wrong impression, and I was foolish enough not to give him a chance to explain things. Things have been cleared up, and I know I was in the wrong. I want to come to tonight's game and let Cole know that I love him."

"Do you want me to stay with Leo tonight?" Aunt Ju offered.

"No, I have a friend that will help me out. The entire town, though, knows about our split. I was hoping that we could sit together at the game. I think I'll need a little moral support."

The older woman laughed. "I will be your Rain, Nova. That mother bear protecting her cub. Anyone wanting to get to you will have to go through me first."

Her eyes blurred with tears. "Thank you, Aunt Ju. I knew I could count on you."

"Honey, you're already like a daughter to me. Cole is a smart guy. Yes, he's been hurt, but he won't let that hurt stand in the way of the two of you being happy."

"I hope that with all my heart, Aunt Ju."

Since the semifinals game was being played at a stadium in Tyler, Nova arranged to swing by Aunt Ju's apartment and pick her up so they could drive to the game together.

She heard the doorbell ring and hurried to answer it, hoping it wasn't friends of Leo's trying to see him a day early. Today needed to remain low-key and quiet for her son.

Opening the door, she was startled to find two men on her porch. One was an older gentleman in his sixties, dressed in a law enforcement uniform and wearing a Stetson hat. The other wore a suit and tie and appeared to be around forty.

"Mrs. Turner? I'm Police Chief Roscoe Hamilton. This is Detective Douglas."

"Oh, you must be here to interview Leo. I know the police

spoke with Teddy in Tyler, and Rilda told me matters would be turned over to the Sugar Springs Police Department. Please, come in."

She offered them seats and told them Leo was resting in his room.

"The doctor wants him to remain in bed a few days because of the concussion. Is there anything I can answer for you, and then I can take you upstairs."

"No, ma'am, we don't need to speak to Leo right now," Chief Hamilton said. "Maybe in a day or two when he's up and about. We're here to tell you that we've arrested a suspect in the hit and run of Leo and Teddy O'Riley."

Nova gasped. "So quickly? Was it the woman who called 911 that helped you find the driver? Rilda mentioned that to me."

"Yes, ma'am," Detective Douglas said. "Mrs. Dunaway was walking her dog Precious and saw the boys on the motor scooter and the car deliberately swerve toward them. She got the first two letters on the plate and thought she saw part of the third one. Either a *D* or an *O*. While Mrs. Dunaway is seventy-five, she's still sharp as a tack. She said the car was a Honda. Knew that because she has one herself. Didn't know if it was an Accord or Civic, but with a partial plate and identifying the maker of the vehicle, we began combing state registration records, starting with residents of Sugar Springs."

"And that's how you found this person?"

"No, ma'am," Chief Hamilton said. "Sugar Springs is a small town. Gossip flies fast. Even faster now with texting. Teddy O'Riley started texting his friends, telling them what happened to him and Leo. Word spread." He cleared his throat. "We had someone call in, telling us he thought he knew who might've been responsible."

She waited, her heart racing.

"Phyllis Arnold," Hamilton said.

Shock numbed Nova. "Phyllis?" she repeated weakly.

"Yes. Her son said he'd seen some damage on his mom's car this morning when he went out to the garage to get into his own vehicle. We immediately looked up her information and saw that Phyllis drives a Honda Civic."

"Keith?" she asked, shaking her head.

"Yes, Mrs. Turner," the detective said. "It took a lot of guts for that boy to come forward."

"I knew... I knew Phyllis didn't like Leo or me, but for her to go this far..." Her voice trailed off.

"We arrested her two hours ago and had the car towed in," Hamilton continued. "Detective Douglas and I interviewed her. At first, Mrs. Arnold denied everything. Then we told her that a witness had identified her car and some of the plate number. That the damage to her car matches what Mrs. Dunaway saw, and it would only be a matter of time before we connected her car with the accident. Once she was confronted, she broke down and confessed. Said you and Leo coming to Sugar Springs had ruined everything. Cost her son his starting position on the football team. Railed about how you'd turned the booster club against her for no good reason."

The chief shook his head. "I'm sorry for what happened to your boy, Mrs. Turner. I can't recall anything so downright mean happening during my entire time on the police force, and I've been here for decades."

Nova asked, "How is Keith? Where is he? This is so terrible for him and Fred."

"Fred Arnold was leaving the station when we headed over here. Looking to hire Walker Cox to defend his wife. If it comes to trial, that is. Phyllis may simply plead guilty. Fred said Keith had gone to school today." Hamilton glanced at his watch. "Should be out by now."

"He's on the football team, though," Detective Douglas pointed out. "He should be with the team."

"That poor boy," she said, shaking her head, knowing how gossip would tar Keith with its ugly brush.

"As I said, we might need to talk to Leo in a few days. Just wanted to make you aware of the situation. The news'll get out soon that Phyllis has been arrested. I wanted you to be prepared."

"I'll tell Leo. He needs to know," she said.

"Thank you for your time, ma'am," Detective Douglas said.

Nova escorted them to the door, seeing them out. She closed and leaned against it for support.

Phyllis Arnold had tried to kill her son. And Teddy. It was unimaginable. Yet it had happened. Phyllis herself had admitted her guilt.

With a heavy heart, Nova went to Leo's room to break the news to him.

26

———

Cole shifted in his chair, trying to concentrate. It was hard to do so. His thoughts all day had drifted to Nova and Leo.

He slipped his hand into his pocket, fingering the ring meant for Nova. He'd carried it in his pocket ever since he'd bought it. Even after she had rejected him, he couldn't help it. It was like having a piece of her with him. He should give up. Take it back to the jeweler's shop in Tyler. See if he could get any of his money back.

Pulling it out, he studied the white gold, slender band, which had five small diamonds running across it. Nova wasn't one who wore rings, due to her artistic work. He'd decided to skip an engagement ring and opt for a simple band with the diamonds in it.

His heart ached as he looked at the ring, knowing it represented hopes and dreams which would never be fulfilled. Then anger filled him.

Cole Johnson was not a quitter.

Why had he quit on Nova then?

He told himself it was what she wanted. Hell, what about

what *he* wanted? He wanted her. He wanted to understand what had changed about her. About them. His feelings for her were still so strong, his love deep and resonating within him. Cole resolved in that moment that he would stop being a meek, agreeable player in this game of life and meet the challenges ahead—straight on. He would get to the bottom of why Nova had rejected him out of the blue.

Maybe if he could understand why, he might be able to move on.

And maybe—just maybe—he could somehow find the way back into to her heart.

The final bell of the day rang, and he rose. His players would be arriving in the gym soon. By now, they would have had all day to wrap their heads around the challenge they faced tonight, missing two key teammates as they faced their toughest opposition of the season. He would need to see they ate and got to Tyler. He hadn't begun to think about what he would say to them in the locker room. He prayed the right words would come.

As he rose, he saw Keith Arnold lingering outside his office.

"Keith? Do you need to talk to me?"

"Yeah, Coach."

The boy rushed by him and plopped in a seat. Cole closed the door and sat next to the senior.

"Are you worried about tonight? How you'll play? If you'll be injured again?"

Keith shrugged.

Cole said, "I've been hurt before and come back. All athletes have injuries of varying degrees. I've broken bones. A broken rib was especially painful. Had concussions. Sprained ankles and wrists. You've done a good, steady job for us since you returned from your injury. We'll be counting on you tonight, more than ever, with Leo out."

"I know." Keith swallowed and finally looked Cole in the eye.

"I had to do something today, Coach. Something that I know was the right thing to do, but it really hurt." His gaze fell to his lap.

"Do you want to tell me about it?" he asked gently, knowing the boy did, or he wouldn't be here.

"I called Chief Hamilton this morning."

"The police chief?

"Yeah." Keith sniffed, wiping his eyes. "I think my mom is the one who ran into Leo and Teddy."

The boy's words stunned him, striking as hard as any physical blow. "What?"

Keith told Cole how he'd seen his mom's front left side of her car damaged when he left for school this morning.

"I thought it was weird until I got to school, and the texts started flying. Teddy said someone hit them on purpose. I... I got to thinking. And I know how much my mom hates Miss Turner and Leo." Keith swallowed. "I don't. I know Leo's a way better receiver than I am. And you've been great, letting me start after I came back from my injury. But I haven't begrudged Leo getting more playing time or being named the starter during the playoffs. That's all my mom's complained about. Bitching all the time—sorry, Coach. But it's like she's crazy mad about it."

He placed a hand on the teen's shoulder and squeezed. "You've given the police information that they need, Keith. They'll check it out. If your mom didn't do anything wrong, it'll be easy to prove. Look at me, son."

Reluctantly, the senior lifted his head, his gaze meeting Cole's.

"What you did was difficult. But you said it yourself. It was the right thing to do. If your mom is responsible for running over Leo and Teddy, then she needs help. You speaking up might be the first step in her getting that help."

Keith broke down, his sobs loud. Cole wrapped his arms around the player, no more words exchanged between them.

When Keith calmed, Cole said, "Pull yourself together. Join the team when you're ready. We'll be down in the cafeteria."

He left his office, still amazed by what Keith had revealed. He had seen the resentful looks Phyllis Arnold had tossed Nova's way. To think, though, that the hair stylist's anger ran so deep that she had tried to kill two teenagers shocked him. He wondered if Nova knew of this latest twist and decided the police would have informed her by now if Keith's information had been verified.

It made Cole all the more determined, however, to see her after tonight's game.

They ate their pregame meal in the school cafeteria, barbeque sandwiches and sides, and then headed to the buses which would take them in to Tyler, where they were playing at a neutral site. They would be the visitors tonight and went to that locker room upon arrival. Usually, the players were talkative before a game. Tonight, the locker room was silent as pads were put on and turf tape pressed into place.

The team took the field for their pregame warmups. Already, the stadium was packed on both sides, Knights fans cheering on their team as their opponents loudly booed them.

Once warmups finished, the players and staff returned to the locker room. Coaches went around giving last minute advice, adjusting players' uniforms, and passing along words of encouragement. He knew it was now time to address his team.

"Gather around, gentlemen."

Cole looked out at these students, wanting the best for them, as he said, "I didn't know a soul before I came to Sugar Springs. I didn't know how good Ida Lou's fried chicken could be. How amazing Romano's pizza crusts are. I hadn't been to Sugar Lake or the gazebo in the town square. I was moving to a new town to take a job I wanted badly."

He paused. "I hadn't met any of you or my coaching staff. But when I did, I knew there was something special about this team. Very special. You listened. You soaked up everything we threw at you. You learned from your mistakes. You remained disciplined and focused.

"I know tonight is a challenge. An uphill battle. It was the minute we learned who our opponent would be. They have six state championships under their belts and are bucking for another title this season. They are smart. Talented. They know how to score—and how to keep the other team from scoring on them."

Cole took a deep breath. "Even with Teddy in the backfield and Leo sprinting down the sidelines, we were facing the biggest challenge of our season. Without those two, the challenge is even greater." He paused again. "But I believe in you. My coaches believe in you. And you need to believe in yourselves. We are going to go out there. Do our best. Fight. Claw. Perform. Execute. Whether we stand victorious when that last second ticks off the clock or not remains to be seen. Whatever happens on the field tonight, though?

"I'm proud of each and every one of you."

Cole fell silent, feeling the air charged around him. "Knights on three. One, two, three!"

"Knights!"

They took the field, running in as the school fight song played. He didn't skim the crowd, knowing Nova wouldn't be there. She would need to be with Leo. Instead, he kept his attention on the field and the sidelines.

At half, the score was tied, ten-all. He thought they might have a chance, even if their rival was bigger on both the offensive and defensive lines and faster coming out of the backfield. He was pleased when Keith Arnold caught a pass on a fourth down they went for at their own forty-eight yard line.

It wasn't enough, though. By the time the game ended, they'd lost by eight points, the other team going for two after their last touchdown, inside of five minutes to play. Jake had done his best to rally the team and bring them down the field, playing his heart out, but the rival's defense proved too much at the end, sacking the Sugar Springs quarterback, who coughed up the ball with less than a minute to go. Out of timeouts, Cole watched as the other team ran out the clock, taking a knee two plays in a row in a show of good sportsmanship.

He congratulated the victor's coach at midfield, wishing him the best in next week's championship game. He signaled for his team to face the fans in the stands as the band struck up the school song. Players all around him raised their helmets high as they sang along, tears streaming down their faces.

He gazed into the crowd and spied Aunt Ju.

Nova stood next to her.

He stilled, his gaze locking on her. Slowly, Nova raised a sign, opening it, holding it high above her head.

A huge, red heart was in the center of the sign.

I love you.

Despite being down from the loss, Cole's spirits soared.

"I love you," he mouthed as the school's anthem came to a close, and the Knights fans cheered.

He turned away, following his team to the locker room, but he pulled out his phone as he went, texting Nova.

Need to talk to the team. Will you wait for me?

THE BLOOD POUNDED in his ears as he saw she was typing a reply.

I'll wait forever.

Cole slipped the cell back into his pocket and pushed his left hand into the other one, toying with the ring again. Hope filled him.

In the locker room, his players remained silent. Some collapsed upon a bench, spent. Others milled around, waiting to see what he would say.

He moved to the center of the room, knowing every eye was on him.

"The tough thing about ending your season on a loss is that loss tends to stay with you until the next year." He looked around the locker room. "I don't want that to happen with us. We are a great team. We went head to toe with the toughest opponent this season and stayed with them the entire game. You have nothing to be ashamed of, gentlemen. You gave it everything you had out there tonight. Yes, we came up short—but look at what a deep run we made into the playoffs. We were a game away from the state championship finals.

"That's what I want you to focus on now. All the good things we did this season. All the things we'll do even better next season. Go home and celebrate—because you earned it. You have more heart than any team I've ever played on or coached. You are an amazing group of young men, and you have even better days ahead of you. Learn from any mistakes you made tonight. We'll talk about what went right and wrong come Monday. Take this weekend and enjoy the fact you were a playoff team. Knights on three."

The locker room resounded not with the voices of players who had lost, but ones who saw a bright future ahead.

As the team hit the showers, he gathered his coaching staff.

"Everything I said to the players was meant for you, as well. I didn't know any of you from Adam, and yet we became a premier coaching staff because you believed in our mission. You are a generous group, giving of your thoughts and time, and putting heart and soul into everything we do. I couldn't be prouder of you. Thank you for everything you contributed to this winning season. I hope you'll all want to come back and do it again—and that it will be a state championship season for us next year."

Cole went around, hugging every member of his staff, even John Peterson.

"I may never like you, Coach, but I respect you," John told him.

"I can live with that," he said, grinning at the defensive coordinator.

He pulled Ben Peterson aside. "Listen, I want you to be in charge. I'm not going to ride back with the team."

Ben gave him a knowing smile. "I saw the sign, Cole. Hell, I think everyone in the stadium saw it." He clapped Cole on the back. "I hope you and Nova work things out."

"I do, too."

Leaving the locker room, he returned to the field. Paper streamers littered the ground. Only a few stragglers remained in the stands.

One of them was Nova.

Cole moved up the concrete steps toward her. She rose, the sign in her hands, folded now as she nibbled on her lower lip. He was going to do a little nibbling on it himself.

He reached her and pulled the sign from her hand, tossing it aside, drinking her in.

"I want to—"

He didn't give her a chance to say anything. Cole yanked her into his arms, his mouth coming down on hers, the taste of her filling him with happiness. He kissed her for a long time, not wanting to end the magic of this moment.

Finally, he broke the kiss. She smiled up at him.

"Do you love me?" he asked, his voice husky.

"More than anything," she told him, her fingers pushing into his hair, pulling him down to her again.

The kiss filled the yearning that had echoed within him,

filling that empty space that had resided inside ever since Nova had shoved him away. He knew it spoke of the promises they would make to one another, now and in the future. Some of those promises would be spoken in front of others as they sealed their vows.

For now, though, Cole was happy to know the woman he loved was his once again.

Nova pulled away, though. "I love you. I always have. And I did an idiotic thing, Cole. I made a snap judgment—when I should have trusted you. Talked to you."

"Do you trust me now?" he asked.

"Yes. I always will. I will never, ever be such a dolt again."

She told him what she had witnessed standing outside Fine Jeweler's that day and how she had misconstrued the scene she had witnessed.

"I threw everything we had out the window. I was so hurt. I was trying to protect myself. And Leo. I should have given you a chance to set the record straight."

He kissed her softly. "Lesson learned. How did you figure things out?"

"Brynn came to the hospital after you left. To see Leo. I was horrible to her, too. Her confusion made me question what I had seen." Nova hesitated. "She told me why she was there with you. What you were doing."

He caressed her cheek. "Yes, Brynn agreed to help me out."

She smiled ruefully. "I guess I ruined that Christmas present."

Grinning, he pulled the ring from his pocket and held it up, hearing her sharp intake of breath.

"It's not an engagement ring, babe. I know you don't like to wear rings when you're working. A lot of the ones we looked at, the diamonds stuck up or out. I knew you wouldn't like that because they might catch on something. Brynn thought you'd like just a band instead. I spotted this one in the display case and had her try it on. The diamonds are flat in the band. It just looked like you."

Tears streamed down her cheeks. "I do like it."

Cole dropped to one knee. "Although I can't give it to you now because we need to save it for the wedding, I do have one very important question to ask you, Nova Turner."

He paused, seeing the love for him in her eyes, knowing his for her was reflected in his own.

"Would you marry me?"

"I will, Cole. And I will show you every day just how much I do love you."

She pulled on him, and he stood again, his lips molding to hers. The kiss was perfect. Absolutely perfect.

Just like Nova.

He broke it. "I wish I could kiss you all night, but it's really cold. Besides, we have somewhere to be."

She grinned mischievously. "In your bed?"

Cole laughed. "A tempting offer, but I had something else in mind. I think besides asking you, I need to ask Leo for your hand. If I get a yes from him, then we can definitely get married."

He swept her into his arms and carried her to her car in the parking lot. Once inside the car, he kissed her again, his need for her so great he couldn't help himself.

"If Leo says yes to me, do you think we can get married over my Christmas break?"

Nova's brilliant smile lit up his world. "Best idea I've heard all night, Coach."

EPILOGUE

FIVE YEARS LATER...

Cole tweaked the last bit of tonight's gameplan and leaned back in his chair, his hands pillowed behind his head. He glanced at the family picture on his desk which had been taken a few weeks ago and smiled.

He liked being a dad. And a husband.

"Looks like you're goofing off, Coach," a voice in the doorway said.

He beamed as he saw his old quarterback Jake Fletcher grinning at him. Jake was accompanied by Leo, and Cole went and gave both bear hugs.

"I see you're using your open week to your advantage," he said, ushering the young men into his office.

These two had been responsible, along with Teddy O'Riley, in helping Cole win his first state championship at Sugar Springs. Jake and Teddy had been a seniors and Leo a junior when that occurred. Teddy had received a scholarship to play running back at Sam Houston State University, while Jake had been offered an athletic scholarship at Stephen F. Austin University. Leo had followed Jake to Nacogdoches the following year and had become Jake's favorite target among a talented corps of receivers.

He and Nova made it to as many home games as they could to watch their son and his best friend play, since Nacogdoches was only ninety minutes away from Sugar Springs. Jake would graduate this coming spring but had redshirted his freshman year, so he still had a year of eligibility left. He was considering returning to play another year while he started grad school, so that he and Leo could spend a final year together on the football field.

"It worked out well with this weekend being homecoming in Sugar Springs," Leo said.

"Have you been by the house yet to see your mom?" he asked. "Either of you?"

"That's our next stop, but we'll be back for the game," Leo told him.

"You know you're welcome to come down on the sidelines," he told the pair.

Homecoming was a huge tradition in Sugar Springs, and many former players came back to visit old friends and watch the game together. Bubba Reynolds had welcomed these former players on the sidelines, and Cole had continued this tradition.

"Think you'll go to state this year, Coach?" asked Jake.

In his years coaching the Knights, Cole had two state championships under his belt and had taken a third team to the finals last year.

"We'll have to see," he said.

Leo laughed. "You always play it close to the vest, Dad." In a gruff voice, imitating Cole, Leo added, "I won't guarantee a win, but I know this team is prepared for tonight's game."

As the boys cracked up, Cole couldn't help but think how proud he was that Leo called him Dad. Being a husband and father meant more to Cole than even being a coach, and that was saying a great deal.

He and Nova had married during his Christmas break five years ago, and Ash had been born the first day of the following October. Nova was into what names meant, and she had convinced him to name their son Asher, which meant blessed, fortunate, and happy. The name had quickly been shortened to Ash, and his boy was already showing athletic talent. Ash had gone around throwing and catching a miniature football since the time he could walk. He also had a set of tiny golf clubs, and Cole thought Ash might even turn out to be a better golfer than football player.

His daughter would be three years old in another month. Since she was born on Thanksgiving Day, Nova had wanted to name her Samoset because it was the name of the Native America tribe who celebrated the first Thanksgiving with the Pilgrims. Her name had been shortened to Sami, and she was all girl, playing with dolls and always wanting to wear dresses. Nova had placed Sami in dance classes, and she also had just started taking skating lessons from Rory Cox. Rory and her husband Walker had become good friends of theirs, thanks to their twins Remy and Jack being close to Ash in age, and they attended the same preschool.

The bell rang, and Cole rose, telling the boys, "Go home and visit with your moms now, and I'll see you at tonight's game."

After Leo and Jake left, Cole was surprised when Keith Arnold stuck his head in the office door.

"Coach? How are you?"

"Keith! It's great to see you."

Once again, he hugged his former player. After Keith's mother had been convicted of attempted murder and sent to prison, Keith and his father had moved from Sugar Springs shortly after the boy's graduation. This was the first time he had had any contact with Keith since then.

"What are you up to these days?" he asked. "You look good."

"I graduated with a degree in accounting, and I've been working as an accountant with an insurance firm." Keith paused. "I got engaged last week."

"That's fantastic," Cole declared. "Congratulations."

Keith frowned. "I didn't know if anyone would want to see me. I've never been back. You know, because of my mom."

He placed a hand on Keith's shoulder. "No one blames you for anything your mom did, Keith."

"I hope not. I took a chance and decided to come to homecoming tonight."

"I just visited with Leo and Jake. They'll be on the sidelines tonight." He paused. "You're welcome to be there, as well."

"I'll think about it, Coach. Thanks."

Keith left and the next few hours went by in a blur as all the pregame meetings and meal took place. Once the team had dressed and gone through their pregame drills, Cole gave them a pep talk in the locker room and they took the field once more as the school fight song played.

As he moved to the sidelines, he looked up in the stands and found Nova sitting with Brynn and the Fletchers. Brynn held her and Ray's two-year-old on her lap, trying to balance the child against her burgeoning belly. He waved and Nova returned the wave, as did Ash and Sami. He motioned for Ash, and the boy scampered down the bleachers to the field. People in the booster club kidded Cole, calling Ash his little shadow, because the boy took every step alongside his father during a game.

Sami followed her little brother, but she joined the cheerleaders down on the track. His daughter was their adopted mascot and wore a miniature version of the school's cheer uniform, even having her own set of tiny pom-poms to shake. At her young age, Sami had already learned the cheers and helped lead the crowd, along with the cheerleaders.

"What do you think of tonight's match?" a deep voice asked.

Cole turned and found Police Chief Gideon Ross at his side.

"Our chances are good," he said. "We're prepared. As always."

They quickly talked about the quarterback battle, which had been raging all season long, and how Smith had pulled ahead in the contest and would start tonight.

"I'll see you later," Gideon said, going into the stands to sit with his family.

"You need anything, Cole?" asked Aunt Ju.

He slung an around his aunt's shoulders, grateful that she was in his life on a daily basis. Aunt Ju had earned her nursing degree and now served as the nurse at Sugar Springs High School, where she was much beloved by the students and faculty.

"No, I'm good," he told her, offering a hand to Ford Carpenter as he joined them.

Ford had replaced his uncle Rex as one of the town's primary care physicians. He'd also taken on Rex Carpenter's duties as team physician on game nights. Ford had married a local girl who had returned to run Romano's, her family's pizza parlor.

"Just wanted to give you an update on Jackson."

Ford told Cole about one of his defensive back's rehab and how he thought the player would be able to take the field next week.

"That's good news, Ford," he said. "Especially since we have the Randolph Raiders coming up next on the schedule."

The national anthem was played, followed by both school songs, and the Knights won the coin toss. By now, Leo and Jake had joined the team on the sidelines, along with many other former players, including Keith Arnold. Both Leo and Jake wanted to get into coaching, and he hoped someday one—or both of them—might join his staff here in Sugar Springs. Like Ben Peterson, Cole's roots ran deep in this community now, and it would take an enticing offer for him and Nova to consider leaving this program and the town they both loved.

The game went as he expected, homecoming opponents usually one of the weaker teams in the district, and the Knights won 41-10. He had been able to play every player who'd suited out, glad he could help them get more experience as they moved deeper into the season.

When the game ended, Cole strode to the center of the field

and shook hands with the other head coach, who told him that he thought the Knights would go all the way to the championship game this season.

"That's the goal," he responded. "Every year."

He congratulated players from both teams and as his own team and staff made their way into the locker room, he saw Nova leaving the stands in order to join him on the field for a few, brief moments. He was fortunate that she understood the life of a foot-ball coach and never gave him a hard time about the long hours he put in.

Cole wrapped his arms around her as she met him, pausing for a long kiss. Other coaches wouldn't have shown any kind of public display of affection in front of their players or fans, but Cole wanted everyone to know how happy he was in his choice of a wife and how natural it was to show affection to someone you loved.

She broke the kiss. "Good game, Coach. It was a great turnout for homecoming," she noted. "The sidelines went from endzone to endzone with players and former players."

"I know you're happy to have Leo home this weekend. So am I."

He kissed her again, the kiss hard and possessive. "Let me walk you to the car."

By now, Sami had joined them, and he scooped his daughter into his arms and placed her so she sat on his nape, her legs hanging to his chest. Ash, who had been running around, pretending to catch passes, ran to them. He took his son's hand and escorted his family to their van.

Cole helped Nova buckle the kids into their car seats and then stood next to her, reluctant to leave her.

His hands encircled her waist, and he brushed his lips against hers slowly. "It's hard to leave a sexy mama," he said, his voice husky.

Her eyes twinkled. "Speaking of that..."

Anticipation rippled through him. "Yes?"

"It looks as if we might be adding to the tribe," she told him, smiling broadly.

He kissed her again, soft and sweet. "When?"

"I think mid-May. We'll have to see. I have an appointment with my OB on Monday to confirm."

"I could win every game for the rest of my career, and it wouldn't make me as happy as I am in this moment," Cole said.

He kissed his wife a final time, knowing in his heart that they were a perfect match.

ALSO BY ALEXA ASTON

SUGAR SPRINGS

Shadows of the Past

Learning to Trust Again

A Perfect Match

A Fresh Start

Recipe for Love

MAPLE COVE

Another Chance at Love

A New Beginning

Coming Home

The Lyrics of Love

Finding Home

HOLLYWOOD NAME GAME

Hollywood Heartbreaker

Hollywood Flirt

Hollywood Player

Hollywood Double

Hollywood Enigma

LAWMEN OF THE WEST

Runaway Hearts

Blind Faith

Love and the Lawman

Ballad Beauty

SAGEBRUSH BRIDES

A Game of Chance

Written in the Cards

Outlaw Muse

KNIGHTS OF REDEMPTION

A Bit of Heaven on Earth

A Knight for Kallen

SECOND SONS OF LONDON

Educated by the Earl

Debating with the Duke

DUKES DONE WRONG

Discouraging the Duke

Deflecting the Duke

Disrupting the Duke

Delighting the Duke

Destiny with a Duke

DUKES OF DISTINCTION

Duke of Renown

Duke of Charm

Duke of Disrepute

Duke of Arrogance

Duke of Honor

<u>MEDIEVAL RUNAWAY WIVES</u>

Song of the Heart

A Promise of Tomorrow

Destined for Love

<u>SOLDIERS AND SOULMATES</u>

To Heal an Earl

To Tame a Rogue

To Trust a Duke

To Save a Love

To Win a Widow

<u>THE ST. CLAIRS</u>

Devoted to the Duke

Midnight with the Marquess

Embracing the Earl

Defending the Duke

Suddenly a St. Clair

<u>THE KING'S COUSINS</u>

God of the Seas

The Pawn

The Heir

The Bastard

<u>THE KNIGHTS OF HONOR</u>

Rise of de Wolfe

Word of Honor

Marked by Honor

Code of Honor

Journey to Honor

Heart of Honor

Bold in Honor

Love and Honor

Gift of Honor

Path to Honor

Return to Honor

Season of Honor

NOVELLAS

Diana

Derek

Thea

The Lyon's Lady Love

ABOUT THE AUTHOR

A native Texan and former history teacher, award-winning and internationally bestselling author Alexa Aston lives with her husband in a Dallas suburb, where she eats her fair share of dark chocolate and plots out stories while she walks every morning. She enjoys travel, sports, and binge-watching—and never misses an episode of *Survivor*.

Alexa brings her characters to life in steamy historicals, contemporary romances, and romantic suspense novels that resonate with passion, intensity, and heart.

KEEP UP WITH ALEXA
Visit her website
Newsletter Sign-Up

MORE WAYS TO CONNECT WITH ALEXA